Poets Pass

A Coal Country Novel

HILLARY DEVISSER

Cover design and formatting by Cassy Roop of Pink Ink Designs
Editing by Sarah West of Three Owls Editing

Poets Pass

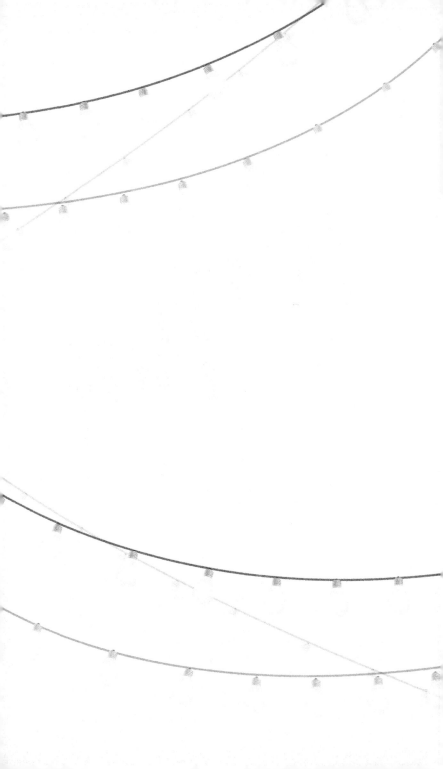

one

J AKE WALKED BACK FROM HIS CRUISER to the driver's side window. Rain dropped from the brim of his hat as he leaned forward.

"Here's your license and registration. This time I'm letting you off with a warning. The speed limit is fifty-five on this highway, not sixty-five. Got it?"

"Got it," the 19-year-old kid in the brand new SUV said with a shrug.

Idiot's going to hurt somebody, Jake hissed internally. He drew in a big breath and exhaled as he rolled his neck, desperate to relieve the tension from an all-night shift. He checked the traffic and eased back onto the highway behind the kid he had pulled over. Newly planted cornfields lined both sides of the road and dark rolling hills rose up against the early morning sky. If he looked hard enough despite the gritty tiredness in his eyes, he could see the rock plateau peeking out of the trees.

Jake smiled as memories from his teenage years washed over him. When he hadn't been at a football game or practice, he'd been roaming around the backroads and hills with his buddies. Most of the guys had moved off for college and never returned to their little corner of southern Illinois. A few were still around, but he hadn't reached out yet. One or two of his old friends that had stayed behind found themselves in the kind of lifestyle that would keep them from welcoming their old friend, a cop, back into the fold. Thankfully, he wasn't much of a social creature anyway.

Really, the only people outside of work that he interacted with were his family. Jake wasn't into the local high school sports scene yet. His cousin's kids played baseball, but he hadn't attended any games. He wasn't a drinker, so that took the bar life out of the equation. His father sure had been a drinker, though. Alek had been meaner than a striped snake. How he ever managed to win over a smart, funny, and beautiful woman like his mother was a mystery to anyone who ever met the couple.

The depths of his father's depravity when drunk led Jake to never touch the stuff. He had watched alcohol turn a quiet but charming man into a scathing, sarcastic son of a bitch more times than he could count. Ruthie, his mother, never spoke about Alek's drinking to either Jake or his sister, but she seemed to have a knack for predicting when he was going to go on a bender. As a little guy, more times than he could count, Ruthie would rush into their rooms or the yard where he and his sister, Mallory, were playing, and announce that they'd be having a sleepover at Aunt Eadie's house with their cousins, Jesse and Anna. Ruthie would keep the mood light as she packed their things and wasted no time driving them to the neighboring town where his aunt and her family lived. Jake didn't think his dad had ever hit his mother, but she must not have thought it was beyond the realm of possibility that he'd start, or turn on the kids.

A sad smile spread over Jake's face as he thought about the way he'd recently turned his life inside out to leave Chicago and move back to southern Illinois. The upside was that he was away from his ex and near most of his remaining family again. The downside was that it nearly killed him to leave his sister alone in the city. He had to make the choice, though. He had to have a change. His dad had finally had the courtesy to die twenty-five years ago around the time when Jake had graduated high school. *Good riddance*, he thought to himself. His mother was doing well but wasn't getting any younger. After the disaster of a marriage he'd just escaped, a change of scenery and fresh start was welcome.

His shift was ending and, as he headed back to the station, his radio went off, "017, Womble..."

"Go ahead, Womble,"

"We just dispatched EMS to 1320 S. Amos Street, possible drug overdose. Neighbor advised unconscious female party on the floor. Door is ajar, no other parties present per the neighbor. We'll stage a block away until you advise location is secure."

"10-4, Womble, en route now," Jake answered, making his way to the address. He arrived at a rundown apartment complex. Some of the units had windows broken out, some had doors boarded up, and others were just hanging wide open. The place brought to mind scenes from horror movies, and a sense of dread welled up in his throat.

Nodding at a few neighbors that had gathered in the yard, Jake knocked on the partially open door to 4D.

"This is Officer Marcovic, everybody okay in there? I'm coming in to make sure everyone's okay," he announced. No response. Jake opened the door fully, and the first thing that struck him was the stench. The next thing that struck him was that a terribly skinny little boy was sitting on the floor next to a woman laid out on the filthy carpet. Jake shot a dirty look at the people who hovered in the doorway.

"Why didn't somebody get this kid out of here?" he threw over his shoulder.

"He ain't our kid to tend to," someone spit back at him.

Jake fought back the need to knock that person on his butt and addressed the boy instead. "Hey, buddy, what's your name?" he asked, taking in the state of the apartment. Beer cans littered the table, cigarettes had been put out on the carpet, and in the midst of this, a little kid lived in the squalor.

Jake could stand a lot of things, but the mistreatment of a kid wasn't one of them. Unfortunately, that was something he encountered often.

The boy didn't answer. "Is anyone else here, buddy? Just you and your mom?" The little boy remained quiet. "Okay, I'm going to try and help your mom, but first I need to see if there's anybody else here, then I'll get her some help." Jake made quick work of checking each room. There wasn't anyone else in the apartment, so he turned his attention back to the woman. He gave her a sternum rub with no response. Jake put his fingers to her wrist to check for a pulse and leaned in to check for a breath and the rise and fall of her chest. There was barely any air moving in her, and her pulse was faint but present.

"Womble, location secure. Have the ambulance come on up, tell them to expedite," he said into the radio. "We've got a little boy here, I'd guess around three or four years old." The dispatcher asked him to bring the boy to the hospital as Jake nodded to the paramedic that came through the door.

The boy still didn't speak, and if Jake had to bet, he'd guess the boy had been taught from an early age that police were the bad guys instead of the people you run to when you're scared. "Come on, buddy. Do you have a stuffed animal to bring with you? Or a special blanket?" The little fella went over to the couch and picked up a ratty blue blanket and stood rooted to the spot. Jake smiled and picked up the boy who couldn't have weighed twenty-five pounds. "I've got something for you in my car. The nice ladies at my church make special bears for special kiddos just like you. Would you like one?"

The sad-eyed boy nodded, looking over Jake's shoulder at the door to his apartment. Jake pulled a patchwork bear out of a sack in his trunk and settled it next to the little boy in the backseat of his cruiser. The social worker met Jake and the boy at the hospital entrance. Before he left he knelt down by the boy and gave his thin shoulders a hug.

"You're going to be okay, buddy. Remember, the police are always here to help however they can, okay?"

The little boy blinked at Jake but didn't answer. Jake shared a sad smile with the caseworker. "Thanks for getting here so quickly."

The kind-looking, sleep-rumpled woman nodded. "You bet, part of the job," she said, eyeing her watch. She bent down to introduce herself to the little boy.

"Hi, kiddo, my name is Mary. What's your name?" she asked.

The little boy looked from Mary to Jake and back. "Toby," he whispered.

"Toby? Nice to meet you, Toby. Let's go in and wait a little bit here in the hospital. Would you like a snack?" she asked, rummaging in her bag as they turned to walk into the hospital.

"Ma'am," Jake said, causing her to turn and look back. "Where will Toby go from here?"

She shrugged. "I'm not entirely sure yet. After the doctor clears him, we'll go to my office. I've got a list of foster homes to go down to see if anyone can take him in."

A pit of dread settled in Jake's stomach. He said a quick prayer that a safe, kind home would be found for the poor little one. "Can I check in with you to find out how he's doing?"

"Sure," she said. She fished around in her purse and handed him her card. "Have you got kids?" she asked, flicking her gaze down to his ring finger.

A pang hit Jake's heart. "No, but not for lack of trying," he said sadly. "Take care, Toby." He nodded to Mary and walked back to his car. Jake's heart broke for the little boy.

It took days for him to shake the weight of that slight-framed kid from his arms. How easily it could have been him and his sister had his mother not stood firm against his father's alcohol abuse. How easily it could have been just about anyone if not for someone or something that stood in the way of utter ruin. Some people just threw their children, or the welfare of their children, out like garbage instead of treasuring them like they were meant to be treasured.

two

A very shut the door to her office, leaning back against it as she closed her eyes and rubbed the wrinkle between them. "That patient is *disturbed*," she said quietly, crossing her office. Being a psychiatrist in a one-horse town was an interesting job, to say the least. While it could be a little overwhelming at times, what she liked most about it was the variety, knowing no two days would be the same. Each patient was like a walking puzzle with moving pieces. They ran the gamut between adults that had been coddled too much as children and lacked coping skills when they faced challenges, to people who were somehow still standing after surviving true horrors.

She took a deep breath, stretched her arms over her head,

and shook off the negative energy from her last patient. She slipped behind her desk to review notes and cranked through the work at hand. Overall, today had been one of the good days, when she felt the patients she saw left her office better than when they arrived. There were some that were on the cusp of burrowing out of the holes they'd been in and were just about ready to taper off the frequency of therapy visits. There were others she figured would hopefully be seeing her - or some other doctor - for the duration of their lives. Mental illness had gained a little more awareness over the last few years, and it was certainly something to be taken seriously, not feared irrationally. Avery took special pride in being one face her patients could trust that would treat them professionally and with gentle respect.

Sure, she could be tough when she needed to be, and God knows she'd had more than her fair share of opportunities to prove it. But when given the chance, at least within the boundaries of that building, she preferred kindness and grace. The colder side of her personality certainly seemed to have free-range outside those walls, once she was far enough from her practice. That's probably why she found herself secluded at her cabin more times than not.

If she didn't have her outlets, she might just end up on the other side of her own therapy couch. Avery couldn't help but get tickled that her two passions were seemingly at opposite ends of the spectrum. When she wasn't travelling to a beach to release tension, she burned it away on her yoga mat or the gun range. She was a mantra-loving, gun-toting, walking, talking contradiction of a woman.

Avery didn't really need much to be content. She needed a hill where she could sit and drink coffee while watching the sunrise and the occasional glass of whiskey to savor while watching the sunset. She needed to be able to see trees, fields, and hills in the background. The sounds of cicadas, frogs, and birds were the perfect way to end her mentally exhausting days. Neighbors and conversation were not required.

Sometimes though, she got lonely. Avery thought she talked aloud to her cat more than was normal while she walked around her garden, but nobody was around to hear, so who cares? Mr. Rochester, Rocky for short, was a part-time mouser, full-time mooch. He patrolled Avery's property in exchange for cat crunchies and specialized in darting in front of her tires late at night when she went to park her Range Rover at the end of a long day. Her phone buzzed at an incoming call.

"Hello, Cade," she answered with a smile.

"Avery, how are you?"

"Doing well, wrapping up a hectic day."

"I'm in town. Want to get together tonight?" She wrinkled her nose as she glanced at her watch. It was still pretty early, but she was too bushed for the kind of get together he had in mind.

"Not tonight, today was a rough one," she answered.

"You sure? I can throw in a massage, the whole nine if you want it," Cade crooned, knowing he was playing dirty. There wasn't much in the world Avery liked more than a massage.

"Nice try, maybe next time. What are you up to, anyway? I didn't think you were due here for another few months," she asked, flipping through her calendar.

"There's a cardio conference in Nashville. I don't have to be there until tomorrow afternoon, and thought I'd spend a little time with you if you were available," he answered, his crooked grin absolutely enticing, even through the phone.

"I can't say yes every time, Cade. You might think I'm easy," Avery joked, slipping her feet out of her heels.

Laughing, he said, "Avery, you might be a lot of things, but nothing about you is easy. I'm leaving around eleven or so in the morning. I'll be passing back through in early June.

"Sounds good, safe travels."

"Take care, Avery."

AVERY LOOKED UP at her diploma, and memories of her time in med school washed over her. She and Cade had hit it off immediately. She'd grown up in the St. Louis area and didn't bat an eye at the traffic, while Cade had grown up in a little town in Texas and was completely out of his element in his new city. He was smart, funny, had a sexy Texas drawl, and he allowed Avery to lead him around by the nose. Their friendship was unique… though they dated in college, she thought of him as an old flame and an occasional indulgence between the sheets. As it was, Avery had zero time to commit to a relationship that would inevitably flounder, and Cade was a no-strings-attached kind of guy. They got together every now and then when he passed through, and it was a nearly perfect arrangement. They were great friends, they more than scratched the occasional itch, and best of all, she didn't have to pick his wet towels up off the floor or remind him to call his mother.

She finished her notes and slipped her heels back on. Avery gathered up her belongings, flicked off the light, locked up, and headed off to her little slice of heaven -- her cabin out in the country. There was acreage for sale next door, and she was tempted to buy it just to keep neighbors from being too close. A house up the road had recently sold, and she had seen a family with a huge amount of kids working on it. A sense of dread filled her as she envisioned listening to four-wheeler motors zooming down her road and invading her sense of peace. "You can't keep everyone out, Avery," she scolded herself. If she wasn't careful, she was going to end up one of those crotchety old women with a bunch of cats. She chuckled to herself at the thought. She didn't mind being alone, but she didn't want to turn into a crazy cat lady.

Maybe a preemptive strike was necessary. To branch out and be a little friendly, she decided to do something outlandish, for her. She'd pick up a pie or something for the new neighbors. They had to get hungry working on that place all the time. She noticed trucks there nearly every day when she drove home. Plus, maybe it would be easier to keep the kids off her property if she cozied up to them a little first.

She decided to do a little recon before swooping in with

a pie in hand. After work, she threw on some tennis shoes, slipped her 9mm into her holster, and went for a walk. She was way out in the boonies and never knew what she'd come across, so she was always prepared. Less than a mile up the road she peered up the gravel driveway. Two pickup trucks and a big Suburban were parked there. A woman with a huge, curly bun of brown hair was on the porch bossing around three teenage boys and two grown men. Avery knew at first glance she liked her.

"For the love of Pete, Luke. If I wanted that dropped on the gravel, I would have tried to carry it myself. Michael, go help your brother, please, and Jake - good Lord, you're going to sprain a testicle. Levi, can you grab the other end of that before he kills himself?" she said, half-laughing, half-disgusted. Ryan, can you grab that box, please?

She caught sight of Avery coming up the driveway and rose to meet her. "Men, they'd be useless without us," she said, shaking her head.

Avery nodded in agreement. "Most of them, yes. Hi, I'm Avery. I'm your neighbor," she said, gesturing with her head toward the direction she'd come from.

"Hi, I'm Jesse Murray, nice to meet you. We're over a month away from getting in this place, but figured it wouldn't hurt to move a few pieces of furniture in so we could at least be comfortable while we're tearing it to shreds. This is my husband, Levi. Levi, this is Avery…"

"Avery O'Gara, I live about half a mile down the road, here."

"Ah! Dr. O'Gara! I'm pretty sure I've heard your name. I think you see my sister's husband, Aidan Doherty," Jesse said with a smile, answered by a non-committal smile from Avery.

"Nice to meet you, Dr. O'Gara," Levi said, extending his hand.

"Avery, please."

"Avery," he corrected.

A man came around the corner, dusting his hands off on his jeans. Avery instantly felt her body react to him. He had thick brown hair, a strong jawline, and his scruffy beard looked like it would tickle against her skin. Even from a few feet away she saw the real draw was his green eyes and grin.

"Avery," she said, hand outstretched.

He stepped up to her and dwarfed her with his size. "Nice to meet you, I'm Jake," he replied, drinking her in with his gaze.

"You're the one whose testicles she's worried about, huh?" she said with a smirk.

Jake's eyes widened, and Levi choked on the beer Jesse had passed him. "No, ma'am, those would be mine, I think. My bride is very conscientious," Levi said with a laugh.

"Bride, huh?" Avery said with her eyebrow cocked toward the oldest boy who appeared to be at least 16.

"Well, second-time bride," Jesse supplied with a happy smile. She wrapped her arm around his side and said, "Levi and I were married last year."

"Gotcha," Avery said.

"Nice 9mm you've got there," Jake said quietly, noting the weapon she thought she had concealed.

Avery wrinkled her brow. "Noticed that, huh?" she asked.

"Cop, twenty-one years," he said with a wry grin.

Despite an instinctive dislike and distrust of most men, she couldn't help but notice the attractive way his eyes crinkled at the corners. Good Lord, what was he? Six and a half feet tall? The man was huge. His shoulders were broad and tapered into a trim waist and hips. His body made her instantly think of sweaty sexual positions. She needed some distance between herself and this guy, quick.

Avery nodded in acknowledgement, not sure what else to say. She felt a panic seize her and needed to get far, far away. "Well, I uh, just wanted to say hello and introduce myself. I'm going to get back to my walk now. Good luck with the house."

Only Jake remained, watching the direction Avery had walked as Jesse barked out orders after the group said their goodbyes. He definitely wasn't looking for anything right now, but man, she was a sexy little woman. Lush curves, blond hair piled high on her head in a ponytail, and a neat little pistol under her shirt. If he were in the market, that's the kind of woman he'd be after. She was sexy, but she didn't have a ready smile. He spent the rest of the evening trying not to wonder why that might be.

three

JAKE'S RADIO SQUEALED AS THE dispatcher announced
that some teenegers were spotted at the abandoned
school in the middle of town. He was just a few blocks away
and responded, "Womble, 017. I'm just a few blocks away,
en route now."

He groaned as he saw the boy loitering around the
entrance, which was a pair of double doors chained together
with the glass busted out. It was his cousin Jesse's boy, Luke.
He slowed his cruiser down and pulled to a stop. Thankfully,
the idiot kid had enough sense to at least stop instead of
running. He met Jake halfway to the curb.

"Dude, what are you doing? There are 'no trespassing'
signs everywhere. You've already been warned once, right?"

"Yessir," Luke answered, eyes to the sidewalk.

"It's 6 AM. What in the hell are you doing out here, buddy?"

Luke outwardly winced at being called buddy. He barely knew Jake, let alone considered him a buddy. "I was, uh, just nosing around before Mom got up."

Lie. Jake knew it, and Luke knew he knew it. He picked up his radio and let dispatch know he'd found the kid and was talking to him.

"Let's walk. Show me what's got you so transfixed with this building, Luke," he said, pulling Luke by the elbow. Luke's feet sprouted roots that went down to the center of the earth.

"Luke. Move."

Luke moved. He ducked through the broken glass, and Jake did the same, placing his hand on his firearm. The building had been abandoned for at least ten years and was a rumored home for vagrants. Shockingly, the police had only been called there a few times over the past several years. It was a thousand wonders the place was still standing.

Inside the doors, Jake inhaled deeply, the institutional smell of a school still coating the area, despite the exposure to the environment and time. He never knew if it was the smell of bleach or the sawdust crap they sprinkled on puke that gave schools that singular smell. Whatever it was, the building still held it. Jake couldn't help but cringe a little at the ruin. That building had held court for 90 years at least, and as far as he was concerned, should've been tended and kept up for decades more. Nothing could be done for it now, though. The damage was too extensive to reverse.

"Why can't you keep away from here, Luke? You know your mom's going to lay an egg when I tell her about this."

Luke shrugged and marched a half-step behind Jake. Jake looked down the hallway and couldn't see much aside from the sunshine spilling through the door with the glass busted out at the end of the hallway. He pulled open the doors to the auditorium and felt a shiver go down his spine when he heard skittering noises from the mice, or rats, or God only knows what else, as it made for the shadows. What a shame to see the floor all torn up, chairs randomly ripped out and the smell was horrific. He'd seen countless abandoned buildings in his time, but this one broke his heart a little. He remembered walking these halls as a kid and watching several plays, school productions, and even remembered the thrill of getting to walk to the building for exhibits in the beautiful auditorium there. Jake noticed Luke nervously glancing at the steps off toward a hallway that led to a different part of the school, so he took off in that direction.

He could feel the nervous energy rolling off his young cousin at this point and gave him one more chance before opening the doors to what used to be the library. Luke stuttered a little, but he didn't get in Jake's way.

The lighting was dim and the shelves were empty and eerie. Books had been cleared out when the school was moved to a new location, but the shelves still stood like skeletons. As Jake walked toward what used to be the circulation desk, Luke jumped in front of him.

"Just wait, Jake. I… um, we…" he sputtered, irritating Jake to no end.

"For God's sake, spit it out, Luke. What's going on here?"

The gangly, sullen kid hung his head for a second. "Follow me. My friend's in here. There's a bedroom, sort of."

Jake looked at Luke for a second, and a sense of dread welled up in him. "What am I going to find in there, Luke?"

Luke panicked at the tone of Jake's voice and the steel in his eyes. "Nothing bad, I mean, my friend is in there. She lives there. She's pregnant. Like, really pregnant," he said with a grimace.

A curse hissed out under Jake's breath. "What's her name?"

"Maggie. We went to school together till she got pregnant. Her mom kicked her out and she ended up here. That was a while ago, though," Luke said, shrugging his shoulders. "I came in here to look around and jerked the door open and scared the crap out of both of us."

Jake knocked on the door. "Maggie, this is Officer Marcovic, I'm here with Luke. Answer the door, please."

He was relieved to see the door open gently and quickly. The last thing he wanted was some kind of standoff with a pregnant kid in an abandoned building. A scared-looking, hugely pregnant girl, maybe 14 years old peeked out at him.

"Luke, why did you do this?" she asked accusingly.

"I'm so sorry, Maggie. Jake, um, I mean, Officer Marcovic, is my cousin. He caught me leaving the building."

Jake looked inside the bedroom, to use the term loosely, and saw that Maggie had been sleeping on an old mattress in what used to be a listening room where kids were allowed to play records or tapes back in the day.

"Maggie, you're not in trouble, but I'm going to need you to come with me. It's not safe for you to stay here. People are in and out of this building constantly, no matter what the city does to stop them. It's a constant battle. We're going to go to the station, get you some food, and find you a safer place to be, okay?"

She turned her nose up at him. "I can take care of myself," she said, tears streaming down her face.

"Maggie, he's right," Luke said. "This place is creepy."

"I know that, Luke," she snipped, suddenly doubling over in pain, her voice morphing into a groan. "Oh no! Not now!" she said, dropping to her knees.

Fantastic, Jake muttered under his breath with a glance at his watch. He was off in five minutes and now this. He didn't mean to be an unsympathetic jerk, but he'd been up for 48 hours. He sighed as Maggie let out a yelp. No matter how tired he was, he wasn't in near as bad of shape as this kid was in.

"Luke, get in her room and grab anything that looks like a personal item. Now!" he said, jerking the wide-eyed Luke out of his stupor and helping Maggie up. "Alright, Maggie, let's get you to the car. Do you know how far along you are?"

"I lost track," Maggie answered. "I've just been trying to get through every day the best I can," she sobbed, stopping to brace her hands on her knees. As he braced her with one arm he grabbed his radio with another.

"Dispatch, we've got a pregnant woman in labor, Maggie..." he paused. "What's your last name, Maggie?"

Maggie shook her head adamantly. "No. I'm not telling you that. I'm not going home. My mom threw me out like a piece of trash. I'm not going back there."

"Last name withheld. We're going to need an ambulance to meet us at the south entrance to the building."

"Marcovic, I can't get it there, we've just had a four-car pileup on Route 109. Every ambulance in the county is there right now."

"I'll bring her in."

"I'll notify the hospital."

Jake sheathed his radio and helped Maggie get through the opening in the broken glass doors. "Watch your head, duck down a bit more," he said as she stopped to clutch her belly. "Come on, kiddo, we're almost there."

Luke was running ahead to the cruiser to open the door to the backseat. "Here you go, Maggie, here you go!"

"Luke, call your mom this instant and let her know where the hell you are. She's got to be out of her mind with worry about you not being home. You ever sneak out like this again and I'm going to kick what's left of your butt after she gets done with you."

"Yessir," Luke replied with eyes as big as saucers. "You're going to be okay," he whispered to Maggie soothingly as he did his best to be helpful.

"How do you know?" Maggie cried. "Where am I going to live now?" she asked, her voice breaking on her pain.

Jake maneuvered the poor girl into his backseat and quickly made his way to his seat. First babies usually weren't in a rush, but who knew what would happen with this kid. Would her lack of prenatal care make it different? The stress she was under? If there was anything he knew less about than the birth of babies, he couldn't think of it.

As he pulled the car onto the street, Maggie let loose a howl that made the hairs on the back of Jake's neck stand up. "How long have you been in labor, Maggie?"

"My water broke last night, and I've been hurting like this all night. The contractions are closer together now," she said, howling again. "I've got to push!" she said, her legs straining against the back of his seat and car door.

Shit, Jake muttered. "Try not to push, Maggie!"

A scream of terror broke the air. "I can feel its head, oh my God it hurts so bad!"

"You can't have the baby in the car!" Luke yelled.

"Shut up, Luke!" Jake and Maggie said in unison.

"It's a ten-minute drive to the hospital, Maggie, I'll get you there as fast as I can."

"I can feel its head!" she screamed again, hands grasping wildly beneath the hem of her long, ratty t-shirt, stunning Luke.

"Oh my God! Jake, the baby's head is out!" Luke screamed in horror.

Jake knew he couldn't make it to the hospital in time and jerked his radio off his belt.

"Dispatch, we're about ten minutes out from the hospital, and Maggie's having the baby in the car. The head is out," he said sternly, fighting his own tide of panic.

"If the head's out, pull over, Marcovic. I'll talk you through this and get a unit on the way," the dispatch operator answered. Jake yanked the car into the first empty parking lot he saw. Thankfully, it was a church. That had to be a good omen.

"It's going to be okay, Maggie," he said as a startled Luke practically fell out of the opened car door. Jake did his best to help Maggie position herself in the backseat of the car with her legs braced against the doorframe. Sure enough, there was a head, but no sound.

"The baby's not crying," Maggie said. "Shouldn't it be crying?" her voice frantic, as she moaned and curled up against the contraction.

With dispatch instructing him from the radio, Jake did his best to appear calm. "Maggie, you're going to need to deliver the baby quickly. On the next contraction, push with all your might."

Unable to answer, she nodded her head frantically at Jake.

"That's it, you can do it." Jake was scared out of his mind and wondered if he'd ever been in a more awkward situation in his whole life. Fourteen years old. This poor kid.

Maggie pushed during her next contraction and Jake guided the tiny, silent baby out of his mother. There was so much gunk and blood on the baby, he knew he was going to have to clean it before he could do CPR.

"Give me your shirt, Luke," he said, his hand outstretched to the pacing teenager. Luke stopped in his tracks and stared stupidly, panic and concern etched into his face.

"Take off your t-shirt right now and give it to me," Jake yelled as Luke jerked from his frozen state, yanking his t-shirt off over his head.

Jake tuned out Maggie's cries as he focused on wiping the baby's face and chest clean as best as he could. He laid the baby on the seat as Maggie tried to scamper away from him, still connected to the baby by the umbilical cord. Jake blocked out everything and placed his fingertips in line on the baby's chest and gently pressed thirty times. Next, he covered the baby's mouth and nose with his lips and very gently blew two breaths, feeling the tiny chest expand. He started compressions again and cycled two more times before he was rewarded with the most beautiful sight. The baby, who had turned blue, rewarded Jake with a deep breath and a tiny wail.

Until that moment, Jake had blocked out every other sound. When the volume in his head switched back on, he heard Maggie's relieved sobbing, the dispatch operator's congratulations, and the blessed sound of an ambulance siren in the background. He wrapped the baby up in Luke's t-shirt and handed him to Maggie.

"Here's your baby boy," he said with a smile, suddenly feeling every minute of the past two days. "Give me your shoe, Luke," he said, outstretching his hand. Dutifully, Luke stripped off his shoe. Jake pulled the lace free and used it to tie off the cord. The ambulance whipped onto the street and in a flash, two EMTs had Maggie and the baby safely loaded.

"Good job, Marcovic," the burly man said. "Not bad for a new guy," he cracked with a smile.

"Happy to help." He nodded. "You did good, too, kid," he said with a slap on Luke's bare shoulder. The boy looked absolutely comical, standing in the parking lot shirtless with a shoe in his hand. All he could do was nod in reply.

"Get in the car, Luke. I'll take you home to your mother."

Jake knew he ought to rip into Luke for hanging around an abandoned building, or not telling anyone about Maggie living there alone and in her condition, but he decided the lecture could wait. Luke had been scared to death for his friend, and if it hadn't been for him getting busted sneaking out of the building, God only knows what could've happened to Maggie and the baby. The thought of what could've been made his blood run cold. Instead of dwelling, he turned his mind to problem-solving mode, wondering what it would take to make his car not look like someone just delivered a baby in it.

"Where will she go now?" Luke asked quietly as Jake turned onto his street.

"I'm not sure, bud. Social services will get involved because she's a minor, so they'll take it from here."

Jake watched as Luke nodded with a somber expression on his face.

"I've got to ask, Luke, is the baby yours?"

With relief, Jake saw Luke adamantly shake his head.

"No, no way. She was just my friend. I'm still a... I haven't ever..." he sputtered. "No."

"What were you doing there so early?"

Luke looked ashamed as he admitted the truth. "I've been taking her food and stuff."

Though the situation was beyond screwed up, and he'd rather Luke not be wrapped up in it, he felt proud of the kid.

"We're going to talk later about this, but for now you've got bigger problems," he said as he saw Jesse standing on the porch with her arms folded.

She didn't say a word as they walked up the steps, but even Jake felt a little afraid for Luke. He watched as she put her hands to his face and kissed Luke's forehead, equal parts fury and relief written plainly on her features. She jerked her thumb toward the door, and without a word, Luke went inside.

Jake watched Jesse sag with relief and worry as she sat down into the adirondack chair, patting the one beside her for Jake.

"My God, I have been so scared for the last few hours. I know you had him call me, but I honestly didn't get much out of him. What in the world has he done?"

"He's actually kind of a hero," Jake answered, "albeit a misguided one. A friend of his, Maggie something, has been living in the old abandoned school. The poor kid turned up pregnant and her mom kicked her out of the house."

Jesse scoffed with disgust. "Who does that?"

"You'd be surprised. Anyway, she found a spot in the old school library."

"Oh my God. That poor kid," Jesse said, motherly ire burning in her eyes. "How could her parents just turn her out?"

"Jesse, I don't mean to be morbid or condescending, but it's way more common than you think. I can't count the incidences of teen girls in the city that were kicked out of their homes. And not just from shitty backgrounds, either. You see all kinds out there without a single soul that cares for them." He shrugged. "It's enough to make you sick."

"Really. I can't even fathom turning your kid out when they need you most. I can't even imagine..."

"Imagine or not, it's what's happening out there. By the way, Luke was helping her out with food and stuff. I'm not sure exactly what he was providing her with, but he was trying to help."

Jesse sat still for a minute. "I'm not sure whether to be proud or pissed, Jake."

"I know, Jess. The baby isn't his, by the way. I already asked."

"Sweet Jesus, I didn't even think of that," Jesse said, growing pale.

A laugh escaped him despite himself. "I asked," he said in a placating voice. "I believe him. Ex-wife notwithstanding, I'm a pretty good judge of character."

With that, Jesse patted Jake's arm. "You look like crap. Go home. I'll talk to Luke. Thanks for bringing him home."

"You bet," he said, as he rose to go. "Take care."

"Jake?" He turned and looked back at his cousin. "What will happen to Maggie and the baby?"

"They'll be assigned a caseworker. If the girl's mom won't take her in, she'll probably end up in a group home or something. There's one a few towns over that takes in new mothers." Jake watched Maggie's grim reality settle over Jesse. She turned and looked back at her house, and he could see the wheels turning.

"Jesse," he said in a quiet voice.

She shrugged. "I know. I can't fix everybody, but damn it. I can't believe someone would turn their back on their own child."

He nodded. "Believe me, I get it," he said solemnly.

Jesse watched him leave and threw up a quick prayer for Jake. She'd never understand how his ex could let him get away. *He'd be a terrific father,* she muttered to herself. Jesse took a deep breath and went into her house, trying to decide how she was going to handle Luke's involvement in Maggie's situation. She couldn't believe he hadn't told her that the girl was living in an abandoned building.

JAKE NEVER COULD wrap his mind around how fast shifts at work went in contrast to how slow the rest of his life passed by. He loved his job to the point he could be single-minded about it. Maybe that was the reason his ex-wife filled more than her hours with other men. He knew he was a perfectionist and blamed a lot of his responsibility issues on his home life as a kid. There was still a part of him that felt like if he did everything the right way, he had a shred of control on the outcome. His mother had done her best to shield him and his sister from his father's drunken rages, but there were memories that still haunted him. Jake had been so excited to have love and a nice, normal home life that he'd been blind to her betrayals.

He'd been with Juliet for years, but she'd traded night-shift boredom for her marriage. How many times had he rolled in as she was leaving for work in the morning and slept on the same sheets she'd shared with other men? As far as he was concerned, he was done with women beyond satisfying basic needs. He could cook for himself, clean for himself. Other things he preferred not do for himself, so he could step out for that. At the end of the, uh, experience he'd be safe and sound, back in his own bed, unconcerned with a single thing.

For months he'd been sickened at the thought of contracting some disease from his whore of a wife. They'd slept together frequently during their marriage. She'd never let on like she was unsatisfied. Maybe their schedule hadn't allowed for the long-winded, seemingly endless marathons that women preferred with dinner, talking, and then hours of lovemaking, but he'd always ensured he was 100% ringing her bell.

Sure, women could fake it, but it was easy to see if the effects were genuine if a man just cared enough to investigate. Jake couldn't claim sainthood, but by God if he knew one thing, he knew how to please his woman really well. If only he'd been as aware of other things as much as Juliet's satisfaction in the sack. The same certainly couldn't be said of her truthfulness, or moral code.

One thing he couldn't wrap his mind around was how she could reconcile being kind and sweet to him while nailing anyone she could find behind his back. Shouldn't there have been some kind of divide of the conscience? The part that let her share her married body with someone other than her husband should've been the part that railed against serving his dinner with a sweet smile, or cuddling on the couch, or even scratching her nails down his back in the shower as he made her see God, right? Months past it all, it still rubbed him wrong.

Jake kicked his pile of laundry across the floor of his mother's house as he cussed himself, gathering the clothes back into a pile before stuffing them into the washer.

"Jake, is that you in there? What the hell is going on?"

"Nothing, Mom, just doing some laundry."

Ruthie stood in the doorway, a frown etched into her sweet forehead. "Let me do that. Son, I'm so sorry things didn't work out how you planned." She gave him a sideways glance and said, "But, I always thought Juliet was a snake."

Jake choked on his spit. "Good Lord, Mom, don't mince words…"

She shrugged. "What's the point of that? I'm not going to live forever," she said.

"Well, if we're being morbid…"

"Morbid? Jake, people my age are dropping dead every day. Why waste time fussing over the perfect words?"

He shook his head. "Mom, got me there."

"Got you there," she said, grinning up at him. "Now look, sit down and eat, then go to bed. I know you're worn out. You look like crap, Son."

"Not crap, Mom, just night shift."

"Got it. Now eat, and get to bed. Let me finish up the laundry."

"Mom," he said.

"What? It'll give me something to do."

"Thanks, Mom. Just so you and I are on the same page, I'm looking into another house," he said, piling eggs and bacon onto his plate. "I still can't believe the first one fell through."

"Well, Son, shit happens. You know that. You'll find the right spot. Just keep looking. I've been on my own a long time now, but I don't mind the company." She grinned, pouring him a cup of coffee.

"I know, I just thought I should keep you in the loop."

Ruthie nodded. "I appreciate it, kiddo. It's been just you, me, and Mallory for a long time now, hasn't it?"

"Yeah, it felt like just the three of us even when he was alive." Jake wished he had a time machine to suck those words back into his lungs when he saw his mother cringe.

Ruthie nodded, her face tight with sadness. Decades had passed, but she still couldn't bring herself to speak a bad word against his father. Jake just couldn't understand it. So much more than years separated their generations. His was one that bled their feelings and opinions all over social media, although Jake had little use for such a thing. His mother's generation was the one that suffered through their hurts with a stiff upper lip. As far as he was concerned, neither one was one-hundred percent healthy. Even now he could hear Aunt Eadie's voice reminding him that his mom had done the best she could with the tools she had. How many times had he heard that reassurance as Eadie tucked him into bed at her house after his mother had dropped the pair of them off while his father raged at home.

There wasn't much in this life Jake could guarantee, but he could promise to live a life free of abuse that would poison him and those he loved. Not much else was said as Jake wolfed down his breakfast and coffee -- decaf. He had to get at least five to six hours of shut-eye before he'd wake up, hit the gym, and do it all over again.

Ruthie let out a heavy sigh. "I sure wish Mallory would move home, too. It would be so nice to have you both close."

"Me too, Mom. Night," he said, putting his dishes in the dishwasher.

"Night, honey, be safe," she said, grinning at his joke. It was nearly 9 AM, and Ruthie had been up for hours and hours by that point. Her day started at the crack of dawn and ended sometime around 9 PM. Ruthie shook her head as she tidied up the kitchen.

"I still don't know how I woke up old one day," she muttered to herself. There were times she literally jumped when she looked in the mirror at the sheer shock of it all. In her mind, she still felt somewhere around 40 or so, but the mirror showed the face of her own mother and grandmother. She was glad she had their nose and blue eyes. A soft smile appeared on her face as she remembered those warm-hearted, generous ladies. Her life with Alek had been a hard one. Rather than dwell on the years of verbal abuse, loneliness, and secret relief once he died, if she was being honest, Ruthie chose instead to remember how instantly she had fallen for him.

———————

ALEK HAD IMMIGRATED from eastern Europe at time of upheaval in Yugoslavia in the late 1970s. Both his elderly parents had died, and when the window opened for him to escape the turbulent country, he took it. A little money and lots of luck, depending on your perspective, Ruthie thought, landed Alek in southern Illinois. No, she chided herself. Without Alek she wouldn't have had Mallory and Jake. Her kids were her very heart.

Ruthie gathered the laundry as her mind wandered back to the day she met Alek. She was a senior in high school and couldn't wait to see what happened next in her life. Unofficial options for women at that time were to become teachers, secretaries, nurses, or wives. She had planned on becoming a nurse until the moment she saw him. She, Eadie, and a convertible full of girlfriends had pulled into the root beer stand and parked next to a car of guys from school. Eadie had been dating Walt by then, so they were side-by-side, flirting shamelessly. Ruthie had walked over to place their order and would never forget the unease that settled over her when a guy from a neighboring town sauntered over to her. Steve had a rotten reputation and even the way his eyes passed over her slowly from head to toe made her skin crawl.

Back in high school Ruthie had been a beauty. She had shiny dark hair and green eyes, and her sister had joked she was built like a brick shit house. This guy, Steve, had snaked his arm around Ruthie's waist as she finished her order and pulled her close up against him.

"Let go of me, Steve," she hissed, not wanting to cause a scene.

"Come on, I know you're not dating anyone. I asked around. Come back to my truck," he breathed against her ear.

Ruthie was repulsed by his suggestion and turned to push against his chest. People were starting to stare, and the last thing she needed was a rumor getting back to her parents that she was letting this loser put his hands on her in front of everyone. "If you don't let go of me I'm going to scream!"

"If I were you, I'd let go of the girl," a stranger said in an exotic-sounding accent. Both Steve and Ruthie turned on their heels to face a dark-headed stranger looming over them. "Right now," he said quietly, anger burning in his eyes as he stared down Steve, a full head shorter than the mysterious giant.

Steve had turned loose of Ruthie and slinked off back to

wherever he came from, and the rest, as they say, was history. Even if he hadn't rescued her from Steve's disgusting grasp, Ruthie would've fallen head over heels for the handsome stranger. She'd always been a sucker for accents, and as far as she was concerned, listening to Alek read the phonebook would've been enough to thrill her for the rest of her days.

Their courtship was brief, and they married after she graduated high school. Her plans of being a nurse were traded for a honeymoon baby and making a home for family. Jake was born a year after Mallory. Sometimes Ruthie thanked God that her second child had been born a boy. In his disgust that his first child was a daughter, Alek had made it clear they would keep having children until he had a son. As little involvement as he had with the children over the years, Ruthie never could figure out why it was he cared whether he had sons or daughters. What difference did it make if he only planned to treat them like a burden? She couldn't imagine how much harder it would have been to protect the children had there been more of them to shuttle off to Eadie's the moment he signaled he was going on a bender.

There had been warning signs aplenty regarding Alek's dark moods and drinking, but she had been young, foolish, and in love. Her parents had been furious that she'd date and marry a *foreigner*, something unheard of in the area and the time, but by the same token, she was of a marrying age and the sooner she was out of the house, the sooner her care would be on Alek's dime rather than her father's, and times were hard back then.

Ruthie's heart lurched as the memories of her marriage washed over her. True to form, she pushed those memories down and focused on her daily routine. Now that Jake was home, temporary as it was, she was overjoyed to have more to fill her day. Before he'd made the move, she had spent most of her days zipping through her tasks then going over to her sister Eadie's house each day. Ruthie hadn't fooled either herself or Eadie. She'd been spending so much time there as a cure for her own loneliness as much as she had to be helpful to her grieving sister.

As Eadie allowed time to slowly lessen the shock and heartache from the unexpected loss of her husband, Ruthie had served mainly as comic relief. Though they sometimes fussed like the Odd Couple, Ruthie's light-hearted personality and tendency toward optimism balanced well with Eadie's often more serious nature. Before Walt had passed, Eadie had been boisterous and busy, but his loss had taken the wind from her sails. Ruthie was confident Eadie would become more of herself over time, but she needed time to come to terms with her new normal. As it was, they balanced each other out nicely and knew when to reminisce and smile, and when to simply be still. Eadie had done the same for Ruthie when Alek died.

At that point in time, Mallory was starting her second year of nursing school and Jake had just graduated high school and went off to college. Ruthie had taken a job the minute Jake had moved out. Alek hadn't allowed her to work outside the home until Jake was gone. "A woman's place is in the home," she heard him say in her mind as clearly as if the words had just left his lips. It had been a little over twenty-five years, but she could still hear his voice like it was yesterday. The sound produced such a contradictory reaction in her. A shiver crept up her spine at the memory. It had been a relief to have a job to escape to. She'd liked having someplace to be, especially because Alek was home during the day. He worked mainly third-shift at the coal mines, so he would work at night, come home during the day either to drink or sleep, or a combination of both. One night she came home from her secretary job at the employment agency in town and found Alek dead in his bed, a half-empty bottle of vodka on the nightstand.

Ruthie rubbed her hands together as the memory of how badly her hands had trembled as she poured the bottle down the sink and removed all evidence of his cigarette and drunkenness from the house before she called 911. Mallory and Jake were called home from college for the funeral, and suddenly her life was very, very still and quiet. Without her job, she might have gone stir-crazy, not to mention hungry. Eadie had been her rock, pulling her out of her confusing grief with constant dinner invitations and little excursions here and there. She was only too glad to repay the favor, sad as they all were that Walt was gone. Walt and Eadie's marriage had been a steady example to both their own children and hers of what married life should be like.

Mallory was still unmarried, a thought that sometimes plagued Ruthie, although Mallory was happy to spend most of her time working. When she wasn't pulling long shifts at the hospital, she was off traveling the world. Ruthie was in awe of her daughter and sometimes puzzled at the path Mallory had chosen. She didn't really mind so much that marriage and babies weren't for Mallory, but she did want to know she had companionship and love around her, especially after Ruthie was gone. Ruthie did her best to refuse to dwell on the fact she didn't have any grandchildren to spoil. Thankfully, she was heavily involved with Eadie's grandchildren. It wasn't the same, but it filled the void.

Jake, however, had married and it had gone down in flames. Though she had never liked Juliet, she hated that Jake's marriage had ended so badly. How dare that little hussy cheat on her boy. She'd never understand it. Jake wasn't perfect - he was moody, quiet, and withdrew when he was stressed out. He'd always been like that. But, he was good. He was good in the way that Alek could've been.

"*Stop it, Ruthie,*" she said to herself. She so easily forgot the horrors Alek had witnessed in his country before immigrating. There were things he wouldn't, or couldn't, talk about. There were some things he had shared about his life there that she had wished he'd never told her. She imagined the same could be said for Jake in his line of work. He had no doubt seen things in his life as a police officer that would make her skin crawl, especially in a big city.

I'll never understand how people can be so mean to one another, she thought. She poured herself another cup of coffee and grabbed her phone. Ruthie jumped when

Mallory's phone started playing music while she waited for her daughter to answer.

"Hello?"

Ruthie cringed as she realized she'd woken Mallory up. "Oh no, honey, I woke you up, didn't I?

"It's okay, Mom. It's time I got up anyway. Long shift yesterday. How are you?"

A smile crinkled Ruthie's eyes as she pictured her daughter as a little girl. She'd always taken a long time to wake all the way up. Her dark hair would be rumpled and her eyes squinched closed as she avoided light at all cost. Ruthie had to wake her up a full twenty minutes earlier than what was necessary in order to give her enough time to wake up and be in a good mood. How she missed those years of seeing her babies every day.

"I'm doing fine. On my way to go visit with Benji. He's the cutest little thing."

"Sure looks like it from the pictures. I'll take a look at my schedule today and see when I can come visit. How's Anna doing with motherhood?"

Ruthie moved around her house as she talked, straightening the already tidy home. "She's doing really well so far. She's tired, of course, but she's handling the sleeplessness and the mess that comes with it pretty well. Aidan takes good care of her, though. He's a big help with the baby."

"I should hope so; he's the father," Mallory replied.

Ruthie rolled her eyes. "Yes, I know, dear, but back when

I was a young mother, men weren't typically very helpful. Their contribution was bringing home a paycheck and that's about it. You didn't often see men changing diapers and helping with bottles."

"I'd have been divorced in that era," Mallory answered sarcastically.   Ruthie wasn't going down that road. Sometimes she felt like she had to defend herself for having stayed married to Alek. She wouldn't mind talking that through, but she'd prefer it to be a face-to-face conversation. She knew she had her baggage from those years, and no doubt the kids did, too. She did the best she could with the tools she had at the time.

"Tell me about your day, dear." Ruthie happily listened to Mallory outline her upcoming week while she grabbed her purse and keys. It was time to go check in at Eadie's and see what trouble they could get into for the day. They were supposed to get to watch Benji, Anna and Aidan's little one. She could use some snuggles. Nothing like a baby to cure the blues.

four

"So, you're really going to do it, huh?" Mallory asked her brother.

Jake sighed and switched his phone to Bluetooth when he got in his truck. "What do you mean? I've been down here for months. I officially live here now."

"I know," she said in a whiny voice. "It's just that building a house down there makes it a permanent thing. I miss having you up here. It was nice having family close."

"I'm on the department down here. Believe me, it's permanent. Besides, we didn't even get to see each other that much, Mal. You work all the time, and I work weird hours."

"You're missing the point. At least I knew you were nearby if I needed you."

"I know, Sis. You know, you could move closer. We do have hospitals and doctors offices here, you know."

"Now you sound like Mom."

He laughed quietly. "I do, don't I? She'd be over the freaking moon to get you back here."

"Believe me, I know. She was working on me even before she started working on you! I think it's because you had the she-monster for a wife. Mom wouldn't have wanted her at her backdoor all the time."

"Thankfully that's no longer an issue." The conversation hit an awkward lull. "Well, if I can't talk you into moving back, I'll get off the phone."

"You pouting?" she teased.

"Nah, just ran out of things to say."

"Oh well, at least you're honest. Take care. Love you."

"Love you too, Mal." He stuck his phone into the console of his truck and enjoyed the scenery on his way to help out at Jesse and Levi's house.

THE NEXT FEW DAYS were a whirlwind of fast decision making. Sick of being in limbo, Jake was ready to put down some roots. He was exhausted from helping out at Jesse's new place, but it was a good kind of tired. They were stripping several rooms in the old house down to the studs and making them energy efficient and roomy enough for what Jake considered a horde of children. He and Juliet hadn't had any children within their marriage, but it hadn't been for lack of trying. Except for the six years they'd been married, he'd lived alone most of his life and preferred quiet and solitude most of the time. Jake loved being around Jesse's family and her sister Anna's baby, but the best part was when he was able to get into his quiet truck and drive home. His mother was one of those women who rarely stopped talking, not because she had so much to share, but mainly to fill the quiet void in the air. She was pleasant and he loved her dearly, but he needed his own space.

Jake's time in Chicago had made him long for a country setting. He'd had his fill of crowded city streets and lack of privacy. A view of the hills and solitude of the country life was much more his speed. Jake couldn't help but be drawn to Poets Pass, the winding gravel road where Levi and Jesse were rebuilding their home. The houses were surrounded by woods and fields. Driving around after work one morning he noticed acreage for sale that lined up next to that cute little doctor's cabin. There was even a view of the bluffs in the distance from the hilltop. He had initially put down an offer on a place on the other end of town, but it had fallen through. A quick call to a realtor hungry for the sale found him with an appointment and absolutely drowning in information about the property. Ten acres, mostly wooded with a small creek. An acre on the hilltop was cleared, mostly level and ready for building. It had belonged to someone who planned to build, but they had trouble with financing and it went belly up. It was perfect. He could pretty much write his own ticket. Even after Juliet had done her meanest in the divorce to bleed him of most of his money, he had enough in savings to put down an offer.

Levi had mentioned the property on Poets Pass a few weeks ago. He and Jesse had considered purchasing it, but then she'd fallen in love with the farmhouse. Jake knew it was impulsive, but he needed to get out of his mother's house and get his own space. This was a gorgeous area to live in, and with his family just up the road, he'd basically be getting everything he wanted. What's not to like?

The neighbor isn't too bad, either, he found himself admitting. Next, he called a builder that Levi had recommended and scheduled a meeting to look at available plans. With any luck, he could be drinking coffee on his own porch by the end of the summer.

———

"Are you sure this is the kind of house you want to go with?" Mark asked.

"Yeah, that's the one. Why? You do build them, right?"

Mark shrugged. "Well, it's actually my design. I'm a licensed architect, but original design doesn't fly much in this area," he added with a laugh. "I've got a portfolio of traditional designs, which seems to be what we sell the most of around here. We can build it, but nobody in this area goes with contemporary-style homes.

"If I'm going to live out in the boonies, I want to see the

scenery. I like all the windows and the boxy style. The views will be great up on the hill."

"Okay, man. If you're sure. I think it'll look great. I'm excited to get a chance to build it." Mark grinned from ear to ear.

"Sounds good to me. I recently moved down here from Chicago, so I'll stick out like a sore thumb for a while down here anyway. Might as well go all the way with it."

"Got it. You grew up around here though, right?"

"Yes, next town over," Jake answered. "I played football against a Williams, but he would've been older than you, I think."

"My brother, I bet."

"Probably so. Anyway, how soon can you get started?"

Mark flipped through the calendar on his desk. "A week from now work for you? We had something fall through, so we can get started right away."

Jake frowned. "I'd be freaked out by that if Levi Murray hadn't recommended you."

"I know, not our issue, I swear," Mark said, standing and offering his hand.

"Sounds good to me," Jake replied, anxious to get going.

THE SATURDAY MORNING sun was just beginning to pour over Avery's deck as she unrolled her mat and began her sun salutation. She got as far as the cobra position before she heard the jarring sound of a piece of equipment roar to life. Determined, she gritted her teeth and progressed to downward dog. That's when she heard the men hollering back and forth. Her downward dog turned into a ticked off, defeated child pose instead of a lunge.

"Damn it," she hissed. Her whole day would be out of whack now. "No, positive thoughts," she corrected herself.

Avery knew yoga was out for the day; once her zen vibe flew out the window it was nearly impossible to get it back. Instead, she threw on her shoes, slipped on her holster under a t-shirt, and decided to go investigate the ruckus.

At the end of her driveway she was met by Jesse and a pretty redhead wearing a baby carrier as they walked down the road.

"Morning," Avery said, forcing a friendly expression.

"Morning! Avery, this is my sister, Anna, and her sweet baby boy, Benji." Jesse cooed at the baby.

Recognition flooded through Avery, and she realized this must be Aidan's wife and son. She saw him occasionally in therapy. He's a vet living with PTSD, and an incredible guy who was over the moon for his new family. She realized she'd have to help him find a new therapist, though. If she was going to be running into these folks often, it could get weird.

"Nice to meet you, Anna, Benji" she said, leaning in to take a look at the sweet-faced, carrot-topped little fellow. "He's gorgeous," she said, trailing her finger over his chubby little arm.

"Thank you. Nice to meet you, Dr. O'Gara." Anna smiled.

"Avery, please." She could see that Anna was unsure whether to mention Aidan, and she was grateful that she didn't. Avery had learned the value of privacy early in life. She'd grown more guarded every time her mother let another near-stranger move into her home. She pulled herself back, unwilling to waste another second thinking about her adolescence. With a jolt she realized that Jesse had been speaking to her. "I'm sorry, what?"

Jesse wrinkled her brow in curiosity and repeated her question. "We're off to check out Jake's progress. Did you know he bought the land next to yours?"

Avery's eyes went round. "Jake? The guy I met at your house the other day? The one with the hair?"

Jesse cackled in response. "Yes, the one with the hair. Gorgeous, huh?" she said, waggling her eyebrows at Avery.

A snort erupted before Avery could stop it. "Yeah, but not for me," she said, heading off any misunderstanding.

Anna's eyebrows snapped up to her hairline. "No? Seeing someone?"

Avery knew she'd wandered into a trap with no escape. These ladies would be like a bulldog with a pork chop, not letting go till they had their answer. Her heart rate kicked up and she felt her palms get sweaty. "No," she said with a nervous smile. She decided to go with the truth. "Just no time for that. My practice keeps me busy and honestly, my bullshit tolerance is at a record low right now."

Both ladies laughed. "You're right. I like her, too," Anna said, nudging Jesse with her elbow.

"How do you feel about wine?" Jesse asked Avery.

Surprised by the question, Avery glanced down at her watch. "What? It's seven in the morning..."

"Not now, later. We're grilling out and having a bonfire tonight. There will be plenty of food and drinks, and you're more than welcome to come over. Should be a nice night for it," Jesse answered, looking around at the gorgeous day.

Avery didn't have anything else planned. Why not step out of the box a little? "Sure, what can I bring?"

"Not a thing. We usually have enough food to feed an army," Anna answered. They were quickly climbing the newly poured gravel driveway of Jake's property. She recognized the crew of men from Jesse's house. The usual suspects were standing near what was clearly going to be a basement. "Look at them. Scratching, spitting, and telling lies, no doubt."

Avery sidled up to Jake, feeling Jesse and Anna's eyes boring into her back. "Hello, neighbor," she said with a smile. "Welcome to the neighborhood."

"Hey, Avery, right?" he answered, a glint in his eyes that made Avery sure there wasn't a chance in hell he was unsure of her name. "Sorry about the noise. I know it's early."

"Yeah, you pretty much killed my yoga mojo this morning, but this won't take long, right? A few weeks?"

"Yoga?" He turned and yelled in the direction of a man driving an excavator. "Hey, Mark, can we change the deck to face that way?" he yelled, pointing toward Avery's property. Mark had on his headphones and pointed, gesturing that he couldn't hear. Jake laughed and swung his hand in the air, dismissing Mark.

"Nice," Avery answered sarcastically, adding an eyeroll to boot.

"It'll be more than a few weeks. Four to six months, I think," he said with a wince.

Avery suppressed her groan and forced herself to adapt to the idea of doing yoga in her living room instead of the deck, something she did in the winter. She could deal; she wasn't giving it up.

Curiosity got the best of her as she peered around the piles of dirt. "What kind of house are you building?"

"One that's quiet. Well, except for the building part," he replied. "I'm currently living with my mother and she talks non-stop."

"Ah, your mom, huh?" Avery said, in an all-knowing, that's-what's-wrong-with-him voice. She knew there had to have been something pretty wrong with this guy. He was hot, but he was surely coming up on forty. Talk about a warning sign.

He stepped closer to her and bent his head down toward hers. In a sexy voice he said, "Yeah, I live with my mom. I have this really great apartment in her basement. Want to come over and see it?" He cocked his head until he was looking her in the eye despite the drastic height difference. She didn't miss a detail about his face. His dark hair swept his eyebrows, his green eyes were rimmed with long, dark lashes.

Still, her eyes bugged out and she looked at him like he had sprouted a unicorn horn. "Are you serious right now?"

Jake threw his head back and laughed, drawing the attention of the rest of the people watching the excavator dig out the walk-out basement.

"Just until the house is built, if I can deal with it that long," he said, his voice lowered. "I just moved down from Chicago." He took a few steps toward the others, and Avery followed. "The house I had put an offer down on before moving fell through; the seller changed their mind about selling. I had to crash somewhere since I was due to start my job. I couldn't find a decent apartment, and mom was happy to have the company," he explained. "Oh, and I don't live in her basement. I have my childhood bedroom back. Full-size bed included," he said with a grin and threw his hand up to emphasize his height. "Now do you want to come over?" he asked, leaning his head toward hers.

"Gross, no," Avery answered, her cheeks pinking up despite herself.

"That's a shame," he said, shaking his head. He put his hand on her shoulder and Avery felt a shiver build at her neck and trail down her spine. "Maybe some other time," Jake said with a wink and he turned to talk with Levi and Aidan.

Avery couldn't bring herself to make eye contact with Jesse and Anna, whom she knew wouldn't have missed that shiver, so she feigned interest in watching the machinery move massive amounts of dirt. Finally, she turned and walked over to the ladies.

"Well, I'm heading back home. Thanks for the invitation tonight. What time should I come over?"

"Six-ish sound good?" Jesse asked.

"Sounds good to me."

"Wear your stretchy pants. Jesse's a heck of a cook," Anna said.

"Stretchy pants. Got it," Avery answered. She wasn't much for socializing, but even she had to admit these ladies were nice. She threw her hand up at the guys and headed back down the hill. She didn't want to admit it to herself, but she was already feeling nervous butterflies wondering if Jake was going to be there tonight. Avery growled at herself. What was the point of thinking about him and his eyes? She wasn't going anywhere near that guy. He did make for some nice eye candy though, she conceded.

WHEN SHE MADE it back to her place she fed and watered Rocky and picked up her phone. She had twenty missed calls from an unknown number and no messages. She checked her office voicemail and had several hang ups there too, but no messages. They were all within the last ten minutes or so; she could see the timestamp on each call. A cloud of unease settled over her. The persistence of the caller brought back an unsettling memory.

Instinctively, Avery went to make sure that the doors were locked after tucking her phone in her pocket. She was fairly careful about that at all times, she was a woman living alone, after all. That, and her small stature accounted for her fondness for guns as well. She was raised in a house where sketchy men came in and out frequently.

Avery had been around ten years old when her mother left her alone in the house for a few hours while she went down to the corner bar. She remembered making her own peanut butter and jelly sandwich for dinner and watching cartoons. Her cartoon had been interrupted by a pounding at the front door. Her mother had told her not to answer the door no matter what, so she didn't. Instead, she ran and hid in her bedroom closet. The pounding seemed to go on forever until she heard the door open. Her mother had made it home again, and the man was yelling as he followed her from the front door to her mother's bedroom. The door slammed shut and didn't open again for a long while.

Once the man had left, Avery tried to go to her mother for comfort, but she was snoring in her bed. After all the years, she still remembered locking the doors and turning out the lights and putting herself to bed. She'd been scared out of her mind from the incessant noise of the knocking and screaming and never got the comfort she so badly needed.

Avery recognized now that her sense of self-preservation and protection was in polar contrast to her mother's capacity for codependency. Relieved that the front and back doors were locked, next she checked the garage. Everything looked fine. Avery stepped out to the deck with a cup of coffee, determined to take back some peace, and saw muddy footprints on the mat, trailing down her steps. Goosebumps rose on her skin and her stomach flip-flopped. She drew her weapon, snapped a quick picture with her phone, and re-entered her house. Forcing herself to breathe evenly, Avery locked the door behind her and checked every single room, closet, shower, and under each bed. The house was clear. She checked the garage again, her Range Rover was empty.

Whoever it was, they were gone. She put her gun back in the holster and felt the tears well up. Her hands shook and she let the fear surge over her. The sooner she gave into it, the sooner it would be gone. She sat on the couch and had a good, purging cry. Flashbacks washed over her from the worst incident in her youth.

Suddenly, she was a teenager again, poor as dirt and sleeping in a tiny bedroom with a locked door. She'd heard the lock click open and when that shadow passed through her doorway, her trust in men was forever shattered. Avery had run away that night, escaping to her grandmother's house. Her mother had never even bothered to come for her, and both she and her grandmother were relieved. With the love and support she found there, she was able to thrive. There were so many repercussions that went hand in hand with that night. Sometimes it felt like Avery had clawed her way out of a suffocating cobweb only to be sucked right back into it at random times. Something as innocuous as a smell, a sound, or even a shadow in the corner of the room at night could throw her right back into that night, despite being in her late thirties.

Once she had recovered from her crying jag, Avery picked herself up by her bootstraps.

Within the hour she had caught up on her chores and started laundry. Finally, she forced herself to make the call to order a home security system.

"What do you mean it will be a month before you can install it?" she said into the phone.

"Ma'am, the system you're wanting is back-ordered, and it won't be available until then," a bored-sounding man explained.

"But the point of ordering a home security system is to get it in place and feel more secure, correct?"

"You're welcome to choose a less sophisticated option. If you go down to the next package, we can get it there next week."

"Forget it. I'll call your competitor. I'll see if they can give me what I want in a reasonable amount of time," Avery said, wincing at the meanness in her voice. It wasn't fair to take her temper out on this poor guy. The system she wanted was out of stock. He wasn't the one leaving muddy boot prints outside her door. Avery exhaled. "Sir, I'm sorry I was so short tempered. Thank you for your time," she said, and then hung up.

Within thirty minutes Avery had contacted another company and had an appointment scheduled for installation within two days. The second company was more expensive than the first, but at this point she was ready to have peace of mind and wanted to put the experience behind her. She was well versed in both her attributes and flaws, and severe impatience was definitely riding high on her list of flaws.

She drummed her fingers on the counter and realized she had time to squeeze in a manicure and pedicure before the cookout tonight. She also wanted to hit the liquor store to at least have a bottle or two of wine to offer up to her hosts. Avery double checked that all doors were locked, and slipped out the door. As she drove into town she tried to convince herself that this episode was a one-time thing. Avery wasn't willing to let her sense of safety and security crack wide open.

five

JAKE WATCHED HIS FAMILY SCURRY AROUND like ants as they prepared for the get-together at Jesse and Levi's ramshackle house. The place was in a general state of chaos, but the bathrooms were functioning and kitchen had been roughed in, with a sink in working order. Plywood had been placed as makeshift countertops, and a few boards across sawhorses were being laden with food. His cousin Jesse was the same fireball he remembered as a kid. Jesse had a red bandana wrapped around her head like a headband with her big, curly hair in a poofy ponytail. He heard her complaining earlier about humidity making her hair bigger. Jake wasn't sure how that could happen at this point. Anna was rocking Benji, looking as content as a cat who's got the cream. He wasn't sure the kid had ever been put down, and he happened to think that was awesome. Jake never did understand that crap about babies being spoiled anyway. Aidan, Anna's husband, roughhoused with Jesse and Levi's boys, four total, while Levi's daughter joined Jesse in the bossing of the menfolk.

From what Ruthie had explained, Levi's wife had died a few years ago, leaving him to raise their twins with the help of his parents. His first wife's family visited when they could, and were down this weekend. Jesse's mother, Eadie, and his own mom were in hog heaven, alternating between watching the kids play and helping cook the meal. Jake marveled at how well everyone seemed to get along. Even Aidan's parents, sister, and family were folded into the mix. Levi manned the grill with Aidan's brother-in-law, Evan, one of the few people in this circus that Jake hadn't met yet. He walked up to the men and offered his hand.

"Hey, I'm Jake," he said with a smile.

"Ah, the prodigal cousin, come home to roost," Evan said with a grin. "Nice to meet you. I'm Sorcha's husband, Evan."

"Aren't you the one who broke his femur?" Jake said with a glance at Evan's leg.

"Yeah, mining accident. Finally got the damned cast off a few months ago. That was torture," he said.

"Torture. That's a good word for it. For all of us," a bright-eyed redhead chimed in, as she handed Levi a platter of burgers to grill.

"Ah, you must be Sorcha," Jake said. "Nice to meet you."

"Nice to meet you, too, Jake. How's the house coming?"

she asked, wrapping her free hand around the shoulders of a sweet little girl, probably no more than three years old. Jake's heart tugged, thinking of the little boy he had handed over to the social worker at the hospital. He couldn't help but wonder what happened to the little guy, trying to push the thought from his mind.

He saw Sorcha tilt her head slightly and wondered if the shadow of his thoughts had passed over his face. "The house? We got the basement dug today. Well, the crew did. I watched," he said with a shrug, feeling stupid and caught off guard. Jake typically felt like he had brick walls sealed around his deepest thoughts, but he had let himself relax around this group. He made a mental note to start building those walls back up. He didn't need a single person to recognize the sadness he carried in his heart.

"Sounds like a good start. What kind of house are you building?" she asked, her gaze probing a little deeper than he felt comfortable with. He started explaining the contemporary design when that hot, little Avery hopped out of her Range Rover and started walking toward them.

"It's basically a shoe box made of mostly windows," he said, suddenly feeling a little self-conscious.

"Shoe box made of windows?" Avery asked. "Is that the monstrosity I'm going to be living next door to now?" She punctuated her question with a faux eyeroll.

"Yes, ma'am. That would be the one," Jake answered with a ready grin, thankful for the distraction. "Nothing too big, just big enough for me. Great views from the hilltop. I can't wait for it to be done already."

Ruthie sidled up to the group. "Don't be in a rush, kid, I'm glad to finally have you home! And without that hateful shrew of a wife," she said with a look of horror on her face.

"Mom," Jake said in an exasperated tone.

"What? She was awful." Ruthie looked around the group until her eyes lit on Avery. "Well hello, dear. I'm Ruthie."

"Hi, Ruthie, I'm Avery. Nice to meet you," Avery said, already in love with the little lady. She glanced between Jake and his mother, and the idea that someone so little could make someone so big was nearly impossible to understand.

"You're a shrink, right?" Ruthie asked, Jake not missing Aidan's shoulders jerk upward toward his ears.

"Eh, yes, but I prefer the term therapist or psychiatrist," Avery said kindly.

"Fine, fine, everyone with their fancy labels now," Ruthie mumbled under her breath. "Nice to meet you anyway, kid. Come grab a drink," the little woman said, hooking her arm through Avery's. "Oh look! You brought the good stuff!"

Avery smiled at the group and let Ruthie lead her toward the house. She glanced back at Jake, and something electric passed between them. She was jerked out of the moment by her tour guide. "The place looks like it's shot to shit right now, but it's going to be amazing," Ruthie said, yammering away about bedrooms and open concepts.

Jake looked down at the ground, feeling like all the air had been sucked out of his lungs. There was something about her sharp gaze that entranced him. It was like she could cut right through the bullcrap and see right into a person's soul. He wondered what those blue eyes would look like filled with passion. Avery's body was curvy and lush, and he wanted to feel it against his. He wanted to fist his hands in her hair and taste the softness of her lips.

"Relax, buddy. It'll be fine. The doc is pretty hot, huh?" Levi said with a laugh, clapping his hand on Jake's shoulder.

Jake nodded, unsure of exactly how to answer. He agreed, she was hot alright, but he wasn't interested in pursuing her for anything more than a night of fun. The way the people in this group paired off and reproduced, he was scared to even comment for fear he'd be married within a month.

AVERY WAS GETTING the grand tour from Jesse, who had rescued her from Ruthie's relentless questions. She tried desperately to focus her attention on where the new walls and closets would go, but her brain was buzzing from the look Jake had given her. She'd always had a thing for tall men, and damn it, he fit the bill. Her fingers itched to tangle in his hair and feel those arms wrapped around hers. Each time she'd seen him he'd looked a little different. Clean cut in the morning, but by evening his scruff had grown on his face. She was just envisioning the feel of him against her skin when she was jerked from her reverie by her phone.

"I'm sorry, Jesse. This stupid phone keeps going off, can you please excuse me for a minute?"

"Sure, sure, go ahead!" Jesse said, fanning her hands at Avery. Jesse had liked her right out of the gate, but Avery was going to have to learn to relax if she was going to hang with their group. Except for her insane planning skills, Jesse had learned to roll with life, something you had to do to enjoy parenting so many kids. As a whole, the family was pretty relaxed and easy going. Most of the members of their family had weathered more than their share of hard times, which seemed to ease them into the mindset of taking life one day at a time.

Jesse caught Avery's expression out of the corner of her eye and watched as the blood drained from her face. Avery looked at Jesse in horror, and Jesse rushed across the room to wrap her arms around her new friend.

"Here, sit down," she said before dashing to the door. "Levi! Come quick!" she hollered, not sure what was happening but knowing she'd feel better with him by her side. Levi thundered up the stairs with others close on his heels.

Avery held out her phone so that Jesse could see the pictures that were being sent to her phone, causing all the alert sounds.

"These are pictures, of the inside of my house," she said, her hands shaking so hard Jesse could barely focus on the photos. "Someone's been inside my house," Avery clarified.

Jesse looked from Levi to Jake, eyes wide.

"I'll call it in," Jake said, pulling his phone to his ear. He was off-duty and would head right over, but he wanted someone else there in case the douche bag was still inside her house. He knew he'd need a witness there if he got his hands on whoever did this.

"Avery, can you read me the number the pictures are sent from?" he asked, crouching down beside her. He gave the number to whomever he was speaking, along with Avery's address and let them know he'd be on the premises momentarily. Once he disconnected the call he stood and offered his hand to Avery to help her up.

"I'm going to head over. Anything else I need to know? Any alarm codes or anything?"

"No, I called a company today, but I don't have one in place. I called them after I saw the boot prints at the backdoor."

All eyes turned on Avery then. "I didn't know what else to do. Earlier this morning after I had been to your property I saw a pair of muddy boot prints at the backdoor. I checked the entire house and didn't find anyone. I called to order an alarm system, but the one I wanted is out of stock. I called another company, and they'll be at my house in two days to install it." She felt defensive, as if she had done something wrong by not having an alarm system already.

"I've never run into this before. I'm not exactly sure what to do!" Avery said in a trembling voice. Her feelings started to shift from fear to a burning fury. *How dare someone make her feel vulnerable like this!* she screamed to herself. Her inner demon started raising its head. Avery had zero tolerance for feeling like a target. Her skin crawled, and in the back of her mind she heard the snick of the door unlocking when she was fifteen. She saw her mother's louse of a boyfriend standing over her bed while she tried to figure out what to do. She smelled the odor of whiskey permeating the air and wanted to vomit from the memory of the stench.

Jake put a hand on Avery's shoulder and she jumped like she was shot. "It's okay, we'll get the house cleared. You'll want to go ahead and head down to the station so you can fill out a report and give them a copy of the pictures. One of us can take you," Jake said, then searched the room for an answering nod. "Can I see the pictures, Avery?" he asked, holding his hand out for her phone.

He thumbed through the pictures and noticed the sunset through the windows. He didn't have the heart to tell her that whomever sent the pictures was probably in her house right now. Just then, he heard a cruiser with sirens blaring fly down the road and he handed her back her phone. "Okay, I'm going. Avery, give me your number, I'll let you know what we find out."

She gave him her number and accepted the hot drink Eadie pressed to her hand.

"Here, honey, here's some coffee," the older woman said, her kind smile a balm to Avery's nervous heart.

"Thank you, Eadie. I'll bring back the mug," she said, looking at Jesse, who nodded in response.

"I can drive your car to the station, sweetie. Jake can bring you home after. You can stay with us tonight," Ruthie fussed. Avery was in a fog and didn't know where the heck she would be staying, but she knew there was no way she was setting foot back in her place till she knew what was going on. Her grandma had been gone for years and she didn't talk to her useless mother. Other than Cade, who lived hours away in St. Louis, she didn't really have any friends she could turn to. His friendship had run the gamut from boyfriend, traveling companion, to occasional hookup and friend. It wasn't so much the crash on the couch type of relationship anyway, though Avery doubted he'd mind. There were hotels in town, but none that she'd willingly stay in. She wasn't the type to easily accept help, but Ruthie was offering and Avery was uncharacteristically terrified.

She nodded her head at the older woman. "Thank you, Ruthie. I appreciate it."

Jesse handed Avery her purse on their walk to the Range Rover, and Ruthie hopped up like she'd been born to drive the fancy vehicle. Avery's hands were still shaking and she couldn't stand to touch her phone, as it if were the offensive object rather than the freak that had sent her the pictures. Even though Avery had liked Ruthie from the moment she met her, she found herself wishing Jesse had come along as well because her presence would have helped somewhat to calm her.

Ruthie was quiet on the short drive into town until they were close to parking.

"This is just the kind of thing that terrifies me about Mallory being alone in her house," she said quietly.

"Who's Mallory?"

"My daughter. She and Jake moved to Chicago years ago. I haven't been able to talk her into moving back yet, but I do my best," she said with a grin. "Let's go, hon."

She walked Avery in and greeted the officers and staff that she saw by name. Jake might be new to the department, but Ruthie was well known in the little town. After she saw her settled in, Ruthie left in Avery's vehicle. With each minute that ticked by, Avery was a little less sure about her plans for the night. At this point it was too late to change them, she just had to hope Jake actually showed up.

Her worries were unfounded. Detective Jones, the man assigned to her break-in, left the room and Jake and another officer stepped in.

"The phone number belongs to a burner phone, so we don't know yet who sent the pictures," the officer said. "We did take some prints, but that's only helpful if whomever it is is registered in the system from a previous crime and the prints aren't a match to your own. We'll have them processed and will let you know as soon as we know anything."

Avery's shoulders sagged at the lack of definitive news. "Whoever it was was in your house while you were at Jesse's, Avery. I don't think you should go back there until an alarm system can be put into place," Jake said. "Do you have someplace you can sleep tonight?"

"Um, well, your mom invited me to her house - your house - for the night," she answered, wishing she had any other place to stay.

The other officer's face colored, and she saw Jake give

him a look that dared him to so much as smile over it. "Okay then. Let's get you home. Joe, is there anything else she needs to sign or fill out?"

"Let me check," Joe answered, stepping out to quickly confer with the detective. "No, we're done here, Marcovic."

Jake walked Avery to the door, fighting his urge to wrap a protective arm around her shoulders. She barely came up to his shoulder, and she was such a little thing. It made him sick to think some pervert was trying to scare her, or worse, hurt her. He opened his truck door and held it as Avery hoisted herself into it. The ten miles to his mother's house had never in his life seemed like such a long drive. Jake wasn't a talkative man by any stretch, but his fear for Avery seemed to lock up all his words. She was absolutely no help in that department, choosing instead to stare blankly out into the night.

As he pulled into the drive and killed the engine, she jumped, jerking back into the present. "I don't do scared very well," she said in quiet voice. "It makes me really angry to have someone make me feel vulnerable on my own turf."

"I get that in more ways than you can imagine," he said, giving her hand a quick squeeze. "Let's get you inside before my mom has a cow. She keeps a spotless house, but I bet you dollars to doughnuts she's cleaned from top to bottom all over again since she's having a guest."

Avery couldn't help but smile. She was happy to have wandered into this big, friendly family. She'd been in this town for around ten years, and it had been bone-achingly lonely at times. Avery detested small talk, which didn't help her out in the friend-making department. Also, she had quickly figured out that if a person wasn't born and raised in the area, they weren't readily welcomed into any of the social groups. Most of the time it didn't bother her. Most of the time.

Ruthie met them at the door. Jake could tell by the smell of Pinesol wafting through the air that he had been right. He exchanged a knowing glance with Avery and knew she was on to Ruthie as well.

"Come in you two. How are you doing, honey?" she asked, taking Avery's purse. "Can I get you some tea?"

"I'd love some, thanks." Avery nodded.

"Good. Jake, I put some clean sheets on your bed, go show Avery up to your room, please. You're stuck on the couch tonight, Son, unless you want to sleep in Mallory's room."

Avery sucked in a breath. "Oh no! I don't want to displace you. I can sleep on the couch for the night. I probably won't even sleep tonight to be honest."

"Nonsense. The couch is hard as a rock. He's tough. He can take it," Ruthie said with a light swat to Jake's back.

"I'm tough, I can take it," he mock-whispered to Avery. "Come on, it's impossible to win an argument with this one. Might as well relent and save your breath."

"Heard that!" Ruthie called from the kitchen.

Avery looked miserable to have them making a fuss over her. "If you're sure..."

"We're sure. Now scoot. I'll have the tea ready in no time," Ruthie hollered.

Jake led Avery up the staircase where the bedrooms were. He hadn't been kidding--every surface she could see was immaculate. Avery was no slouch in the cleaning department, it sort of went with her slightly neurotic rebellion against being like her mother, but she didn't hold a candle to Ruthie.

"This is your room for the evening," he said with a grand sweep of his hand. "See, aren't you glad I don't really sleep in the basement?"

Avery groaned. "You remember that, huh?"

A sultry smile appeared on his gorgeous face. "I remember everything. Mind like a steel trap," he said, tapping his temple with his finger.

"Full-size bed, huh?" she said, eyeballing the room that seemed too small to accommodate a man of his size. "How in the world do you sleep in that thing?"

"Not easily." He sighed. "Like I said, this was not part of the plan, but," he shrugged, "I'm thankful to have it." He sat down on the edge of the bed. "Mom is happy to have me home, and I've been able to help her quite a bit with projects since I've been here. I seem to be working mostly nights for now, so I pull the shades and make the best of it."

Avery nodded in response. She couldn't imagine a time when she had felt more awkward than she felt at that moment. "Well, thanks for, uh, letting me stay here. I mean, I know it wasn't your idea, but I'm thankful to have someplace safe to be for the night."

Jake rose and put his hands on her shoulders and gave them a squeeze. "I'm glad you're here." He lingered for a second too long and Avery felt her cheeks start to burn. "Here, let me get you something to change into," he said, digging around in his chest of drawers. He pulled out a pair of sweatpants and a gray t-shirt. Unfolded, the sweatpants came practically to her chest and they both laughed quietly.

"Okay, maybe that won't work," he said quietly. "How about this?" he asked, holding his t-shirt up for her. It came to her knees and her head dropped in defeat.

"It'll be great, thanks."

"One more thing," he said, causing her heart to nearly stop in her chest. "These are a must, she keeps the house like a meat locker at night." His eyes crinkled in the corners in a kind smile as he tossed her a pair of socks that would no doubt reach her knees.

"Again, thank you, this is more than thoughtful."

"Glad to help. I'm going to grab a shower then head for the couch," he said, gathering a change of clothes for himself and snagging one of the pillows from his bed. "Holler if you need anything, okay?"

"Okay," she said, waiting a beat before she followed him out of the room. She had every intention of thanking Ruthie profusely, chugging her tea, and returning to bed. Her adrenaline had buzzed through her system and she could feel herself starting to sag. She might just sleep after all.

A FEW HOURS LATER, Avery was slowly dragged awake by an annoying sound. Her phone was buzzing against the bedside table. She had switched it to mute but had left the vibration setting on. Another text came through as she blinked herself awake and Avery felt her heart stop.

You aren't home. Who are you with?
AVERY, WHO ARE YOU WITH?

Bile rose in her throat and she barely made it to the bathroom across the hall before she lost the meager contents of her stomach. She borrowed some toothpaste and freshened up as much as possible with cold water on her face. When she swung the door open, Jake was standing in the hallway, which made her jump.

"Jesus, Jake, you scared me," she hissed, trying not to wake Ruthie.

"Are you okay? I heard you run to the bathroom," he asked, his eyes searching hers.

Avery sagged against the doorframe of the bathroom. "I got another message."

"Let me see," he said, following her into his bedroom with his hand outstretched for the phone. "Son of a bitch," he said quietly, causing Avery's blood to chill. She was glad to be on Jake's side instead of against him. The shift in his muscles and the tone of his voice could be positively frightening.

He picked up his phone and called the department.

He shared the information and asked to be transferred to Detective Jones' voicemail. Beyond that, there wasn't much else that could be done right away.

"They're sending two patrolmen out to see if the person is still around. I'm so sorry, Avery."

She took her phone back and switched it off. She couldn't handle any more messages tonight. Tears welled up in her eyes and she laid back against the bed.

"Mind if I just sit in here for a while?" Jake asked, thankful that she nodded her consent. Avery slipped under the covers and Jake sat on top of them, not wanting to spook her or make her uncomfortable.

Avery flicked off the light and closed her eyes, willing her tears to stop. He heard her sniffing quietly and leaned over her, grabbing a tissue from the box on the far night stand. When she took it, her fingertips grazed his. The heat he felt from that small touch burned up his hand and arm like a jolt of electricity. He stilled his movement and paused there, wishing he could take her in his arms and comfort her like he wanted so badly to do. She looked small and vulnerable and he wanted to wrap himself around her and make her feel safe.

When the dawn broke through the space between the wall and the room darkening shade, Avery felt warmth like a heater snug against her back and hips. Jake was spooning her with his arm draped across her breasts. She had snuggled her arms around his, pinning him in place while his head nestled above hers. The door was open and Ruthie had no doubt seen the whole thing when she passed by to go downstairs. By the level of light seeping through the shade it was definitely not early morning.

The smell of bacon and coffee drifted up the stairs, confirming her suspicion. *Great*, Avery thought, *now she's going to think I'm a psycho magnet. And an easy one at that.* The internal comments took Avery by surprise, she wasn't typically one to care what other people thought. But, she argued with herself, these were good people that welcomed her into the fold, so to speak. They didn't know her from Eve, but they knew she was in trouble and they helped. It was okay to care about people, she reminded herself.

After allowing one more minute to pass tucked into his arms, Avery tried to maneuver away from Jake as gently as possible. As soon as she started to stir, he pulled her back close to his body.

"Mmm," he murmured against her hair. Avery nearly gasped when she felt the length of arousal pressing against her from behind.

Heat burned through her body as her mind warred with what to do with that sensation. "Jake… Jake. Wake up," she said, scooting farther away from him as she turned back to the bed.

His eyes snapped open in sleepy surprise and he looked utterly confused. "Avery?"

She opened her eyes widely and nodded, waiting for him

to catch up and explain why he was wrapped around her like the world's sexiest body pillow.

He grinned. "Ah. I must've fallen asleep. The bed is little, but it's way more comfortable than the couch." He raked his hand through his hair and revealed nicely sculpted arms.

Avery felt her mouth go dry at the sight of him all warm and rumpled from sleep. She wondered exactly what she looked like. Mornings weren't really her thing. The whole "I woke up like this" movement was less sexy than comical when it involved hair sticking up all over her head. She patted her hair and said a prayer for makeup that wasn't smeared all over her face as she plucked a tissue from the box on the nightstand.

"How do we explain this to your mother?" she hissed.

"Well, I'll tell her this way. When a man and a woman really like each other…"

"Jake!" she whispered.

"I'll tell her the truth. You got another creepy message, I sat up with you for a bit, and I fell asleep."

She looked him dead in the eye. "And she'll buy that?"

He looked a little exasperated. "I'm on top of the covers, Avery. Plus, we're both plenty old enough to get naked together, if we wanted to anyway."

Avery shut her eyes and let that comment sink in for a second. The combination of his voice, gruff with sleep, and his body so close to hers seemed to fog her brain. Fine. He was right. She was thirty-seven years old. He seemed to be a few years older. But, this was his mother's house and she was a guest. Guests don't mind-bang their host's son, even if they are a sexy, smart-mouthed cop.

She piled her hair in a bun and blushed when his eyes drifted to her breasts covered in his soft t-shirt. "Fine. Can you go down first and explain? I'll get dressed real quick."

"Yeah, just give me a minute to... settle down," he said with a crooked grin. "It'll go away on its own, but there's a faster, more fun way to handle it if you're interested."

Before she could stop herself, Avery's eyes dipped down and took in the view. "My God," she said quietly, mostly in annoyance at him. Mostly.

"Suit yourself," he said. Jake stood and turned to the closet, robbing Avery of a view she would tuck away into her memory for a long while. He grabbed a sweatshirt out of his closet. Give me a few minutes to relax. I'll go set her mind at ease that you didn't take advantage of her son."

"You're gross," she whispered.

"You're not," he replied, dropping a kiss to the top of her head. "Your hair is a trainwreck, though," Jake said with a chuckle.

17

Six

JAKE HAD HEARD BACK FROM DETECTIVE Jones early in the morning and filled Avery and Ruthie in over breakfast. Two patrolmen had gone to Avery's house and looked around after the call had come in about the message, but they didn't find anything suspicious. The best guess at this point is that whomever broke into Avery's house was lurking in the woods.

The thought of some weirdo watching her completely unnerved Avery, but she couldn't just avoid her responsibilities. She had a business to run and patients to care for; they depended on her. She needed to get her things and get to her office. "I've got to get to work soon."

Jake watched the wheels spinning in Avery's eyes. "I'd like to go with you and check the house if you don't mind,"

Jake said. For a half-second Avery was tempted to dismiss his offer. She already felt like she had imposed on their generosity, but the fear in her belly was louder than her pride.

"That would be great, thank you," she said with a smile. She saw Ruthie's face light up and a sense of alarm sounded. All she needed was this sweet lady to start making plans. "I need to grab some clothes and get to my office. I'm not seeing anyone today, but I need to move some appointments around before ten. I've got a security company coming early tomorrow morning to install a system."

Jake nodded. "I'm glad to hear that. I'm going to be over at Jesse and Levi's for a little bit this morning to help haul some of the stuff we've torn out to the burn pile, so I'm going that way anyway."

Ruthie popped up and started clearing away dishes. "I'm heading over to Eadie's house. We're in charge of Harry, Oscar, and Benji today, and I can't wait!"

Avery's eyes bugged out. "Good Lord, you're a prodigious bunch, aren't you? Do you have an army of kids I haven't heard about yet?" she directed at Jake.

He choked on the mouthful of coffee he was trying to swallow when Ruthie answered matter-of-factly. "Nope, no kids here," she said with a slap on Jake's shoulder. "Maybe he shoots blanks, who knows?" she said with a shrug. Stunned into momentary silence, Avery chose to quickly clear her plate. Placing the dishes in the dishwasher, she turned to find Jake's smiling eyes trained on her face.

"Aren't you glad you asked," he said quietly with a grin,

brushing her arm with his as he placed his dishes in the sink. Avery felt heat pass from her arm all the way down her body. She wanted to deny how he set every nerve ending of hers on fire, but she was a realist. Fine. She was attracted to Jake. He was sexy as hell and looked like the kind of man strong enough to actually pick her up and nail her against a wall like in the movies. She swallowed an involuntary moan. His body completely turned her on. Jake, however, lived with his mother, came with a crazy and loud, albeit awesome, family, and had his own baggage.

It's not like you want to marry him, though… Avery felt her cheeks flame up as the little devil on her shoulder whispered in her ear. Desperate for a distraction, she turned to Ruthie.

"Thank you so much for taking me in last night. I appreciate it," Avery gushed.

"Absolutely, dear. You're welcome here," Ruthie said with a smile. "By the way, Benji is Anna's baby, I'm sure you remember. Harry is Anna's Standard Poodle and Oscar is Jesse's Great Dane. We're Methodist, not Catholic, so you don't have to be scared, honey."

Avery's eyes darted to Jake in time to see him roll his eyes to the ceiling. She imagined that happened a lot.

***

AVERY'S HEART HAMMERED in her chest as Jake went first into her house. At his insistence, she waited at the doorway as he cleared every room and waved her in from the door.

He even washed away the muddy footprints, knowing they had been documented. Even though he'd cleaned up the traces of an intruder out here, she knew a mess would await her inside. That fingerprint powder multiplied like rabbits no matter how careful they'd been.

"All clear," he said, angling his body close to hers as he sheathed his weapon. How do you feel about closing all the blinds and curtains for now?" he asked, frowning a little as he watched her.

Something flashed in her eyes and she quickly blinked it away. Jake could tell she was putting up a brave front, but he could see that she was nervous at being back at her home. "I would be completely fine with that," she said, stepping past him as if she'd be burned if they touched. "Actually, I'm probably going to be a big wuss and turn every light on for good measure."

"Makes sense to me," he said. "I'll help."

Avery watched Jake move around her home like he knew it well. *Of course he does*, she realized. He'd been through a few times by now thanks to some crazy person stalking her. Her stomach flipped at the thought of it.

"Are you going to keep your gun on you?" he asked as they stepped into her bedroom.

"Definitely," she said. She crossed to her bedside table and placed her hand on the safe. Jake stepped beside her as she checked that her gun was loaded and pulled the holster from her top drawer.

"This is a first," he said.

"What?" she asked with a frown.

"Well," he said as he stepped a bit closer to her, "I've been in a few bedrooms, and you might be the only the only woman I've known who keeps a gun in her nightstand instead of... other things."

"Oh, that? I have *that* hidden in my closet," she shot back casually, the tone of her voice suddenly sultry.

A big laugh escaped Jake, and Avery realized how much she liked the sound.

"Man, thought I'd get you with that one," he said, placing his hand on her shoulder as he edged passed her in the tight space to look out the window of her bedroom. Her shoulder practically stung from the contact.

"Nah, I'm hard to ruffle. I'm a therapist, for Pete's sake," she said sarcastically.

"Makes sense," he said quietly.

"What does?" she asked quizzically.

He smiled. "Well, you have to admit. You're on the somber side..."

She shrugged with one shoulder. "True. It's just my nature."

Jake nodded, opening her large walk-in closet and examining the attic access panel there. No signs or marks. He looked closer at her closet and saw all the clothes were organized by color. "Organized, aren't we?"

"What? It makes it easy to get dressed in the morning," she said defensively. He raised an eyebrow at her answer. "Fine." She glared. "I'm a bit on the neurotic side when it comes to organization. Everybody has their quirks..."

He nodded in a teasing way. "Right. Have you got a stepladder handy? I'd like to look up here."

"Yeah, give me a sec. Avery trotted off to her pantry and fished out the one she kept there to reach the high shelves.

She awkwardly dragged it down the hallway to her bedroom where Jake was waiting, pushing her bangs back from her forehead. "Here you go."

"Perfect, thanks." He touched his hand to the firearm at his his side. Avery winced as alarm bells clanged in her head. Jake had his gun out when he cleared the house, but she'd forgotten about it. She was totally comfortable with guns, but she was nervous around other people wearing them.

He's an officer, she reminded herself. *He's safe*. She silently reprimanded herself for her skittishness. Avery watched as he placed the gun on the shelf before he moved the attic access panel to the side. With his height, the stepladder put his head at ceiling-height with the opening. Jake braced himself on each side and Avery watched as he used his arms to raise the rest of his body into the attic opening. His t-shirt raised with his shoulders and she saw the sexy v-line of his ab muscles disappearing into the waist of his jeans.

"Oh my God," she murmured, heat pooling in places she desperately tried to ignore.

"Hm? Did you say something?" Jake asked, ducking his head down from the opening.

"No, nothing," Avery said, feigning great interest in the shoe-covered corner of her closet.

"Everything looks good up here from what I can tell,"

Jake said, lowering himself down inch by delicious inch from the attic. A mist of sweat coated Jake's forehead from being in the attic. Spring was developing into a very warm season that left Avery wondering if summer would be unbearable. It would be a sweltering one, for sure.

"That makes me feel better. Thanks for checking. What do I do now? Act like everything's normal?" she asked with a forced smile.

Jake folded up the little stepladder. "I guess so. Can I stay until you're ready to go to your office?"

"Actually, that would be wonderful. Thanks," she answered automatically. Surprised at her response, Avery scolded herself for falling into the 'damsel in distress' role. Truth be told she was more than freaked over the turn of events.

Jake nodded. "Will do. I'll be in the living room snooping," he said with a grin. Avery couldn't help but smile as he left the room. Her life may be going to hell in a handbasket right now, but the view was nice.

She gathered her things and took a quick shower, never quite losing the feeling that she was being watched. Avery was a little insecure knowing there was a man in the house with her while she was naked. *Release the baggage*, she sighed to herself. No matter how much time passed, she wondered if she'd ever get over her anxiety of being completely alone with a man in the house, except for Cade, but that's only because he was her best friend. It certainly didn't bode well for her love life to be so nervous with men. She scoffed to herself at the thought.

Avery admonished herself. She was just fine without a steady man in her life. She finished getting dressed to spend a few hours in her office. She could fake fashionista when she wanted, but left to her own devices, she was typically a hot mess. She dried and tossed her hair into a bun, threw on a pair of shorts and a "proud supporter of messy hair and no makeup" tank and meandered into the living room.

Jake's eyes traveled up the rather short distance of Avery from head to toe. He smiled a huge, wolfish smile and nodded his approval. What Avery didn't know was that Jake's ex, Juliet, was a total glamor-gal and never left the house without the full extent of highlighter powder and fake lashes. Truth be told, Jake was one to appreciate all walks of beauty, high-maintenance to low, however recent experience had sort of embittered him toward the glittery end of the spectrum.

"I'll be down at Levi and Jesse's for a big part of the day. I'm on thirds, but I'll keep my ears peeled and be close by as much as I can. You okay with that?"

"Of course," she answered, feeling a little bent out of shape. She'd been on her own for years and didn't like the feeling of being needy or a pain for Jake, or anyone for that matter.

"Well, guess you're as settled here as I can get you," Jake said, his green eyes betraying the concern he had for her.

"Guess so," Avery answered, her feet leading her to the door, Jake following in her shadow.

"Let me give you my number," Jake said, flipping his

phone out from his pocket. "I'll send you a message so you can save it."

"Got it, thanks," Avery answered. Jake nodded, making his exit toward his vehicle.

"Have a good day," she yelled out, feeling like an awkward teenager as the words left her lips.

"Nice sleeping with you," he answered with a grin. Avery blushed from her head to her toes, which made Jake laugh as he got into his truck.

HE WAS STILL smiling as he backed out of the driveway. It would be a long time before he forgot the sight of her at her backdoor in a white tank and a pair of shorts. Something about the mixture of emotions in her face gave her the look of a woman on the brink. He saw nervousness, desire, and indecision all right there warring for dominance. No matter what defenses he threw up against her, something about her eyes and lips burned right into his soul.

OVER THE LAST few months Jake preferred his female acquaintances to be more the showy type, promising no commitment but lots of fun. Since his marriage had died out, he met his needs with ladies who knew the score - one night stands with no expectations or regrets. Avery was different, though. He'd had no prior attachments to her, but he couldn't shake the feeling that her brand of strange was one that he could get used to over time.

As he drove down the road toward home he felt a little paranoid about leaving her alone. He knew that he had to put in his time at the department and that the detective had considered her place free of threat. He also knew that the way her cheeks flushed pink at the mention of anything stupid he came up with was the most endearing thing he'd ever seen. Truth be told, he'd been trying to embarrass her for two days to see that blush and was only partially successful. The woman was damned near unflappable.

He tried to block out the mental images that assailed him as he drove. Flashes from various crime scenes passed through his mind. He kept picturing Avery being overpowered in her home, of her crying out for him. He pushed all of it deep inside that cold, quiet place where a person put things they don't want to think about. Jake did his best not to touch the contents of that place. He'd seen enough horrible stuff in his occupation to fill it up.

The afternoon passed quickly and his night shift flew by in a whirlwind of routine driving and checking his phone at stop lights for messages from Avery. Thankfully, or regretfully, nothing came through. Jake managed his six-to-six shift without going insane for lack of feedback from her. He'd just met the woman, but he couldn't quite shake the feeling that he wanted to be her protector. The feeling was foreign to Jake because honestly, his experience with Juliet had been so awful he was nearly a woman-hater. There was no small part of him that considered most women to be money-hungry opportunists. Juliet certainly hadn't been after much more than his money.

Jake had spent six years with that woman and had been absolutely crazy about her. Jake had stuck by her side with baited breath for years. He'd taken the "for better or worse" vow to heart and had tended her through good moods and bad, up days and down. He'd been her emotional punching bag through every unsuccessful attempt at starting a family, and born the scars from each heartbreak. She'd done the same for him, so he thought. His love hadn't been enough to stop her from screwing that personal trainer.

Eventually he figured out her obsession with getting in great shape "for him" actually had nothing to do with Jake. He'd reassured Juliet over and over that he loved her, body and soul, but she'd always been chasing some unattainable goal. Finally, Jake checked out and withdrew once he realized the fight was something that couldn't be won. There was a storm brewing within Juliet that Jake's love couldn't calm.

The failure of his marriage weighed heavily on him. He'd grown up with a totally screwed up paradigm of love and marriage in his mind. His experience was that the bride was wholesome and good, and the groom was an unworthy screw-up. Jake did his best to be a good husband, and Juliet's betrayal was a complete shock. He'd given everything he had to that relationship and it still failed. While he wasn't much with words, he did his best in actions. Jake took every available bit of overtime during the years they were trying to start a family.

At first, he was working to sock away money for the extra expense that comes with having a child. Then, when they weren't getting pregnant and Juliet wanted to try fertility treatments, the money was funnelled into that process. It certainly wasn't cheap.

He did his best to be supportive however she'd let him. Beyond the initial appointments where his sperm sample was collected, one of the most awkward moments of his life, she preferred he not go to the appointments. She wouldn't even let him be beside her while she gave herself the shots. When Juliet told him it was because she was ashamed about her inability to conceive it broke his heart. He did his best to reassure her that they'd have a family when the time was right. No matter what words he said, nothing was ever enough. Since she shut him out in person he tried to show his love by financially providing. He'd wanted to be involved in every step, but Juliet wouldn't let him be with her while she'd give herself the injections. She preferred to hide away in the bathroom behind a locked door. She got so freaking moody when she took those shots that he was darned near grateful for the work time away from home. At least he had a job he loved. He was lucky to have that and realized not everyone knew what they wanted to do from the time they were kids.

Yet another night shift behind him, Jake settled into his bed for some shut-eye. He set his alarm so that he'd have time to work over at Jesse's for a few hours before his next shift and his phone buzzed.

"Hello?" he answered with his eyes closed.

"Hey, Jake, it's Avery. I just wanted to thank you again for your hospitality. It was really kind of you and your mother to take me in. Please pass along my thanks to her as well."

"You bet, glad to help. How did the night go?" he asked, his voice rough with sleepiness.

Avery sighed. "Well, I had the place lit up like a lighthouse and dozed on and off with

my gun on the pillow next to mine."

His hand moved from his eyes to muffle the curse he nearly spat out at her. "Be careful with that thing."

"I know." She sighed. "That was stupid. It's just eerie, you know?"

With eyes closed, he nodded. "I do. Is the security company coming over to install the system this afternoon?"

"Yes, early afternoon, thank God. I think that will help a little."

"Hope so. Care if I come by to check it out before I head to work?"

"Sure. I'll be home around four or so," she answered.

Jake smiled. "I'll see you around then." He didn't even try to fight the fantasies that popped in his mind at the thought of being alone with Avery again. It was a good recipe for interesting dreams.

seven

THE CALENDAR WAS FLIPPED OPEN TO the next two weeks' worth of appointments as Avery chewed on the tip of her blue ink pen. Yesterday she'd made her way through the majority of her calls rescheduling standing appointments with the exception of one. Most had taken the news like a champ. Mrs. Fritz, however, had been beside herself at the change. She was highly neurotic and very compulsive about her schedule and was convinced something terrible would happen now that she didn't have her regular appointment. For all the time Avery spent on the phone reassuring Mrs. Fritz, she could have just done the whole therapy appointment by phone and at least made some money for her time.

She dialed the last patient on her list, Anthony Jase.

"Hello?"

"Hello, this is Dr. O'Gara, is this Anthony?"

"Yes, doctor. Are we on for this afternoon?"

"Unfortunately, I need to reschedule. Do you have any time available on Thursday at 2:00 PM, or would you prefer to skip to next week?" Avery pulled the phone from her ear in response to the loud exhale on Anthony's end of the phone.

"I don't understand," he said with an edge to his voice. "I've got a standing appointment each week."

"I apologize for the change, however I'm not available as expected. Would you like to reschedule or reconvene next Tuesday?"

Silence hung in the air as Anthony made his decision. "You going out of town or something?" he asked, an overly personal inquiry as far as Avery was concerned.

She was trying to decide how to respond when he seemed to realize he had overstepped. In a wheedling tone he said, "I'll come in next week. Sorry for overreacting, I'm just used to seeing you on Tuesday."

A feeling of unease passed over her and Avery decided to follow her gut. "Anthony, we have reached a point where we need to dissolve our patient/therapist relationship. I have three names I'd be happy to share with you that take your insurance. I will mail the list to you today."

"Dr. O'Gara, please don't say that. I'm sorry I was hateful about the appointment changing. I'm just, I don't know, overly reliant on my schedule, I guess. Please don't give up on me."

The pleading in his voice did more to turn Avery's stomach than elicit her sympathy. "It's better this way, Mr. Jase. I'll send the list today," Avery said, hanging up the phone. She'd been a therapist for a lot of years and never had she had to eliminate a patient based on a yuck factor. It was her prerogative as a small business owner to continue or discontinue services as she deemed fit. Anthony rubbed her wrong and had for a few months. With all that was going on her patience was wearing thin and honestly, she just didn't have it in her to continue working with him any longer.

Next, Avery had to call Aidan and let him know he needed to contact someone on her referral list. She wasn't comfortable continuing as his doctor now that they were moving in the same social circles. Avery laughed out loud to herself at that thought. She was still getting used the idea of having a social life to consider. She dialed Aidan's number but got voicemail. She left a message for him to be in touch and closed her planner, relieved to have those tasks behind her.

Not excited about hanging out her house alone, Avery did something completely out of character. The phone rang three times before answering.

"Hello?" Jesse answered, sounding winded.

"Hey, this is Avery. I was wondering if you'd like to grab some lunch at…"

"Yes! Wherever you want, just promise no men or kids allowed."

A chuckle erupted from Avery. "You're on. No men or kids allowed."

"Thank goodness. Where do you want to meet?"

"I'm dying for a good hamburger. How about Mountaintop Bar and Grille?"

"Yum, that sounds perfect," Jesse answered. "It's almost lunchtime now, meet you there in fifteen minutes?"

"See you then," Avery answered, proud of herself for stepping outside the box. Her intentions weren't totally unselfish. She was avoiding being home, and she wanted to learn a little more about her new neighbors.

⎯⎯⎯

THE LADIES CHOSE to be seated in the new beer garden area outside the restaurant. The sun was shining down and the weather had taken a warmer turn.

Jesse sipped on her beer and leaned her face back into the sunshine. "This is just what I needed. Thanks for getting me out of the house. I took a day off from work, but so far it has been a total waste."

"Move getting overwhelming?" Avery asked, stirring some sugar into her iced tea.

"Yes, I'm packing and sorting out what we don't need, which is the ultimate way to reinstate interest in long-ignored possessions with the boys. We haven't even been here long and we've still managed to accumulate..." she held her hands in the air, fingers splayed with a wild look in her eye, "so much stuff! I don't even know where it all comes from. The clothes, sure. They are growing at an alarming rate, but the stuff. It's a mess."

Avery smiled despite being unable to relate. She tended toward the minimalist side and donated one item for everything new she brought into her house. It was a trick she figured out long ago when she was in college and limited both on funds and space.

"How are things progressing at the house?" Avery asked, smiling her thanks to the waitress as she served their lunches.

Jesse popped a fry into her mouth as she deliberated on her answer. "It's somewhere between a labor of love and a total shit show."

Tea nearly shot out of Avery's nose. She dabbed her face with her napkin and nodded. "That good, huh?"

"Yeah. The kitchen and bathrooms are coming along, but the rest is a mess. Levi thinks it'll be livable in a little over a month, but I'm not sure I'm buying it. That big pole barn sure is coming in handy. We've got all the supplies stored in there, so at least we're not having to travel back and forth to the home supply store and lumber yard anymore."

"That's good to hear."

"Seriously, we're crammed into my house like ten pounds of poop in a five-pound bag. It's ridiculous," Jesse said, shaking her head. "Thank goodness for our high-capacity washer and dryer, or I'd never survive the laundry. How are you doing? Last night go okay, I guess?"

Avery shrugged. "It went fine. I didn't sleep much,

though. It's incredibly creepy to think some freak was in my house. I hope the cops can figure out who did it."

"Do you have any idea who it is?" Jesse asked between bites of her lunch.

"I'm driving the police crazy by not having an answer. I don't have any sadistic ex-boyfriends. I pretty much keep to myself. I'm a fairly boring person and honestly, I like it that way. I don't understand what is going on," Avery answered.

"That's so scary," Jesse said. "I had someone enter my house uninvited a few times, but at least it was a, um, friend of mine. It unnerved me, though. In my case I had left the door unlocked, a mistake I haven't made since."

A shiver passed over Avery. "I hate feeling like I'm not in control," she admitted. "I'm a bit of a control freak."

"Join the club," Jesse joked. "I drive my family crazy, but it's just who I am."

"To Type A's everywhere," Avery said, holding her glass in the air.

"To Type A's," Jesse echoed, clinking her beer against Avery's tea. "I've got to tackle the kids' closets when I get home to weed out what they've outgrown. What have you got set for the rest of the day?"

Avery looked at her watch. "The security company will be at my place in half an hour, so I'll be dealing with that for the rest of the day. After that, hopefully I'll crash and get some real sleep."

"Poor thing," Jesse said as she gave Avery's arm a squeeze. "We're full to the gills at my house, but my mom would gladly let you stay at her house, or her sister, Ruthie."

Avery felt her cheeks get hot as an image of Jake in bed flashed in her mind. "Ruthie is so kind. And funny."

"She is a wild woman. She has been so good to my mom since we lost my dad. She's helped keep Mom from drawing into herself, I think. She was lost for a while after," Jesse shared.

"I'm sorry to hear about your loss," Avery said quietly.

It was Jesse's turn to shrug. It definitely taught them some important lessons. In answer to Avery's questioning face she said, "Life is terribly short, and it's important to let your friends and family know they are loved."

Avery nodded in acknowledgement. "I'll take that," Avery said when the waitress brought the bill.

"Thanks, I'll leave the tip," Jesse said, fishing in her purse for some cash. "Next time is on me."

"I just hope you'll invite me back out after the circus last time," Avery said, eyes bugged out.

"Hey," she said, swatting Avery on the arm. "We've all had our run-ins with crazy," Jesse said, pushing her chair back under the table.

"Sounds like you have a story I need to hear," Avery said, eyes narrowed with interest.

"Someday," Jesse said with a smile. "Thanks for the lunch date. See you soon, I hope."

"See you soon."

AVERY CHECKED HER watch again. She had plenty of time to make it home before the security company arrived. She took her time winding down the country roads and enjoyed the feel of the breeze against her skin. Her nerves were threatening to take over at the thought of having someone else in her house, but she thought it would help make her at least feel safer.

As she pulled into the driveway, a white service truck pulled in behind. Her stomach lurched until she saw the company logo on the truck. The uniformed installer hopped out and walked over to introduce himself.

"Hello, ma'am, are you Avery O'Gara?"

"Yes," she said, extending her hand. He introduced himself and reviewed the specifications of her order. Once she confirmed that he had it correct, he went to work. Avery followed him around as he explained how the system worked as he fit the windows and doors with sensors. The keypad was installed by both doors, cameras installed on the exterior and in her living room, with a control panel in the garage.

"Ms. O'Gara, if you'll download the app on your phone while I finish up here, I can show you how it works before I go," he said, gratefully accepting the bottle of water she offered.

"That would be great, Rusty. Thanks for all your help." She wished she'd had the foresight to bake cookies or something. The kid wasn't very old, but he was incredibly polite and informative. Avery got the rundown on how to set the alarms, what to do if it went off, and how to control virtually everything from when the lights turned on to lowering the garage door from her phone.

"This is incredible," she said. "Thanks so much for the help."

"Yes, ma'am. Here's the number you call if you have questions," Rusty said, pointing to the service number on the pamphlet. "That should just about do it."

Avery saw him out and drew her first easy breath as she set the alarm after locking the door. She double checked that the door to the deck was locked as well and set off toward her bedroom. She knew just how she was going to spend the next few hours, taking a much-needed nap.

Throwing on an old college t-shirt and pajama shorts, she snuggled under her fluffy white comforter and flicked off the lights as the ceiling fan whirled overhead. The delicious feeling of her extremely tired body giving over to sleep settled over her as a flash of warmth flooded her. A few short hours ago she'd had Jake alone in her room. Avery drifted off to sleep fantasizing about what she'd do to him if she managed to get him in her room again.

eight

AVERY WOKE TO THE SOUND OF HER phone buzzing on her nightstand. A lump of fear rose in her throat as she prayed it would be anyone but whoever had been harassing her. Her chest was flooded with relief when she saw it was Jake's name flashing on her phone, followed by a sudden jerk of shock - it was already four in the afternoon.

"Hello?" she answered as she jumped out of bed and threw the covers back into place on her run to the bathroom.

"Hey, it's me. I'm outside, but the place looks pretty quiet. You home?"

"Yes, give me a few minutes and I'll be at the door," she said.

"Will do," he said, ending the call. A smirk settled over

his face. She sounded flustered, and he kind of liked that. Jake took the time to walk the perimeter of her house. The yard itself was pretty small; the woods encroached on Avery's property on several sides, affording shade and beautiful scenery. As he rounded the steps to the front porch Avery swung the door open.

"Hey, Jake. Come in," she said, holding the door open for him.

"You sounded flustered when you answered. Busy doing something you shouldn't have been doing?" he teased, raising his eyebrows at her.

Avery threw her hands up in mock surrender. "Hey, a woman has needs." As his eyes went wide, she laughed. "You should be so lucky," she answered. "I actually fell asleep. Might've even died for a few hours."

Jake nodded, wrapping an arm around her shoulders. "It's no wonder, you've been through a lot," he said, his breath tickling the hairs on the back of her neck. The contact of his arm and the brush of air sent a shiver down Avery's spine. When he felt it, Jake turned her toward him.

She felt a flush steel over her cheeks as she took him in. "This is the first time I've seen you in your uniform." God help her, she'd always been a sucker for a hot cop. Something about the uniform screamed power, bravery, and capability.

He locked eyes with her and said, "Avery, you feel this too, right?" as he moved his hands to her shoulders.

She nodded, willing herself not to say something rude or stupid. She wanted this to happen. His hands slowly moved from her shoulders down her arms and back up. Avery relished the feel of his work-hardened hands against her naked flesh. One hand moved slowly to the nape of her neck, where the stray curls that had escaped her ponytail gathered. The other moved to the base of her back, pulling her in close. He bent to kiss her, and she rose on her toes to meet him.

She'd kissed many men before, but Jake's lips felt like liquid fire, branding more than her mouth. A mix between firm and soft, he sampled her kiss before moving to that perfect spot beneath her ear and down her neck. His fingers roamed her arms and back as she arched against him. Avery was so carefully guarded much of the time, it felt absolutely glorious to take what she wanted for a change.

Her hands took in the sheer size of his shoulders, feeling turned on by the difference in their stature. She was curvy and petite, and he was her polar opposite, lean and broad. Settling her hands against his biceps, a thrill raced through her body as she imagined him filling her, stretching her body, and touching every inch.

A wanton sound escaped her lips and brought him back to her mouth. Jake hauled her up against him as Avery obliged, wrapping her legs around him. He grunted in approval and carried her through the hallway to her bedroom. His kiss shaped into a grin when he saw her covers tossed haphazardly into place.

"Let's get you back into bed," Jake said as he lowered her onto the mattress.

Rising to her knees she nodded her approval as she helped herself to the buttons on his shirt. Jake took over, quickly working his way down his shirt, pulling it loose and tossing it to the floor. He discarded his gun belt carefully, kicked off his shoes, and stepped out of his pants in a surprisingly graceful manner.

"Your turn," he said, climbing onto the bed, hovering over her. He peeled off her t-shirt slowly. Avery mentally high-fived herself for her lingerie selection this morning. Beneath her shirt and shorts she wore a pink blush colored bra and panty set. The silk caressed her body in a way that made her feel powerful and sexy. Jake's breath left his body in a gust as he took in the sight of her, beneath him on the bed.

"You're even more beautiful than I imagined," he said, grinning wickedly. "And I imagined it, a lot."

Avery smiled at the compliment, letting it soak in. She liked that he'd been thinking of her as she'd thought of him. Late afternoon sunlight shone through the window, cutting a line across the bed. Normally, the space seemed so big, but with Jake there eating up all the extra room, her bed felt cozy and something else. *Homey*, Avery thought. She chafed at the idea. Jake wasn't there to play house, and that wasn't why she was glad to have him in her bed.

She pushed against his chest and enjoyed his surprise as she guided him onto his back and he acquiesced. Heat built inside her skin as she looked down at Jake. His hand reached up to cup her breast, thumb moving against the curve, just grazing her peak, visible through her bra. His other hand settled against her rear, pulling her down to feel his body more than ready for her.

Avery felt the ridge of him against her center, and moved against him there as the pleasure of being touched filled her. She trailed her fingers from his shoulders down and enjoyed the tickle of his chest hair as it narrowed to a trail disappearing under the waist of his boxers. She adjusted, pulling the fabric down. She eyed him happily and flicked her gaze to his smug, self-satisfied smile. A laugh escaped her. Men. So proud of themselves.

She leaned across Jake to pull a condom from her bedside table drawer. Her breasts brushed against him in a teasing way, which proved more of a temptation than he could withstand. He rolled Avery to her back and moaned as he kissed his way from her lips to her belly. Jake's fingers expertly released the clasp of her bra, freeing her from the silky restraints. Kneeling between her legs, he teased her. With strong hands Jake touched her every place except for where she wanted him most. His tongue trailed her body, his teeth nipped at her skin. Once he found his mark, she laughed as she watched the silky garment sail through the air. The throaty sound was the last coherent one Avery made over the next hour.

JAKE LOOKED OVER at the clock and sighed heavily. "I've got to get to work."

Avery's head rested on his shoulder. She nodded her agreement and raised herself on an elbow. "Duty calls?"

"Duty calls." Jake rose and walked gloriously naked to the bathroom, snagging his underwear off the corner of the bed along the way. Avery was confident in her own skin, but she never failed to marvel at men walking around naked. It was as if at some point someone pulled all females aside and said, "Listen, when you're naked with someone, you have to wrap yourself in a sheet and skitter around like you're terrified of your own body." Men apparently didn't get that lesson.

He reappeared in his boxers and smiled as he dressed in his uniform. Avery pulled the sheet around her as he dressed. Jake was strikingly handsome. His muscles bunched against his shirt as he put on his shoes. She wondered if she'd ever see him without remembering the feel of his hair brushing against her skin as he moved slowly down her torso.

"What are you smiling about?"

"Just wondering if I'll see you again without thinking of you naked," she answered matter-of-factly.

Jake laughed to himself and crossed over to her as he strapped on his belt. "I hope not. I'd like to have that experience many more times."

"Many more," she agreed with a nod. Avery jumped out of bed and threw on her t-shirt and shorts.

"Commando? That'll keep me warm tonight."

"Wouldn't want you any other way," she said, giving him a playful slap on the butt.

He shook his head at her. "What am I going to do with you?" he asked, cocking his head to the side as they reached the door.

"No clue, I'm an enigma," she said, reaching up on her tiptoes to kiss his lips. Jake wrapped her in his arms and gave her a big hug.

"Lock up behind me," Jake said as he looked into her eyes.

She nodded. "I will."

"I'm off tomorrow, want to go on a date?" he asked.

"Tomorrow's Tuesday," she answered like he had lost his marbles.

"We can't go on a date on a Tuesday?" he asked, dark eyebrows quirked.

"We can. Just not my typical Tuesday pastime."

"What is?"

"The usual. Get up early. Go to work. Come home. Go to bed..." she said, eyeing him flirtatiously.

He bent and kissed her slowly, setting her on fire. "Tomorrow, then. I'll call you once I'm up."

Avery smiled her answer and closed the door behind her, resetting the alarm. She went about her night feeling a sense of safety and peace of mind that had eluded her over the last week. She would have felt differently had she looked out her sliding glass door to see the fresh pair of dirty footprints marring the deck.

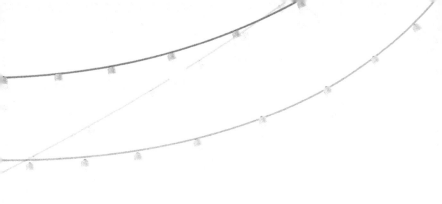

nine

J AKE BERATED HIMSELF AS HE AND Avery walked down the storefronts, checking out the window displays. They had eaten dinner at a little Italian place downtown, and he wasn't ready for the night to be over. What was he doing taking her on a date? He didn't do dates. He did occasional late nights where the expectations were simply that, a late night and a good time. Jake didn't do the thing where you change your shirt a few times to find the right look and stop to double check that the shoes went with the clothes.

He looked down at Avery, dressed in a little black number, and smiled. She wasn't his usual fling either, he admitted. The fact that she was a psychiatrist was a little off-putting. Jake tried to not let himself wonder what she was thinking, or rather if she was evaluating him during their conversations. If he was honest, Avery was a bit arrogant and had a smart mouth. The woman had brains, though. He was a fast processor, but she was faster. During dinner they had traded little bits about their history. She knew how long his father had been gone, that they had never been close, and that he worried about his sister. Now he knew she didn't speak to her mother and had lost her grandmother, her only family. She didn't do serious relationships and never had. She clearly had some kind of boundary issues. He didn't miss her self-disgusted look when she put her hand on his and then jerked it away.

He knew one thing, she wasn't a cuddler. If he read her right, she was about as self-sufficient as he was. Jake liked seeing the conflict cross her features throughout the evening. Avery didn't seem to want to admit it, but she was having fun.

He pulled her into a loose embrace and asked softly, "You don't have a lot of fun in your life, do you?"

"Excuse me?" she asked, annoyance showing clearly on her face.

Jake rolled his eyes. "What I mean is, you don't seem to do much in the way of recreation. You said you pretty much go to work and that's it, right?"

Avery stepped out of the embrace and slowly continued their walk as she thought. "Well, mostly. I do travel some," she said, neglecting to mention most of the trips had been with her friend, Cade. This time she didn't balk as he took her hand.

"What's been your favorite trip so far?" he asked, enjoying the expression on her face as she thought.

"My favorite has to have been visiting the Galapagos Islands," she said, adjusting her purse on her shoulder.

"Seriously? With the dragons and everything?" Jake said, turning toward her.

"Yeah, it's cold as hell to dive there, but the sights can't be beat."

"No kidding," he said. "I'd have never pegged you for a daredevil."

Avery smiled. She liked very much that she took him by surprise. "What's your favorite vacation spot?"

"I'd have to say Mount Rainier in Washington state."

"Mount Rainier?" Avery asked, her forehead wrinkled incredulously.

"Yeah. I went there on a family trip when I was about ten years old. I remember we were on a picnic. We had some food from a drive-through, and I'll never forget I lifted a fry to my mouth and a huge bluejay ripped it right out of my hands. I screamed like a girl," he said, a boyish smile forming on his face. "My sister still teases me about it. My mom laughed so hard she nearly keeled over. I think that's the hardest I've ever heard her laugh," he said with a sideways smile.

If Avery had considered letting her heart flip-flop over Jake, his consideration of his mother did the trick.

"You're really crazy about her, aren't you?"

"Who? My mom?"

"Can't believe I'm saying this, but yes," she smiled, "your mom."

"Yeah, she's dealt with a lot for us, I imagine," Jake said, his smile playing on his lips. "My dad was a drunk," he said, by way of explanation.

"Is that why you had a tonic and lime tonight?"

"Yeah. I've always been a little afraid to touch the stuff, for fear I'd like it," he answered.

Avery nodded with understanding. She'd grown up with a weak parent and understood the fear that went along with codependency. "I get it."

Jake hooked his arm back around her shoulder as they strolled. "My father was like two people trapped in one body... completely unpredictable. He could be clever and fun one minute and then it was like a switch would flip if he was drinking." Avery wasn't sure what to say but she gave his hand a pat where it rested on her shoulder. They had walked the length of town square and were about to head back to his truck when a man stepped out of the darkness between two buildings. He was big, and the stench of alcohol wafted off of him even from the distance between them. Jake's spine stiffened as recognition hit him.

"Walk away now," he said to Avery in a serious but low tone as he pressed his truck keys into her hand.

She looked up at Jake like he had lost his mind. She was blocks away from their truck and a little afraid to take off walking in case that creep had friends. Avery mentally cussed herself for leaving her gun at home. She never intended to use it on anyone, but it certainly made her feel safer having it. She knew he had his weapon on him. She'd felt it under his shirt when she'd wrapped her arm around his waist.

Jake's expression had shifted to something she'd seen only in a brief flash the night someone had taken pictures of her home from the inside. Avery jerked her head in a nod and crossed the street, making her way back to his truck at a run.

"Remember me?" the man said with a sneer, his mouth revealed proof of his drug habit that had led to Jake arrest him.

"Yes I do. Out already, huh?" Jake asked as he scanned the street to see that the piece of trash was alone. "The name is Rogers, right?"

"Yeah, that's right. You've got a good memory for a piece of shit cop," he said, closing the gap between them.

Jake tensed himself, preparing for a fight. "You better think this through, Rogers. You sure you want to risk another arrest over this? Threat of bodily harm is a pretty good charge."

"I ain't getting paid to let you kick my ass," Rogers said, throwing his fist into Jake's jaw.

Jake's head whipped to the side and he felt the punch all the way down to the soles of his feet and tasted the tang of blood. Rogers drew a knife and Jake saw the silver flash in the streetlamp light. Before Rogers knew what was happening, Jake grabbed him by the shoulders and drove his knee into the man's solar plexus. Rogers gasped for air, and Jake threw him on the ground with his arm twisted up behind him. The knife clattered to the ground and Jake kicked it further down the alley.

"I told you you should have thought about it, asshole," Jake hissed as he yanked his phone from his pocket. With a knee in Rogers' back, Jake called dispatch.

"Yeah, it's Marcovic. There's been a 10-10, fight, and 10-78, need assistance, a block down from Aspen and Main. I've got Dan Rogers down, he took a swing, drew a knife, and is now disarmed and held down." He looked down at Rogers' face. "Blood present on both of us, mostly him," he said with a smile as dispatch laughed.

"10-04, sending backup immediately," dispatch replied.

Bright lights lit up the alley as Avery pulled his truck up to the entrance, the engine rumbled loudly. He saw her staring out from behind the wheel, and damned if his heart didn't do a flip seeing her concern flooding through her eyes despite the darkness. Within seconds, red and blue lights lit up the alley as a cruiser closed in on the other entrance to the alley.

"What do we have here?" another officer asked, stepping up with his cuffs in hand.

"Dan Rogers, restrained for officer safety," Jake answered. "The knife he pulled is over there, Jake gestured with his head.

"Not smart, Rogers, not smart. This isn't your first…"

"He mentioned he wasn't being paid to let me kick his ass," Jake said.

Officer Williams' eyes flew up to Jake's. "That right, huh?" he said, jerking Rogers up to a standing position. "I just love a good mystery." Williams walked Rogers to the cruiser. "Can't wait to learn more about that," he said, turning to look over his shoulder to nod at Jake.

Jake answered the nod, then walked toward his truck.

"What the hell was that about?" Avery hissed as Jake pulled open the door.

"Prior arrest and a grudge," Jake answered, neglecting to mention the "paid to kick ass" portion of the conversation. Avery scooted over to the passenger side as Jake settled in.

"I didn't like being run off like that, you know."

Jake turned to her and exhaled. "I had no idea what that scumbag was about to pull. What do you suggest I should've done?"

Avery was surprised by her physical reaction to Jake's aggression. Stress radiated from his body, shoulders locked up tight, veins visible near both his temple and neck. A flush came over Avery as she wondered where else his body might have reacted. It was a long drive back to her place, and she certainly didn't plan to go back to his. The sound of her seat belt unbuckling made a snick against the tense night air. Jake's attention jerked toward her. One look was all he needed before pulling into the nearest alley. Avery was across his lap before the gearshift landed in park.

Jake was on fire as she straddled him effortlessly in the cab of his truck. He was fascinated by the conflict within her. Avery was reserved and analytical outside the bedroom, but with a few well-executed kisses, she transformed to a woman-on-fire. There was a huge difference in their size, but she fit nicely against him, lips crushing his, curves pressing into his body. There was nothing tentative about the way she explored his mouth, her tongue pushing into his as her hands tangled in his hair.

His hands slipped up the curve of her legs as the hem of her dress raised higher. He moved slowly, each inch exaggerating the thrill of what they were doing. He teased her and Avery nearly growled against his mouth as he resisted giving her exactly what she wanted.

Without breaking the kiss, she slipped her fingers between them and freed him from his jeans as his hips lifted to assist her. Her rear brushed against the wheel and the horn sounded.

"Shh! You're going to get us arrested." He laughed.

"Scandalous…" she whispered as her lips found his neck. Jake fished around in his glove box until he produced a condom. The rush of breath that Avery exhaled against his skin as he filled her raised every goosebump on his body. Thankfully, the big truck swaying with a tell-tale rhythm and fogged up windows appeared to go unnoticed.

"DO YOU WANT ME to come in," he asked, eyebrows raised hopefully.

Avery looked up as his smile nearly swayed her from

her position on the internal argument she'd had on the drive home between conversations.

"Nah, thank you for the offer, though." She could go a few more rounds with him, but she didn't want to form a habit of him sleeping over. This wasn't something she was interested in getting serious about, and frequent sleepovers might blur the lines.

Jake tilted his head and his hand enveloped her jaw as his thumb grazed her bottom lip. "Can't blame me for asking," he said with a devilish smile. "Want me to check that the coast is clear?"

Avery peeked in the window where lights had been left on throughout the house. "Thank you, but no. I've got to make friends with this security system and stop freaking out."

"Can I see you again soon?"

"I'll give you a call," she answered.

Jake narrowed his eyes for a second. He knew this move, but it was usually him giving that answer before a brush off. She was a stubborn little thing. "Okay."

"Thanks for tonight, I had fun. Attack and arrest aside," she said, reaching up to press one more kiss to his lips.

"Me, too." Jake slipped his hands into his pockets and walked back to his truck. She was unlike most of the women he'd ever known. She didn't seem to be playing a game. They were clearly really, really good together in the sack. She was prickly, but fairly easy to talk to. He didn't want a clingy woman, but it kind of set his teeth on edge for her to climb all over him in his truck one minute and seem to reject him in the next. She was hard to read, he decided.

His headlights focused on her door until she was inside and gave a little wave through the window before pulling the curtains. A shadow flickered to the side of her house that drew his eye, but then a rabbit scurried across the yard. The light sliced through the trees and Jake made a mental note to talk with her about a motion detection system. As many animals as there were in this area, the darned thing would be going off all the time. He would certainly be installing them next door. Next door to Avery, he said to himself with a grin. Could be worse.

ten

"**WE COULDN'T GET MUCH OUT OF HIM,**" Officer Williams explained to Jake early the next morning at the station.

"What *did* you get, then?" he responded, exasperated.

Williams shrugged. "Only that someone had hired him to kill you."

"Did he think I was just going to stand there and let him hit me?" Jake asked, eyebrows raised. "If he was trying to kill me instead of beat me, you'd think he'd have started off with the knife instead of a punch."

Williams pulled a chair and sat down across from Jake. "Look, that guy has done so many drugs his brains bounce around like two beans in a tin can. He's not firing on all cylinders. He's not a freaking professional hitman, he's a back-of-the-bar piece of trash. We'll get it figured out."

"Fill Jones in on this, please. He's assigned to Dr. O'Gara's case, and we were out together last night when this happened. Can't imagine it's linked, but I haven't been here long enough to piss off too many people yet," Jake explained.

Williams stood. "Will do. Now go home and get some rest."

"Will do." He'd gone in around five o'clock in order to catch Williams before he got off shift. His eyes were gritty from lack of sleep through the night. Between replaying the altercation, wondering if Avery was safe, being utterly perplexed with her moods, and mad at himself for caring, he was exhausted. He decided to take a drive out to the property to check the progress.

Without intentionally doing it, Jake felt himself slow down when passing the drive to Avery's house. He couldn't see much beyond trees, but he had to look anyway. His lane was next. The foundation was poured, and this week the framing would go up. On his way back down the road he saw Avery pulling out of her drive.

He waved and pulled over to the next lane.

"Hey," she said, her expression a bit wary.

"Morning. You okay?"

"Yeah. I didn't sleep great last night. I kept thinking I was hearing things."

"That sucks."

"Jake, I found some muddy footprints outside my window on my deck this morning."

"What?" Jake said, cursing under his breath. "Did you call it in yet?"

"Yeah, and I took a picture and sent it to Detective Jones. This is starting to make me feel crazy," she said, rubbing the wrinkle between her eyebrows.

What the hell was going on at her house? He hated seeing her afraid. "I'm off again tonight, do you want me to come over? Keep you company?" Jake asked, thinking she'd feel better with someone there.

Avery's face reddened and what little patience she had completely shattered. "No, damn it. I don't need a babysitter, and I'm not available for sex every day," she snapped.

Jake recoiled like he had been kicked in the stomach, then his face became impassive. *Who did she think she was?*

"Look, Avery. I wasn't asking because I'm after sex. I was asking as a friend." He stared at her like she was an alien from a different planet. What was her deal?

A mock laugh erupted from her lips. "Right."

He couldn't feel any more offended. "Suit yourself. We're done here." Jake hit the gas and his truck kicked up gravel as he moved his vehicle ahead of hers. He'd been screwed over before. He wasn't out to do that to her. As far as getting laid, he could find that anywhere he wanted. He was good looking and knew it. That wasn't what he had been after.

"Screw her," he said aloud to himself, annoyed that she was taking up any space in his head. He wasn't even looking for anything. He was just getting out of a mess and didn't need any complications. He needed a house. He needed a freaking nap. He needed to chill out and go fishing. That used to relax him back in the day. Anything to get his mind off that irritating little woman. Jake could fix a few of those things. The house was in progress, but of course it was next door to a spiteful woman. "What other kind do I attract?" he scoffed to himself. He needed some peace and had an idea who could help him find a place to go fishing.

Jake pulled his phone from his pocket and hit a button. "Call Levi Murray," he practically yelled into his phone.

"Hello?" Levi answered after three rings.

Jake winced at the scratchiness in Levi's voice and belatedly checked the time. "Hey, Levi, it's Jake. I'm sorry, I didn't realize it was still so early," Jake said, embarrassed to see it was only a little before six o'clock.

"Don't worry about it, we're up getting the kids ready for school and all. What's up?"

"I have the sudden itch to go fishing. Want to go sometime soon?"

"Yeah, I'm always up for that. I need a short break from the house stuff anyway. Fish are biting already over at my family's farm. Let me check with Jesse on our schedule tonight and I'll get back with you toward the end of the workday."

"Sounds good, man. I'm off tonight and tomorrow night, then back on for a few nights."

"Got it, I'll give you a call later on, Jake," Levi answered.

There. One more thing he actually could control, Jake thought. Next stop, his bed to try and at least get a little sleep.

HOURS LATER, JAKE tapped his fingers irritably on his knee as the breeze drifted through the open windows of the truck. He stared into the woods, unseeing, as Levi unlocked the gate to his family's old piece of property.

"Dude, I can't wait to find out what the hell is wrong with you," Levi said as he climbed back into the cab and guided the truck down the narrow, rutted road.

Jake shot him a confused look and Levi chuckled. "You're as nervous as a whore in church. It's a wonder you haven't dislocated your thumb drumming on your knee like that."

Instinctively, Jake jerked his hand from his knee, embarrassed. He kept such a tight lid on his emotions most of the time, he couldn't help but wonder how many times they seeped out unbeknownst to him.

Levi pulled the truck to a stop several yards away from a large pond. Jake nodded his head in appreciation. "Nice pond, man. This place been in your family for long?"

"Yeah," Levi said, exiting the truck and reaching in the bed for his chair, pole, and tackle box as Jake did the same. "It's been ours for several generations, but no matter how long he's been gone I'll always think of it as my grandpa's."

Jake nodded in understanding. They set up on the sunny side of the bank to make the most of the remaining sunlight.

"We'll only have three or four hours at best, I think," Levi said, looking up at the sky.

"That's good, man. I just needed a break. Want to tell me why your ears are blazing red, by the way?" Jake asked, directing his gaze to where his bobber danced on top of the water.

Levi shifted in his chair and tugged at the bill of his ballcap. "Way to let nothing slide, you observant bastard."

Jake shrugged a shoulder as his mouth quirked up in a smile. "Part of the job, man. You don't just turn it off."

Levi rolled his eyes. "Jesse and I used to come out here often when we were dating. The first time around, I mean. We've been back a few times. We, uh, rechristened the place recently and did our best to scare the fish."

Jake laughed despite himself. "You two are pretty happy, huh? That's awesome. It doesn't seem like most folks get a second shot at something like that."

"I don't know, Jake. Isn't that why we're here right now?" Jake shot a pointed glance at Levi and said nothing. "Are you going to tell me what's going on or make me drag it out of you like some sulled up woman?"

Jake sighed and stood to pull in his line and recast. "That's the damndest part of all of it. When I got screwed over by my ex, and I literally mean screwed over, I swore I'd never get into the weeds with any woman ever again. I mean, they are vile creatures who only want to take. They see an opportunity for sex, or protection, or…"

Levi didn't stand or clear his throat, but a shift in his mannerism stopped Jake's words as they spewed from his mouth. Levi shook his head softly before he started, "Let me stop you right there, man. Yes, there are takers, and poisonous people, poisonous women, in the world. Some are opportunists, but Jake, man, most are just people with their own baggage.

"I was, and probably still am, a bad bet for Jesse. Frankly, she's probably a bad bet for me. She's got her own fears to deal with. Have you heard any of the hateful crap her ex-husband pulled on her and the boys? He's straightened out quite a bit now, but I think that's only thanks to therapy, probably some medication, and a near-death experience with a guy she was seeing after I totally screwed her over."

Jake's head whipped to the left and he glowered at Levi. "What? Haven't heard that story? I'll save it for another day. My point is, every danged one of us is a freaking disaster waiting to happen. After I lost Emma, the term 'emotional landmine' didn't even touch my situation. Who was here for me right after the accident? Who took a risk and gave me another shot after I did something incredibly stupid? Jesse. Sometimes people are worth taking a chance on, baggage aside."

Jake sat back down in his camping chair and fiddled with his fishing rod, eyes widening slightly as the bobber dipped below the surface. He stood to begin reeling in his catch. Silence permeated the pond with the exception of the splashing water as the small fish put up its best fight.

"She thinks I'm only after sex," Jake admitted. "I'm not perfect, not by a long shot. I have the communication skills of a caveman, at best. But..." he said, trailing off.

"But what?" Levi asked, recasting his own line.

"But, I can get laid anytime I want. I hate that she's getting to me, but there's something about Avery that makes me crazy. She's infuriating and condescending, but she's all I can think about. When she's not looking down her nose at me, I can't get enough of her."

Levi chuckled to himself as Jake vented. He nodded rather than spoke. He didn't want to interrupt the verbal diarrhea his friend was finally spewing.

"Avery has a gun and, from what I understand, knows how to use it, but she's freaked out because she keeps finding footprints outside her house. It's making me insane to think some pervert is watching her, or trying to watch her. Or that some psycho is trying to freak her out. I don't know. We've got someone on it, but it seems like they're doing nothing. At least they're not doing whatever they are doing fast enough to suit me," Jake said.

"That's scary. I don't blame you for being upset. Have you offered to stay over there?"

Jake let loose a hateful laugh. "Yeah, that's what got me into this. I offered to stay over tonight because I'm off and she accused me of only being after sex." He raked his hand through his dark hair. "She's making me insane."

"She's prickly," Levi said in agreement. "Sounds like she resents feeling like she needs help."

"Yeah, she's not had many people she could actually trust, from what I understand."

Levi sighed before answering. "If that's the standard she's used to, maybe that's why she's so defensive."

Jake nodded his head. "I don't know whether to grab her by the shoulders and shake her, or tell her I love her, throw her over my shoulder, and take her to bed."

Levi laughed. "I definitely wouldn't go with either of those options, dude." The silence stretched between them for a few beats before Levi continued, "Just curious, but did you catch what you said, just then?"

"What?"

Levi looked at the water before turning to Jake. "That you said you love her."

Jake's eyes bugged out for a split-second before looking back at the pond. He had no plans of qualifying that statement.

Levi shrugged and let it go, and they fished for the next few hours in relative silence, except for the racing thoughts inside Jake's head.

⎯⎯⎯⎯⎯⎯

As Jake laid down on his bed he compulsively checked his phone just one more time, half hoping Avery would call or text to apologize for being a jerk earlier. Instead, what he saw made his gut twist. He had missed two calls from his ex-wife. No way he was going to return those calls. Their business was done. A fitful sleep claimed him as his mother paced through the house, worrying over what had him so cranky.

Later, at Eadie's house, Ruthie shared her concerns.

"Jake kept some strange hours last night, and he's meaner than a biting sow today."

Eadie shook her head at her sister. "He's 41, sweetie. He's going to keep odd hours from time to time," she said with a smile.

"Oh, Eadie. I know. He was up before I was, then came home a few hours ago almost as cantankerous as Alek used to be. Whew, could he be such a hateful son-of-a-gun."

Eadie patted her hand on her sister's knee. Eadie had always hated Alek for the way he kept Ruthie all twisted up with worry. It was impossible to guess what kind of mood he'd be in when he'd get home from work. He could be charming and wolfish with those dark eyes and intriguing accent, or distant and cold. It was worse when he was drinking, though. Those were the days when a look, Mallory singing or running through the house, or one of Jake's little toys out of place could send him over the edge. She'd never forget how Ruthie would show up with Jake and Mallory and their little suitcases for a last minute sleepover. The children were always so quiet for the first hour or so, like they felt out of place in a noisy, boisterous home.

Ruthie would bustle them in cheerfully, kiss their cheeks, and promise they'd have fun with their cousins. Eadie would give her hand a squeeze and Walt would give her a reassuring smile. Her Walt had not been much for words, but his presence in itself was more calming than any conversation ever could have been. God, how she missed him. Ruthie would be in and out within five minutes, nervously making her way back to her home to withstand the upcoming storm.

"Are you sorry you stayed with him all those years, Ruth?" Eadie asked, finally feeling as if it were okay to talk about.

Ruthie heaved a sigh. "It's hard to say, Sis. Divorce just wasn't done then, remember? Not like it is now. If it was, the woman missed her children's childhood busting her hump at a crappy-paying job. I was able to be there for all of Mallory's recitals and Jake's games. I put dinner on the table and kept as calm of a house as I could for them. I took more than a fair amount of trouble for it, but I did it. It was worth it to get to watch them grow. God bless those women who had it much worse than me. I can't complain, really."

Eadie felt a bit of guilt for having had such a wonderful marriage. Her sister had deserved to be treated well. She'd been so poisoned by her experience with Alek that she'd never dated again, even years after Alek had been gone. Suddenly, Eadie had an idea.

"Ruthie, I've had an itch to make Mother's chocolate chip cookies. Will you help?" she asked, her blue eyes twinkling.

"Of course, I'm always up for baking," Ruthie answered, jumping up from her seat on the porch swing. She looked at her watch. "We've got just enough time to get a few batches in before Jesse's boys come to help with the yardwork."

"Perfect, let's get moving," she answered with a smile, the wheels turning in her mind. She wasn't ready to think about romance, but her sister had been single for over twenty years. Surely it was time for a friend.

eleven

AVERY SAT AT HER DESK, DREADING her clients for the day. Her fuse was super short from lack of sleep and stress, and she felt like an absolute heel. She'd been horrifically rude to Jake, and if there was anything she hated, it was having to apologize. He was probably sleeping, she guessed, checking her watch. She'd have to call him later. He had mentioned that his schedule got pretty screwed up switching from working nights to days off. She tapped her fingernails on the desk and tried to decide which task to tackle before her appointments started up for the day.

She checked her messages and had one from Aidan, returning her call. She'd take care of that first. There were messages from Mrs. Fig, neurotically checking and rechecking the rescheduled appointment. Avery figured she'd be paying for rescheduling her Monday session for a while. There were also six hang-up calls with no messages. *Why do people bother doing that? Either hang up before the recording kicks on or leave a damned message*, she fumed.

Picking up the phone, she dialed Aidan's number.

"Hello?"

"Hello, Aidan?"

"This is Aidan," a deep voice confirmed.

"This is Dr. O'Gara. Do you have a minute?" she asked, pulling out the list of referrals.

"Sure, what's up?"

Avery took a deep breath. "Since I'm now going to be neighbors with Jesse's family and seeing you socially a bit more, I wanted to offer a list of referrals for therapists nearby who specialize in PTSD. I wouldn't want it to get awkward, and I think that would be the best approach. What do you think?"

"Sure, Doc. I'd be fine with that. I don't come often enough for it to be a big deal where I go, as long as whomever I'm talking to knows their stuff. Who do you recommend? Let me grab a pen..."

If only all the conversations could go like that, she thought with relief. She read off the handful of therapists in the area who might be a good fit. She wrapped up the call as her first appointment of the day came through the door.

"Have a seat, I'll be with you in just a minute," she said, gathering the patient's folder from her file cabinet. *Okay, Avery, time to focus*, she told herself, settling in for another long day.

HOURS LATER, EADIE's house smelled like heaven. The ladies bustled around the kitchen, tidying up and setting the cookies out to cool on all available surfaces.

"The smell of homemade chocolate chip cookies takes me back to being a little girl again. Lord, that's been awhile," Ruthie said with a laugh.

"I know just what you mean. Smells are funny that way. I think of Grandma Sary every time I smell lilacs. Do you remember that?"

"Sure do. Remember seeing her go out and grab a chicken for dinner?" Ruthie cackled.

Eadie laughed. "How could I forget? She'd walk out into the coop and swoop one up. When she got to the yard she'd wring its neck, swing it around, and let it flop around on the ground."

Ruthie shivered. "Once it was dead, she'd chop the head off with that little hatchet. Remember how she'd fill that old metal tub with boiling water and pluck the feathers off right there in the yard?"

Eadie nodded and wiped tears away with the hem of her apron. "Do you remember the time I put my new patent leather shoes in the chicken feather water? I was sitting beside her on the steps watching her pluck that chicken and decided just to stick my little foot right in. She put me to bed after that! I was in big trouble!"

"Oh mercy, I had forgotten about that. I loved those days. I loved when the house would be filled with aunts, uncles, and cousins. The men would nap and the women would talk and clean up the kitchen. Grandma would throw a big table cloth over the table so we could come back for leftovers at suppertime."

Eadie sighed. "My word, it's a wonder we didn't all die of food poisoning back in those days."

"Lord, if that isn't the truth."

"Ruthie, if I bundle some of these cookies up in a tin, would you run some out to Anna's office at the mines? If I remember right, it's her supervisor's birthday today. He was so good to her the day of the accident. What's his name again?"

"Oh, that Mr. Darby? He was so kind. I'd be glad to run some out. Let me go freshen up a little. I think I've got flour all over myself. Can't ever keep myself clean whether I'm baking or painting."

"Okay, kiddo," Eadie answered, excited that Ruthie had remembered Anna's boss's name. The fellow was very kind-hearted and had taken great care of Anna the day she went into labor with Benji. Eadie's heart squeezed at the memory of that day. A rock fall had occurred that day, and it was a terrible accident. Anna was scared out of her mind, fearing that Aidan had been hurt or killed, and the stress threw her into early labor. Mr. Darby helped get her on an ambulance despite the chaos going on, and even checked on her in the hospital. If Eadie remembered correctly, he had been widowed for years.

She had just stuffed a tin with two dozen cookies when Ruthie stepped into the kitchen. Ruthie's hair was cut in a flattering bob and had a wave of curls. It had been red in her youth but was now a snowy white, thick and healthy. Ruthie dressed in comfortable but flattering clothes, as she was never one to stay put for long. Even before Walt had passed, Ruthie had popped in several times a week. She was always flitting from church, to the store, to visiting with friends here and there. Once Alek's reign of oppression had ended, and after a period of grieving and adjustment, it was as if she had decided twenty years was more than enough to spend lonesome and under someone's thumb.

"You look pretty today, Sis," Eadie said, placing the tin in her hands. Ruthie started at the compliment.

"Oh stop, two minutes ago I had flour on my nose and you didn't even tell me," she answered, wrinkling up her nose at her sister.

"Just say thank you and move on," Eadie fake-scolded. "Do you remember which office is Anna's?"

"I think so, dear. See you later," Ruthie said, giving Eadie a one-armed hug.

Eadie smiled, locking the door behind her and returning back into her kitchen, her little safe-haven. Her eyes wandered over to Walt's old chair at the table and her heart twinged at its emptiness.

twelve

J AKE WOKE UP A BIT DISORIENTED. He was always a trainwreck the first few days after being off night shift. Annoyance gnawed at him over Avery's treatment, as well as his nagging concern for her. He didn't need anymore crazy in his life, especially with Juliet flaring up again. He pulled his phone up to his eyes and winced, two more missed calls.

He jumped like he'd been shot when his phone went off again. On instinct, he thumbed the answer button.

"Hello?" he answered, registering that the number was blocked.

No answer came from the other end of the phone, but Jake could hear the person making noise of some kind -- tinny sounds like silverware clinking in a sink or something.

"Hello?" he repeated, giving ten more seconds before disconnecting the call.

Seconds later the phone rang again.

"Hello?" he answered, regret choking his words.

"Jake? Thank God. It's Juliet. I've been trying to reach you for days," she said breathlessly. "I've got to talk to you. Jake? Are you there?"

He exhaled and counted to ten, trying to remember every anger management technique he'd read as a law enforcement officer and beyond.

"Juliet, did you just call and not answer?"

"Why would I do that, Jake?"

He exhaled. "Nevermind, what can I do for you?"

"I don't need you to do anything for me," Juliet said in a bitchy tone, then caught herself. "I just want to talk, Jakey. I miss you."

He winced. He didn't even like that nickname when they were happy together. "I think the time has come and gone for that, don't you?"

"That's not fair. You were the love of my life, and I completely screwed it up. I'm so sorry, Jake."

He couldn't help himself, he laughed out loud. "Juliet, if you'd not raked me through the coals, tried to screw me over financially, not to mention sleeping with other men during our marriage, that might actually mean something."

She had the audacity to sound contrite when she answered. "I'm so sorry. I was so lonesome. You left me alone almost every night, Jake!"

"I was working, Juliet. I wasn't hanging out with the guys or slumming in some bar. I was working as a freaking police officer. What's so hard to understand about that? You knew I was a night shift cop when we got married."

"I know, Jake. It was all me. I'm so sorry." Silence hung in the air. As he was about to hang up, she spoke again.

"Can I see you?"

He laughed. "Hell no. We're finished."

"Is there someone else?" she shrieked. "Did you find some little small-town slut, Jake?"

He didn't even miss a beat as he said, "Take care, Juliet. Get some help." Jake ended the call and tossed his phone across the room.

Ruthie entered the office at the coal mine with a bright smile on her face. She was so happy now that most of the kids had returned home. It had just about broken her and Eadie's hearts when they were scattered all over. Mallory and Jake had been in Chicago, Jesse was near St. Louis, and Anna was way off in Denver. Now they were able to spend so much time together and make memories, like it had been when she and Eadie had been young. If only she could get her stubborn daughter to give up on Chicago and come home and settle down. She chuckled to herself. Mallory might come home one day, but nothing about her would ever settle. That girl was as independent as Alek had been mean.

Anna's desk was empty, and there was nobody in the outer officer. "Hello?" she called, stepping a bit further in. Mr. Darby stepped out of his office and blinked in surprise.

"Well hello, may I help you?" he asked with a kind smile on his face.

"Yes, I'm Anna's aunt, and I was hoping to see her and leave her some cookies."

He nodded. "Yes, I believe we met when Little Benji arrived, didn't we? I'm Mr. Darby," he said, hand outstretched.

"I'm Ruth Marcovic, Eadie's sister."

"Nice to meet you, formally I mean, Mrs. Marcovic."

"Oh please, call me Ruthie," she said, feeling a little foolish. "May I just leave these cookies on her desk? Would you like one?"

He grinned and she pried off the lid, losing her grip on the tin in the process. Mr. Darby made a lunge toward the container and caught them as Ruthie leaned down. When they raised up they were inches away from one another as the door swung open.

Anna was more than surprised to see Ruthie and Mr. Darby head to head across from her desk. Ruthie had bright pink cheeks and Mr. Darby looked embarrassed.

"Thanks for the cookies, Mrs. Marcovic," he stammered. "Ruthie, I mean. Have a nice day, now."

"You too, Mr. Darby."

"Hank, ma'am. Please call me Hank." He turned on his heel and fairly scurried into his office.

Anna raised her eyebrows. "Hank, huh?" she asked quietly, in a teasing tone.

"Oh hush," Ruthie scolded. "Eat your damned cookies," she said, grabbing her purse from the corner of Anna's desk.

When Ruthie made it to the door, she turned and grinned at Anna with her hand over her mouth. Her eyes were a bright blue, and Anna suddenly realized how attractive Ruthie was. She'd always just been "crazy Aunt Ruthie" for as long as she could remember, but now Anna saw she was just as pretty as her own mother.

Anna walked into Mr. Darby's office and knocked at the door.

"Come in," he answered.

"Would you like another cookie, Mr. Darby?"

"Sure, those are terrific," he said with a smile. The man had a sweet-tooth a mile wide.

"My aunt is quite a good baker," she said nonchalantly. "Her son has moved closer to home now, so she's getting to cook and bake up a storm again now." His eyes had returned to the endless piles of papers on his desk. He didn't throw her out of his office, so she continued on with her little scheme. "She's been widowed for a number of years now, so I'm sure she's glad to have the company," Anna hinted, risking a glance at Mr. Darby.

"Widowed? What a shame," he said, his surprise overshadowing his sentiment. "I've been a widower myself for nearly ten years. Time goes by quickly," he said, a hint of sadness shadowing his eyes.

"Sorry to hear that, sir," Anna replied. "You know, life's awfully short not to have a little romance sprinkled in here and there…"

Mr. Darby's head jerked up and he looked at her like she'd suddenly sprouted a second head. "Anna, I think I hear your phone ringing. Better go check."

"Yes, sir," she said with a glowing smile. Seed planted, she thought. He was a funny, sweet-hearted man, and Ruthie had been alone a long time. Maybe they could be friends. She looked forward to the day her mom would be ready to consider someone else to pass the time with. Her mother seemed so lost without her father.

Life really *was* awfully short, she thought as her heart warmed, reflecting on how much change she'd undergone in the last year or so. Her father had passed. Her engagement had failed miserably. She'd moved from Colorado to southern Illinois, had a whirlwind romance, two marriages (if you counted Mexico), and a son. Life was good again, finally.

Once she was back behind her desk, she picked her phone out of her purse and saw a text she'd missed earlier from her mom.

I think Ruthie should meet that nice Mr. Darby, see what you can do. - Mom

I'm on it. - Anna

thirteen

AVERY JUMPED WHEN HER PHONE RANG. She fished it out of her bag on her way to the car and a grin spread over her face.

"Hello?"

"Meet me for dinner," Cade drawled into the phone.

She sighed, checking her watch. "Thanks for all the notice, Cade."

"What? You have someplace you've got to be?" he asked, faking offense at her crabby tone.

"Now that you mention it, I don't. I do have a story to tell you, though. Where do you want to meet?" she asked wearily.

"How about the Hawk's Nest? We haven't been there in ages."

"See you in ten." Maybe Cade could help her figure out how to apologize to Jake for snapping earlier.

AVERY WALKED INTO the bar, and Cade's waving hand shot into the air from a booth in the back.

"What are you doing in town? I thought you weren't passing through till summer?" she asked, reaching across the table to give him a hug. He'd always been able to put a smile on her face. He was handsome, with short, dark hair and blue eyes. Cade wore horn-rimmed glasses that made him look a bit older than his years, and they accentuated his intellect. He'd been the smartest student in many of her classes, and her sapiosexual side had homed in on him from the start. Nothing lit Avery on fire like a smart, witty man. *Smoldering green eyes and powerful shoulders aren't too shabby either,* she thought, her mind drifting to Jake. *He is the total package, humor, brains, that body… focus, Avery.*

"I had to run home for the weekend to visit my sister. She's had another puppy," he explained, rolling his eyes.

Avery made an awful face at him. "What the hell are you talking about?"

"A kid. She's had another baby, so I had to go see him." Cade feigned disinterest in kids, but Avery knew he'd have one in a heartbeat, if it didn't mean having to permanently attach himself in some form to just one woman. He liked variety, as much of it as he could get.

"You're almost disgusting," she said, swatting his hand

away from the pile of cheese curds on the appetizer plate. "Don't take all of them!"

"I thought you were on some 'deep fried things are the devil' kick a while back?" he remarked, rolling his eyes.

"Screw it," she said as she popped the hot, cheesy goodness into her mouth. "I might not be getting naked for a while, so why bother?"

Cade's eyebrows shot to the ceiling. "Present company excluded, of course?"

Avery frowned and wrinkled her nose. "Not even you, I'm afraid. I might go on strike."

"This sounds like a terrible idea, but a good story. What have you done?" he asked, leaning in so he didn't miss a thing.

Avery quickly caught him up on the surprise attraction to Jake and the break-ins, including the creepy pictures and phone calls.

"Wait a minute, Avery. You don't 'do' relationships." Cade's eyes were huge with concern. "And what the hell are the police doing to catch the loon?"

She felt herself sink back in her seat. "The police have been very responsive. The detective checks in with me often, and I've had a security system installed at home. I'm not sure what else I can do."

"And the relationship part? What the heck is that about?"

Avery shrugged, her eyes flashing with hurt and pent up emotions. Cade was around to her side of the booth in a flash. He threw his arm around her shoulder and gave her a squeeze.

"Listen, I don't know what your deal is with boundaries. I know we have fun," he said, leaning his head toward her for a second. "But more than that, we're very good friends. Hell, you might even be my best friend," he said with a smile.

A little laugh escaped Avery, and he interrupted her when she started to speak, "I know it's because I'm a pompous ass without friends, but still, I care about you, Avery. I want you to be safe. And if you like this guy, I mean even enough to consider having a relationship, grab it."

Cade kept his arm around her and gave her another smile as a shadow crossed over their table.

Jake walked into the bar with Joe, a fellow officer, both dressed in their uniforms, about to go on shift. A laugh caught his ear and his attention jerked to the back corner. "I'll be there in a second, Joe." While Joe walked on to the bar, Jake stood near the door and took in the little scene before him. Avery sat tucked into a booth smiling into the face of some guy with his arm wrapped around her shoulder. Jake felt his temper rising, and he steeled himself against it. He hadn't expected to have feelings for the mouthy little doctor, but something made his blood boil at the sight of her snuggled up with another man.

"Jake," Avery said, attempting a smile. "This is my friend Cade."

Jake jerked a nod in Cade's direction.

"I was hoping to talk with you tonight," she said solemnly.

"Looks like you found other plans," he said without any hint of emotion.

Cade rose from his seat on the booth and offered his hand. "That would be my fault. I was passing through town and asked if she'd meet me for dinner."

For half a second Jake considered not shaking Cade's hand. The guy looked alright, though. He was meeting Jake's gaze directly. He didn't look cocky, like he was happy about mucking up Avery's plans. Jake offered a firm handshake to Cade and then walked past the booth to sit at the bar with his friend.

"Isn't that the chick you took out on a date?" Joe asked, a grin plastered on his face.

"She's a doctor, not a chick, but yeah," Jake answered with a glare.

Joe nodded with his lips pressed into a line to keep from laughing. "Guess that date didn't go real well…"

"Shut up, Joe."

"Got it," he said into his water.

Jake ordered a soda, burger, and fries, and never looked back to the corner where Avery and Cade were sitting.

"Yikes, he's huge," Cade said, eyes round after Jake left their booth. "And pissed, huh?"

Avery narrowed her eyes at Jake's back. "He has a right to be pissed over me being rude to him earlier, but not about us hanging out."

"Look, he doesn't know we're friends, or, um, the extent of our friendship," he said with a waggle of his eyebrows. "If you don't think he's going to be pissed or jealous about you sitting here with another guy, then you're not as smart as I thought you were," Cade said, wincing when Avery smacked his arm.

"You're a cardiologist. You don't think anyone's smart compared to you, you smug bastard."

"Right, right. Well, anyway," he said, looking at his watch, "I need to get back on the road. I'm glad we could at least see each other, although I'd rather see you naked."

She exhaled. "Safe travels, Cade. I'll let you know how the saga unfolds," she said, throwing her hand up in Jake's direction.

"Seriously, if you like him and he's decent, quit fighting it. Time to throw out your baggage."

"I'm the shrink," she reminded.

"Take care," Cade said, leaning down to plant a kiss on Avery's forehead.

She gave him a little wave and watched him walk out of the bar. Cade was a total pain, but he was just about her only friend in the world. Avery watched Jake's back for a few more minutes, wondering if he was going to turn around again. When it was clear he wasn't, she released a breath she didn't realize she'd been holding. She gathered her things and left the restaurant, more convinced than ever that men were much more trouble than they were worth.

AVERY BALANCED HER grocery bags on her knee while entering the code to her backdoor. Time had slipped away from her while shopping; she'd thumbed through several books in the limited grocery store display to find just the right one to pass the time. She was sick of medical journals and needed a little comic relief in her life. The outside lights usually flickered on when she drove up, but tonight they were dark.

She refused to live her life completely spooked, so she ignored the prickle of unease she felt as she entered the darkened kitchen. Avery never left the house without turning on the range light in case it was dark when she got back home. Had she been so shaken up about the boot prints that she'd forgotten? What good were these extra safety measures going to do if she didn't remember to take them?

Avery flipped on the light and unloaded her groceries. She could argue with herself all night long, but she knew she had to say something to Jake. It was going to eat her up inside to just leave things the way they were. She had thought they could have some fun together and just leave it at that, but if he was going to act like a caveman, she wanted no part of that action, no matter how good he was in bed.

And he was good in bed. Avery closed her eyes and recalled the feeling of Jake moving over her as his green eyes melted into hers. Remembering how he expertly worked her body made a shiver run down her spine. A smile flitted over her face before she brought herself back to the point that it just wasn't going to work with Jake. She had enough on her plate right now to worry about without dealing with Jake's inability to actually verbalize what he was thinking.

THE NEXT MORNING was warm and bright. Avery had actually slept a bit more and felt good enough to take her yoga out to the deck. Each time her eyes turned to the spot where she had scrubbed away the dirty footprints she made herself focus on the sound of the birds. Finally, she quieted down her mind and wrapped up her last movement, stretching out on her mat and focusing her attention on the way the sunlight heated her skin, when she heard footprints on the gravel.

Avery jerked her head up and felt her heart nearly catapult through her chest.

"It's just me," Jake said, hands up in the air in surrender. He still wore his uniform. "I was looking around my property and saw you outside."

"Can you seriously see my porch from your place?" she asked, annoyed, whipping her head around in that direction.

"Binoculars help," he said with a shrug. In answer to her bugged out eyes he added, "Just kidding. Yes, I can see from my place."

A sigh escaped her as she dreaded the conversation to come. She hauled herself up to her feet and sat down in the Adirondack chair.

Jake raised his eyebrows as he stepped up on the porch. "May I?"

"Of course," Avery said as she wiped her face on the folded towel she'd left on the little side table next to her water. She glanced at Jake, who had stretched his long legs out in front of him. He gazed off at the trees before rubbing his hand over his tired, closed eyes.

"Rough night?" she asked.

"Long one. Yesterday got off to a crappy start."

"About that," she started. "I'm sorry I was short with you." Jake raised an eyebrow at her choice of words.

"Short? Is that what you call it?"

Avery felt her temper starting to rise and willed herself to stay calm. "I was rude, and I apologize for that. You were rude as well, at the bar last night."

He didn't even try to stifle his glare. "I was pissed at you, of course I was rude," he said, turning his body toward hers. "Did you even listen to what you said to me about just wanting sex?"

Avery felt her ire rise as her internal flags went up. She was well-versed on her own shortcomings, one of which was zero-to-little tolerance for confrontation. Part of her knew that's why she kept people, men especially, at a distance. They can't hurt you unless they get close. She shook her head and threw her hands up in the air. "We don't have to do this. We don't have to make it a thing and analyze it. We tried to have something casual, and it's clear it's not going to work."

Jake looked at Avery like she had lost her mind. "There's no need to get your dander up over this…"

Avery interrupted. "I think you should go."

He stood and turned on her. "You know what, you're right. This isn't going to work. I've already wasted too much time on a moody woman who blows hot one minute then cold the next." Jake took off on down the steps and made his way down her driveway.

She stood fuming on the porch and paced back and forth once Jake was out of sight. "Good thing I wasted time getting centered today, Jesus," she said as she walked. "Blows hot and cold," she said to the cat as she walked into the house. "Screw him," she said, dramatically dragging out the words. She rifled through her cabinet to find her favorite "hello gorgeous" mug that Cade had given her years ago on one of their many trips. It wasn't in the usual place, so she checked a few more cabinets. She used the stupid thing nearly every morning, so it was either in the sink, the dishwasher, or the cabinet. It was nowhere to be found, but she was too mad to expend any more energy. She plucked a plain white mug from her cabinet and poured a cup of coffee to drink while she got ready for the day.

AVERY WAS FOUR patients in before she calmed down completely for the day. Between patients she checked voicemail and had hang-up calls each time she checked. The light flashed to alert her to another message, so her sadistic nature made her check it again.

A woman's voice left a message. "Dr. O'Gara, I heard you were a filthy homewrecker, and I hope you get what you have coming to you."

Avery dropped the phone in the cradle and stared at it for a second. *Who the heck was that?* Tears welled up in Avery's eyes before she could shut them down. The fear was making her weary. It wasn't like she could run to her mother for comfort. She didn't have anyone to turn to. She put her head down on her arms and gave herself permission for a quick cry. Avery didn't really *do* emotions lately, beyond bitchy, that is. She was so tired of being strong all the time and having to keep everything inside. After a few minutes of self pity she splashed some water on her face in the bathroom.

She locked the office and decided she was beyond cranky and well overdue for lunch. The Hawk's Nest was off limits after her last experience there, no matter how delicious the food was. Deciding a salad was the way to go, she headed toward a little cafe in town. The place was frilly and feminine, and made a salad chock full of meats and cheeses - enough of the good stuff to compensate for the pesky, leafy greens. She placed her order and walked toward a table near the window.

"Hey, Avery, over here!" Anna called out. Avery turned her head and saw that Anna, Jesse, Eadie, and Ruthie were all snuggled in at a table for four and were waiting for their meal.

"Pull a chair up, we'll scoot over," Eadie said, gesturing for everyone to make room.

Avery shook her head. "I don't want to impose, or make you all move around."

"Nonsense, kid. Pull up a chair," Ruthie said as she made a gap for Avery right next to her own seat.

Avery forced a smile while exhaling deeply through her nose. She was stuck. "Thank you," she said with a smile. "So, how is everyone?"

"We're all doing pretty good. Especially Aunt Ruthie," Anna said with a grin.

Avery turned to Ruthie. "Well good, what's going on?"

Ruthie adjusted her napkin nervously in her lap. "The girls are giving me trouble. One of Anna's coworkers called last night and asked me to dinner this weekend."

A devilish smile lit up Eadie's face. "Yes, and we're thrilled that she accepted. Mr. Darby seems like a wonderful fellow."

Ruthie let out an exasperated breath. "I haven't been on a date in forty-some-odd years."

"It really hasn't changed much, Aunt Ruthie. Just make sure you use a condom if you do it," Jesse said.

"Oh my God," Eadie said quietly when Ruthie busted out laughing.

"Enough about this, talk about something else," Ruthie threatened.

"Fine. So, Avery, how've you been?" Jesse asked, starting in with questions. "Any more craziness at your house, or has it settled down?"

She shrugged. "I found some shoe prints on my deck yesterday. That scared the heck out of me. Today I've had a bunch of hang-up calls and a voicemail from some woman screaming that I was a 'filthy homewrecker.' Otherwise it's been quiet." She listened to the gasps of the women and a muttered curse from Jesse and realized it felt good to have a clutch of ladies to talk with. Annoying and unfair as it was, there was a certain amount of vulnerability to being alone in a house, and as far as Avery had learned, each lady at the table had been through it at one time or another.

"Hang on, kid. She called you a homewrecker?" Ruthie asked, blue eyes wide.

Avery nodded. "That's not even the scariest part. She said she hopes that I get what I have coming to me. I don't have a clue who it was. The only person I've even gone on a date with recently was Jake," she said, her hand thrown up in the air. "He's divorced, so that doesn't make any sense."

Silence hung in the air, and Avery noticed that all eyes were on Ruthie.

"Ruthie, he is actually divorced, right?" Avery asked, a knot tightening in her throat.

The older woman nodded emphatically. "Yes, God yes. We damn near threw a party when that one was final. He's divorced, but his ex-wife is a nut!" Ruthie said, hands gripping the edge of the table. The server arrived to deliver their food, and they all acted normal, like they weren't discussing psychopaths, ex-wives, and adultery.

Once the server had left the table she leaned back in and

hissed, "I feel guilty saying nuts to you, being a psychiatrist and everything, but truly. She's a user. An opportunistic whackjob." She was quiet for a moment as everyone tucked into their food. Avery let the comment soak in as her appetite dissolved into nothing.

"Oh, shit," Ruthie said in a low tone. Eadie jerked her head toward her sister.

"Ruthie!"

"Give me a break, Eadie. This is serious." She winced at Avery. "I just remembered something. Last week Juliet called and tried to talk to me about Jake. I told her to leave me alone, that Jake had moved on with a nice doctor and didn't want to be bothered. And then I hung up on her."

Eadie gasped.

"Well I did. She hurt my boy, Eadie! I have no sympathy for that woman. And, I wanted to rub it in her nose that he was dating a doctor. Sorry, but it's true," she said with a shrug of her shoulder.

Jesse put her hand on her forehead in disbelief.

Anna looked confused. "Did you tell her which doctor? How could she get Avery's number?"

"The internet," Jesse said with an eye roll. "It probably wouldn't be that tough between an internet search and social media to figure out who might be single."

"Right. I'm so tired," Anna said, leaning her head on her sister's shoulder. "I didn't believe 'mommy brain' was a real thing, but I am not myself."

"Sis, you were crap with technology before Benji came along, don't blame the baby."

Anna smacked Jesse on the arm, and Eadie said, "Girls, behave."

Anna and Jesse chuckled, and Avery felt a little twinge of envy that they had each other to lean on. She truly liked these people. Too bad she and Jake just called it off this morning. Her hands shook a little as she reached for her tea, and it didn't escape Ruthie's notice.

"I'm sorry, hon. I didn't mean to get Juliet fixated on you," Ruthie said as she took Avery's hands in her own and gave them a squeeze.

"It's alright, Ruthie. I'm just getting overwhelmed with it all. It feels like things are spinning out of control, and I..." she shrugged her shoulder, "I like being in control."

Avery's voice was trembling, and tears erupted from her eyes, sliding hot and wet down her cheeks.

Ruthie pulled Avery into a hug, and Avery allowed herself to relax into it. "Why don't you come stay with us for a little while. It would be so nice to have company," Ruthie insisted.

She shook her head gently and left the kind woman's embrace. "Thank you so much for the offer, but I don't think that's a great idea. Jake and I, well, we decided that we won't be spending any time together."

Avery saw the disappointed faces around the table and looked down at her plate. What a day, she thought. Her appetite was gone, but she wasn't going to look like she was upset over the Jake-thing in front of the women. She didn't want to advertise that it was her idea not to see him anymore, but she didn't want to look like her heart was shattered, either. She faked a half-smile and took another sip of iced tea.

"Well that's too bad. I was hoping there was a spark there," Jesse said, shrugging a shoulder.

"Me, too," Anna and Ruthie said at the same time.

"I've got too much going on with all this craziness to start something even casual," Avery stated, then mentally questioned if the word casual made her sound a bit slutty. *Eh, what the hell. I'm an adult*, she chided herself.

"Famous last words..." Jesse said, her voice trailing off as she took a bite out of her lunch.

Anna smirked at Avery's annoyed expression.

"I'm sorry, what did you say?"

"Famous last words," Jesse said with a smile. "When I got back together with Levi, high school sweethearts, blah blah blah, I was freshly divorced and had just moved back home."

"Don't forget about Cole," Anna supplied.

"Oh Lord, don't remind me. Brief, torrid, toe-curling affair," she said with eyes bugged out. "Sorry, Mom." A nervous laugh escaped both Eadie and Ruthie.

"Anyway, we hadn't planned on anything happening," Jesse said with a shrug.

"And Aiden, dear," Eadie said as she patted Anna's arm.

Anna's eyes lit up with her smile. "Yeah, that wasn't planned. Well, it kind of all wasn't planned. One-night stand, pregnancy, marriage, revealed the pregnancy, marriage didn't count, surprise attack wedding ceremony."

Avery's head was spinning with the ambush of information she was getting.

"Oh come on, you knew you were getting married, you just didn't know where," Jesse scolded.

Anna rolled her eyes. "Got me there. Anyway, the point is, sometimes things just happen regardless of whether it's good or bad timing."

"I'll keep that in mind, Avery said as she fidgeted with her purse. She pulled out a twenty dollar bill and placed it on the table.

"I need to get back to the office; I've got an appointment in ten minutes."

Ruthie rose with Avery and pulled her into a quick hug. "Take care, kiddo."

"I will, thanks," Avery answered. She hustled back to her office and did her best to avoid looking at the blinking light on her voicemail. As threatening as the message had been, she wasn't going to remove anything that might be considered evidence.

fourteen

IT WAS A LITTLE BIT OF AN adjustment having Jake back at home, Ruthie thought. She was thrilled to have him there, to have someone to cook for and eat with again. The adjustment was learning to give him his space. He was protective of her and didn't want to be an inconvenience. Jake wasn't a parent yet--Ruthie wasn't giving up on that idea--so he didn't seem to grasp the concept that she wanted to do things for him. For years, her home had felt so empty without the kids there. Eventually she got used to the quiet, but she preferred a bustling home. If she were honest with herself, she'd admit that's why she spent so much time at Eadie's. When Jake became a police officer, Ruthie thought her heart would burst with pride. It had taken years for her to give over her fear for him to the Lord. Every day she prayed hard for him to be safe from harm, to be able to do good, but she had finally had to hand over her fear. It was too immense to carry every day and frankly, Ruthie finally hit a point where she couldn't live with fear any longer. Life was going to happen whether she worried over it or not, so she decided one day after her morning prayers that she wasn't going to carry it anymore. During her marriage to Alek she had experienced tremendous worry, all tied to how much he would drink. When he was sober he could be so charming, but once he crossed that line... Ruthie shook her head a little, letting her mind clear of the painful memories.

When Jake had decided to move up to Chicago near Mallory, she had been so proud. He didn't even blink at the chance, not at all intimidated by the tremendous differences between a big city and their little ten-stoplight town. Ruthie had been up to visit the kids plenty over the years, and to be honest, the city scared the hell out of her. She was more comfortable in a small town where everybody knew everybody.

She craved time with him, but Jake was tired when he was home thanks to his work schedule, so she tried to give him space. After Avery's revelation at lunch, she was going to see if she could get some details out of him, plus she had some news of her own to share. Mallory was a little more predictable, so she decided to start there. Ruthie picked up her phone and called Mallory.

"Hi, Mom," Mallory answered, out of breath.

"Did I catch you at a bad time, kiddo?"

Huffing, Mallory paused a second before answering. "No, just got off the treadmill at the gym. What's up?"

"Well, I've got some news, kid. A man asked me on a date, and I decided to accept." Ruthie jerked the phone from her ear as Mallory woohooed into the phone.

"That's great, Mom! I'm happy to hear it. Give me all the details!" Ruthie's shoulders sagged with relief as she faced her biggest hurdle, wondering if her children would approve. She shook her head at her own silliness. Of course they would. They'd been trying to get her to go out and socialize for years now. It just felt odd. She'd practically sworn off men altogether after her marriage, though it would be nice to have a friend to have dinner with from time to time.

"I'll tell you all about it, but first, I have something else to ask about. Wait, let me go into another room," she said, her voice dropping to a near-whisper.

"Oh, this will be good…" Mallory joked.

"Shh! You know how prickly Jake can be. Well, he's met someone. Has he told you about her yet?"

"What is it about that place here lately? Something in the water?"

"Come on, kid. Spill, he's going to be awake soon."

Mallory sighed. "He hasn't been very loose-lipped with me. He admitted that he was seeing someone but wouldn't give an inch when I tried to find out if was serious. Jake said she was a shrink, and then I kind of pissed him off."

"What did you say?"

"Well," she answered, her voice going a little higher than normal. "I made a crack about it being good, that I'd always thought he needed to see a shrink."

"Mallory Jane!"

"What? I thought it was funny. He didn't... anyway, he didn't say much after that. Why? Is it getting serious?"

"That's what I'm trying to find out. She's smart as a tack. She's almost as prickly as him, which makes me a little worried. You should see him with her, though. It's like he's awake again. His eyes almost never leave her when they're together. Not sure if it's an alpha male thing or what."

"Mom," Mallory hissed.

"What?"

"Have you been reading those romance novels again?"

"Why?" Ruthie answered, defensively.

"You just said alpha male," she said sarcastically.

"So what, Mallory. They're hot. I could use a little hot."

Mallory answered with a groan.

"Anyway... what do you mean when they're together? Do you hang out with them or something?"

"No, smart aleck, but he brings her to the family gatherings. She's actually friends with Jesse and Anna, too."

"Hmm," Mallory said. "Sounds like it could be serious, then. Also sounds like it could be a flaming trainwreck if it blows up."

"That's the thing. I think they've blown it up." Ruthie recapped Avery's admission from lunch. "What gets me, though, is that she's a handful, but he eats it up. I think she's good for him. She makes him laugh. It's been a long time since he's been happy."

Mallory agreed. "I'll see if I can get anything out and let you know."

"Okay. I'll get off the phone. I need to get some cookies out of the oven." She laughed as Mallory groaned something about Jake being the favorite.

"You're both my favorite, don't be stupid. Love you."

"Love you, too, Mom. Talk to you later."

Ruthie put her phone away and glanced down the hall and listened for footsteps.

"Jake, are you up?" she called up the stairs.

"Yeah, Mom, be right down," he answered. She let herself give in to the thoughts of the hundreds of times over the years they yelled the same words to one another. She could always count on him to help her carry in groceries or help if she needed to move something. He'd always been such a good kid.

"I've got some cookies coming out of the oven. Want some?" she said with a smile. He couldn't resist oatmeal raisin cookies.

He sniffed the air appreciatively. "Sure, thanks."

As she puttered around the kitchen, he sat down at the table. "Son, I have to talk to you about something." Ruthie couldn't believe she felt nervous broaching this topic. Jake's serious eyes looked so much like his father's in that moment, she was nearly dumbstruck.

"What's up?"

"Well, someone has asked me to go to dinner, and I decided to accept," she said with a slight nod, as if she were still convincing herself.

She watched as Jake tilted his head back and looked at the ceiling. "Thank God, Mom. I thought you were going to tell me you were sick or something."

"No, Jake. I'm as healthy as a horse! Don't be silly."

"I think it's great, Mom. Who is it?"

"What, are you going to do a background check on him or something?"

Jake let out a laugh. "No, but I'm glad to hear you're going on a date. It's about time."

"Well, to be honest, I think it took me this long to be ready to entertain the idea. I've been asked on dates over the years, but the idea kind of turned my stomach. My marriage wasn't a happy one, as you know, and that did a number on me."

Jake was a little stunned. Though she would listen to him and was always available to talk with him, as far as he could remember, she'd never said a negative word about his father, no matter how hard he'd tried to drag her true feelings out of her. He didn't want to interrupt the flow, so he just nodded.

"Alek was a good man, as long as he wasn't drinking. Lord, he had charisma and could charm the bloomers off a nun with those eyes. You look so much like him, honey. So handsome," she said, giving his hand a pat.

"Anyway, I had taken the brunt of his addiction and

outbursts for so many years, that I wasn't about to open myself up to being someone else's punching bag. Figuratively, Son. He shoved me a few times, but he didn't hit. It was the way he talked to me that beat me down."

"Is that why you took us to Aunt Eadie's so often?" he asked, looking down at his plate, afraid she'd stop talking even though deep down he already knew the answer to that question.

Ruthie sighed. "Yes. Poor kids. You two probably feel like you were raised there more than here."

"No, Mom. I'm glad you got us out of it, but it makes me sick to think you stayed."

"Things were different then, Son. There may be people who take marriage a little less seriously now because it's so easy to get out of, but I for one am glad people can get out. It would've been harder, financially. Even socially. I didn't want you and Mallory to be left out or frowned upon because of having divorced parents. Maybe if I had it to do over again I would do things differently, but I'm not one for dwelling. I did the best I could at the time."

"We were still happy, Mom. You did a fine job." He watched as she dabbed a tear from her eye. "Now, tell me more about this date."

Ruthie shared what she knew about Mr. Darby, including their plans for Saturday night. While she talked she was building her counterattack. The moment she saw an opening, she went for it. "Today at lunch, Avery came into the cafe and sat with us." She watched his eyes. Nothing.

"She's such a smart cookie, isn't she, Son? Maybe a little tense. She seems like she can't relax."

Something between a sigh and a laugh escaped Jake. "You can say that. Of course, having someone stalking her could explain that, however I suspect that 'tense' is her usual state."

"Speaking of stalking, has she mentioned she got an alarming phone call today?" she fished.

"No, I spoke with her this morning, but not since."

Ruthie sighed. He wasn't making this easy at all.

"What phone call?" *Ah ha, he is interested at least,* Ruthie thought.

"She had a voicemail from a screaming woman that called her a homewrecker, and that she can't wait till Avery 'gets what's coming to her.'"

"Jesus," Jake whispered. "Homewrecker?" he repeated, a sense of dread building in his stomach.

Now it was Ruthie's turn to squirm. Ruthie grimaced. "Did I tell you I talked to Juliet last week?"

Jake rested his elbow on the table, and his fingers massaged his forehead. "Tell me everything, Mom."

———

THE NIGHT HAD been mostly quiet, which Jake appreciated. He needed time to mull over the conversation he had had with his mother. The threatening phone call to Avery was certainly within Juliet's wheelhouse. Amazing how such a beautiful woman could be hiding so much poison inside.

The radio pulled his attention back to the present. "017, Womble…"

"Go ahead, Womble."

"Possible 10-31 at Flannell's Pharmacy on the town square reported by passerby."

"On my way, Womble. Hold radio traffic, set additional car."

JAKE DROVE HIS cruiser a block away from the pharmacy, eyes searching for moving shadows. Dim lights were on in the back of the store, a familiar sight. The custodian worked nights so that the place was ready for business in the morning. He pulled his car in the alley behind the pharmacy and walked to the front door. He gave it a push and the door opened. Jake stepped inside and saw what he guessed was the custodian's feet and legs on the floor, half-hidden behind the counter. He dropped down to feel a pulse at the neck of the custodian despite a dark stain of blood pooling around his head.

A towel was lying on the counter where the custodian had been working, so Jake grabbed it and wrapped it around the man's head to hopefully stop the bleeding. He heard a noise come from the back and crept silently toward the door marked Employees Only. Just as he reached the door, it swung open into the main part of the store. Jake was suddenly face to face with a huge man carrying a box stuffed with medicines.

Silently, he drew his weapon then yelled, "Police! Get on the floor!" The thief threw the box on the floor and rounded on him. "Get down on the floor, now!" Jake ordered.

The man charged Jake and was met with a fist to the jaw.

"Get down, now!" Jake bellowed as the man returned a punch, solidly connecting with Jake's cheek. The taste of blood filled the inside of his mouth, and it pissed him off completely. Adrenaline coursed through his body, and he grabbed the man's shoulder as he drove his knee into the man's stomach. The thief doubled over, but not without slamming Jake into the wall with his shoulder.

He took the quick upper hand he was given to deliver a solid punch to the ribs in order to get behind the massive man. "Get down, now!" he yelled as he threw his weight on top of the suspect and felt for his cuffs.

The man kicked at Jake and did his best to turn over, connecting his elbow with Jake's eye. Jake landed a few more punches into the side of the suspect's head as he did his best to get him cuffed. Once he had him down and secure, he grabbed his radio.

"017, Womble."

"Go ahead, 017."

"Send EMS staged, we've got an injured party with a head wound, pulse confirmed. One suspect detained and cuffed. Continue backup, the rest of the store hasn't been cleared."

"We've got another unit on the way," dispatch answered as he saw the lights flash in front of the store.

"10-4, Womble."

When the other officer hit the door, Jake felt a surge of relief. The man down behind the counter had a pulse, but it had been minutes ago. When he had handed over the suspect, he drew his weapon and cleared the rest of the rooms while announcing his presence.

"017, Womble."

"Go ahead, 017."

"The pharmacy is secure, send EMS in for the injured party.

"10-4, Womble."

It took hours for the adrenaline to burn off from the attempted robbery and arrests. Jake tenderly felt his eye where the thief had managed to land a punch. His eye was already swollen and sore, and the knuckles of his hand were a bloody mess. He wasn't ready to go home and face the barrage of questions his mother would have over the ordeal, so he let his mind wander as his cruiser took him automatically to Avery's driveway. He wouldn't have pulled in for a million dollars, but he did slow down and look in the direction of her house. Just a bit down the road was his own driveway, in need of more gravel already. It was thrilling to drive up and see the house, or at least the bones of the house, in place.

He sighed to himself, turning the car around in his driveway, ready to cruise the streets for a while longer before his shift ended. The town looked peaceful at this sleepy hour of the early morning. Cats scampered across streets, and lights slowly flickered on as families got up to start their day. The adrenaline drain from the robbery coupled with the peaceful scenery had Jake so relaxed that he jerked when the radio went off. Dispatch described a report of a man peeping in windows and walking half-naked down a nearby street.

Two blocks down, Jake saw a short, round man with a bright red shock of hair wearing only pajama pants. He stood on the tips of his toes as he peered into the half-circle window of a home's closed door. As the man shifted to lean and look in the front window. Jake pulled his car to the side of the road.

"017, Womble."

"Go ahead, 017."

"Half-dressed individual found at 1230 S. Grover, appears unarmed. I'm about to go talk to him."

"019 is close by if you need assistance."

Jake couldn't help but chuckle. He rubbed his hands over his tired eyes and braced himself for what was about to happen. "10-4, Womble." He added, "Good to know, my guess is this guy's as drunk as Cooter Brown."

"019, here. I'm coming to watch the show."

"10-04, 019."

JAKE SAT IN HIS car and watched the man continue to peep from window to door. As Officer Henderson pulled up beside him, he got out of the car.

"Excuse me, sir. Can I help you with something?"

The man muttered and began to pace across the porch of the house.

"What is that you're saying?" Jake asked, standing at the bottom of the stairs.

"I said," the man yelled, "that I'm looking for that lady who has the kittens." He whipped his head back and forth as he seemed to notice for the first time that there were two police officers staring at him.

"Alright, alright, no need to yell," Henderson said to the man. "What is this about a kitten?"

The man sat down on the top step and with utter exasperation answered, "Well, yesterday I accidently killed my grandma's kitten, and I'm trying to find another one to, you know, make it up to her. I want to make it right. And there's a lady around here somewhere that's supposed to have a kitten, but, she don't answer the door when I bang on it."

Jake and Henderson exchanged a creeped out look. Henderson mimicked drinking from a cup and Jake nodded. The odor of stale beer surrounded the man in a fog.

Henderson propped a foot on the bottom step. "Killed a kitten, huh? Bummer. How'd that happen? Oh, and what did you say your name was?"

"Rudy. Anyway, it was the cutest little kitten. I accidently ran over the poor thing when I went to take my girlfriend home from my grandma's birthday party."

"Party? Was there drinking at the party?"

"Oh yeah," Rudy said. "I can drink a whole case of beer myself," he said as he patted his protruding belly, "but I ain't got nothin' on Grandma. She might have herself a problem."

Jake nodded solemnly. "Listen, Rudy. We got a call from the owner of this house. She said you've been peeping in her windows and door and won't stop knocking despite the fact she isn't answering."

Rudy nodded. "Yeah, she's supposed to have a kitten for me to replace the, you know, other one."

"There aren't any kittens here, and it's bad manners to pound on doors this early in the morning. You're going to have to get on back to your house. You live around here?"

"I'm a few blocks down the road. A buddy said someone on Grover Street in a white house was supposed to have some to give away. Or maybe it was Garner Street. I always did get those two confused. Hell, I don't know. I'm drunk." Rudy punctuated his sentence with a noisy burp. "What time is it again?"

Henderson answered, gesturing to his cruiser, "Too early. Get in the back of my car, and I'll give you a lift home."

"Thanks," Rudy said, ambling down the steps toward Henderson's cruiser. "It's been a long time since I've been in the back of one of these!"

"That's a surprise," Henderson muttered. "Thank God he just ran over the kitten, I was half afraid to hear what he was going to say.

Jake nodded in agreement. "Thanks for running him home. I'm going to explain to the homeowner what the hell this guy was doing knocking on her door.

fifteen

THE PLANNER SHOWED AVERY a very full day of patient appointments. She pulled some blueberries and yogurt out of the fridge and wolfed down some breakfast before her first patient was due to arrive. Thankfully, she noted there were no messages blinking up from her phone. A sense of irritation piqued as she allowed herself to briefly focus on how much fear was intruding into her daily life. She was afraid of every noise she heard at home, and now she dreaded phone calls in her office, a place where she usually felt very confident and strong.

Her arms stretched out and she intertwined her fingers behind her head, enjoying the stretch of her muscles as she took a grounding deep breath. *"Today will be a good day,"* she said aloud to herself. She heard a car door slam in the parking lot and prepared herself for Maggie, her favorite patient.

To her shock, the woman that walked through the door wasn't Maggie, the nervous teen mother struggling to work through postpartum depression and anxiety from living in a group home. Avery sucked in her breath as she realized the woman standing before her was her mother. Despite the toll two decades of hard living takes on a body, Rose O'Gara was still a beautiful woman. Her posture was straight and her long hair remained auburn, shot through here and there with streaks of white.

"Mother," Avery breathed, as if whispering to herself.

"Avery."

She couldn't bring herself to invite her mother in. Avery didn't want her there. Seeing her reminded her of the rape so long ago, and she felt red begin to climb up from her neckline to color her face.

"You're not asking me to have a seat. I would've thought my mom would have taught you better than that."

"Well, I was fifteen when I went to live with her. Manners are typically taught during the more formative years. You were pretty busy back then."

Rose had the audacity to look offended. "You listen here, little girl. You were the one that decided to leave."

"You didn't even come to check on me!" Avery said, her volume climbing. For a second she was struck with the realization of how badly it still bothered her.

"If you didn't want to stick around, who was I to make you?"

"Who were you to make me? You were my mother! You were the one that should have been protecting me against the groping, slapping, raping hands of your disgusting boyfriends!" Avery roared.

The tight expression on Rose's face turned into an ugly grimace. "Sure, blame me! Like it was my fault you looked like a little slut back then. Men are stupid, they can't resist a tramp."

Avery took a deep breath and fought to compose herself when she heard a car door slam in the parking lot. "I wasn't a little slut, Mom. I was a teenage girl. I had to lock my door at night to keep them out - until that last night when he got in. You need to leave. I have patients to see."

Rose's nose jerked in the air. "I'm not done with you yet. I'll be back."

Avery forced a smile as Maggie walked through the door, giving a wide berth to the woman who was obviously out of place in a professional office. Rose glared at Maggie so hard that she winced in response.

"Maggie, please have a seat. Excuse me for a minute, please." Avery closed the restroom door and braced her hands on the cold, porcelain sink. She closed her eyes and willed her heart to stop pounding. She soaked a paper towel in cold water and held it against the back of her neck for a brief minute as she fought to regain her composure. She couldn't believe her mother had found the resources to travel so far away from the city where they had lived.

———

WITH A SENSE OF dread, she surfaced from her office after six o'clock. She wasn't surprised to see her mother waiting for her. Rose was leaning against the hood of a rusted-out car, facing Avery's office door.

"I see you're still here," she said, holding her keys and phone in her hand, ready to run or call for help in an instant.

"I told you we weren't done here."

"How is that, exactly? What is this sudden appearance trick about?" Avery asked, shaking her head at the strangeness of the fact her mother was standing in front of her.

Rose glared at Avery like she was an imbecile. "It's about money, Avery. What else could it be about? For a shrink you're not very insightful."

Money. Of course. "And why do you think I'd give you so much as a dime after the way you allowed me to be treated?"

"Because no self-respecting doctor wants her dirty laundry aired in a little backwater town like this," her mother said as her eyes filled with a self-satisfied smirk.

"Backwater town? This town is incredible! The people are warm and kind here. They take care of their own. If someone's kid is being mistreated, they speak up. They don't just ignore it." Avery's temper flared as she realized this town and its residents had truly become home, especially after the last few months. She knew Jake's crazy family had a lot to do with that.

Rose's eyebrows soared up to her hairline. "Oh, everything's perfect here, huh? Let's see how perfect it is when they all find out their little doctor screwed her mother's boyfriend."

"How dare you?" Avery hissed, as she advanced on her mother with her finger pointed at her face. Her voice grew louder as her eyes bored into her mother's. "I was raped! I was fifteen years old, Mother! If you think for one second that I have a single thing to be ashamed of for being attacked, you are horrendously mistaken."

As her mother visibly grappled for words, Avery turned to walk to the driver's side of her Range Rover. "You know what?" she said, turning back to Rose. "I take that back. The only thing I have to be ashamed of about that time in my life is you. You were a deadbeat parent then, and you're a deadbeat parent now. Go to hell." With those final words, Avery got in her vehicle and drove away.

MALLORY ANSWERED HER phone on the first ring. She rarely thought about leaving the city that she had made her second home, but she would've liked to have been nearby as her mother got ready for her first date in a hundred years. Instead, she had to hear about it secondhand from her cousins. Frankly, she was a little bitter about it.

"Well, how did it go?" she asked in place of a proper phone greeting.

Jesse answered with a laugh. "It went fine, hang on. We're just getting in the car. Let me switch to Bluetooth."

"Hey, Mal!" Anna chimed into the phone.

"Hey, girls. Tell me all about it."

Jesse answered first. "She looks pretty. We helped her narrow her outfit choices down. I don't know what it is about our moms, but they hit a certain birthday and automatically started shopping in the old lady section. You wouldn't believe the sequins in both of their closets."

"Don't forget about Grandma. She was flat-out flashy," Mallory answered.

"You're right," Anna said. "I forget about that. Man, I can't believe she's been gone so long."

"She was a pistol," Jesse said. "Anyway, Ruthie seems excited and nervous as a long-tailed cat in a room full of rockers. We tried to loosen her up with some jokes, but I think it only made it worse."

"Can't blame us for trying!" Anna hollered.

"Seriously though, how is she?" Mallory said. "I wish I was there."

Jesse exhaled. "I get it. It tore me up when I was away, too. She's going to be fine. Anna knows Hank and likes him a lot."

"He's a sweetheart. His wife passed a few years ago, and this is his first date since then," Anna volunteered.

Mallory was quiet. Her emotions were all over the place.

"How was Jake? Did he behave or act like an idiot?"

"You haven't talked to him?" Jesse asked, her surprise clear in her voice.

"Jesse, I've had 12-hour shifts several days in a row. I barely know what day it is. We talk often, but not daily."

"Sorry," Jesse answered. "I just meant that I was surprised. He's going through a lot with Avery right now, and I figured you were right in the middle of it. I know you two have always been so close."

Mallory exhaled slowly. "Usually we are. I need to catch up with him. What do you think of this chick, anyway? She seems like a lot of trouble."

"Oh, she is," Anna answered, earning a dirty look from Jesse. "What?" Anna asked defensively. "She is! She's got a lot going on. She's gorgeous, crazy smart, almost a little stuck up, but I think it's more that she doesn't know what to say than isn't willing to talk."

"Not everyone likes small talk," Jesse said with a shrug.

"Maybe so, but you have had the chance to talk to her a little more than me," Anna told Jesse with a poke to her arm. "Don't get me wrong, Mal, I like her. I think she's good for Jake. She doesn't mince words and cuts right to the chase. As little as he talks, it's a wonder she doesn't scare the heck out of him."

Mallory couldn't help but laugh. Jake never did have much to say. He always seemed more content to take in the surroundings than to get in the middle of whatever was going on. It probably made him a very good cop, she thought.

Jesse spoke up, "I really like Avery. She seems like she's been through the wringer, and honestly, she's in the middle of it now. Some jerk is creeping around her house and scaring her to death. The police are looking into it, but you know how it is, nothing is ever fast enough when you're the one who is afraid at night."

"I let Mom know I'm going to try and come down soon. It's been too long." Mallory's heart sank the minute her words left her lips. The last time she had been home was for Jesse and Anna's dad's funeral. She didn't know what to say, so she let the words hang awkwardly.

"We would love to see you, so please make sure to let us know when you're coming in," Jesse said, the first to speak around the lump in her throat.

"Love you, Mal," Anna threw into the speaker.

"Love you, girls," she answered, flicking off her phone. Mallory went to her bathroom sink to wash the day off of her skin. She paused, bracing her hands against her counter and stared hard into the mirror. How much of her happiness was tied up in her location? Was it time to think seriously about making a change? Could she go back to living in a tiny town?

AFTER CHANGING HER dress several times, Ruthie sat and nervously drummed her fingernails on the table. Hank was due any minute now, and it had been a lifetime ago since her last date. Her nieces had been absolutely no help easing her nerves. If anything they just made it worse with their jokes about safe sex and not putting out on the first date. Ruthie got tickled thinking about how Eadie had accidentally laughed out loud when Anna cracked a joke about how to put a rubber on a banana. Her sister was slowly getting her sense of humor back, God love her.

The doorbell chimed, and Ruthie took a stabilizing breath. *Get it together woman, you can do this*, she pep talked to herself. Hank stood on the other side of the door in a shirt and tie. Ruthie couldn't help but smile in response - he was more dressed up for their date than he was for work the other day when she dropped off the cookies.

"Hello, Ruthie. You look lovely."

"Thank you. You look nice as well," she said as she pulled the door shut and locked it.

"I made reservations for us at the steakhouse in town, does that still sound alright to you?" Hank asked as he opened the car door for her.

"Sounds fine to me, I haven't been there in years."

Ruthie found that she and Hank settled into conversation fairly easily. Hank seemed to do all the polite gestures that she vaguely remembered from her courtship with Alek. He opened doors, pulled out chairs, and asked the young waitress to please take her order first when she asked him before asking Ruthie. *Etiquette seems to be lost on the young, but they don't know unless they're taught*, she mused.

"You know, I was pretty nervous about tonight," she said after a sip of white wine.

"You were? Me, too. I haven't been on a date in years. My wife, Clarissa, died almost ten years ago. Cancer," he said with a sad nod of his head.

Ruthie's hand shot out and covered his briefly. "Hank, I'm sorry to hear that. I haven't been out on a date since my husband passed, either."

Hank smiled in thanks for Ruthie's pat. "Oh? Has he been gone for long?"

"Only a little over twenty years."

Hank choked on the sip of water he'd taken.

"You haven't been out on a date in twenty years? Someone as pretty as you?"

Ruthie blushed at his surprise and compliment.

"Not a single one. My husband was mean as a striped snake. I haven't even been interested in a date. Till you," she said with a grin.

sixteen

A S SHE LOCKED UP HER OFFICE the following day, Avery scanned the parking lot and felt relieved that the day had not included any more unpleasant visits from unwanted guests. She couldn't quite put into words how upsetting it was to have encountered her mother without any warning, but she knew once she put some distance between herself and the incident, she'd manage to sort out her feelings.

Avery was more concerned with her reaction to the stress. She had immediately wanted to contact Jake and confide in him, not only about the attempt at extortion, but about the attack itself. She had never shared that with anyone with one exception. Cade. He had walked a strange line between best friend and hookup for so long, she'd allowed her all-important boundaries to blur when it came to him.

It had been Cade that she called last night on her drive home to vent about her mother's strange appearance and outrageous demands for hush money. She was out of her head if she thought Avery was going to give her one single penny. And, it wasn't even about the money. What bothered her was her mother's lack of concern about failing to protect her own daughter. For years the sense of abandonment had nearly broken her. She wanted so badly for her mother to track her down, hold her, and promise her that she'd be okay. Her grandmother had been the loving arms that comforted Avery through all the nightmares, panic attacks, and therapy appointments. As a matter of fact, it was that horrific experience that drove Avery to become a psychiatrist. She knew the power of words and retraining thought processes. She was living proof that therapy could turn a person right side out again.

She was replaying Cade's words of reassurance and like-minded disgust in her mind as she pulled into her garage. Her nerves were so shot that she nearly jumped through the ceiling when Rocky darted past her feet in his rush to get outside. Avery could've sworn that she had let him out in the morning. When the weather was nice, she let him have his freedom during the day and brought him in night to keep him safe from coyotes.

"Let it go. You've been a zombie for days," she said to herself as she popped a frozen meal into the microwave and prepped a little salad to go with it. She'd get him back in before bed. She poured herself two fingers of bourbon and then paused. She splashed two fingers more into the glass and figured she deserved it after the way the week was going.

After closing the curtains in the downstairs windows, she opened the door and called for Rocky. He didn't waste much time coming inside since he knew where the food came from.

"At least I can count on you, huh, little guy?" she crooned as she filled his bowl and scratched him under the chin. His purr set off a relaxing vibe, no doubt the bourbon helped, too. She flicked on the TV and decompressed watching a rerun of a sitcom she'd liked in college. She couldn't do reality TV because she saw enough stupidity and drama in real life. Avery couldn't stomach house shopping shows because she constantly got frustrated at the people who couldn't see past the paint color or flooring. She also exhausted herself wondering what it was people on those shows actually did for a living that allowed them to shop for homes in the million-dollar market.

Relaxed, tipsy, and bone-tired, Avery double checked the locks, set the alarm code and trudged back to her bedroom. Usually fastidious, Avery broke her own rules by dropping her dirty clothes in the bedroom floor and pulling on pajamas. She quickly washed her face, brushed her teeth, and collapsed into bed next to the happy cat purring noisily beside her.

THE ALARM CLOCK sounded early, and Avery immediately regretted pouring that big drink so late at night. She wasn't hung over exactly, but she had certainly felt better. Rocky followed her into the bathroom and then to her walk-in closet. Avery's fingers brushed against something unfamiliar as she flicked on the light. She turned to look and saw a note taped to her light switch that read: DON'T BE AFRAID - YOU'RE NEVER ALONE.

A blood curdling scream escaped her lips, and her body began to tremble as she noticed that her clothes were no longer arranged by color like she liked it. Someone had been rifling through her things. She ran to her bedside table and dialed 911. Her voice trembled so badly as she gave her address and reported that someone had been in her home that she had to repeat the information three times before the dispatch operator could figure out what she was saying. She was assured that help was on the way.

When the call came over the radio, Jake had just crawled into bed. His radio had been silenced because he was off duty, but his phone was still on. When he saw Williams' number flash, he answered.

"This better be important. I'm in bed."

"It is, Marcovic. A call just came in. Your girl's had another visitor."

A curse escaped him as he got out of bed. "Avery? What happened?" He dressed as quickly as he could while

Williams filled in what few details he knew. Two officers had been dispatched there and he'd just happened to overhear before going off duty.

"I'll be right there," Jake told his friend. "Thanks for letting me know."

"No problem, man. Be safe."

WHEN JAKE ARRIVED, Avery was sitting at the kitchen table staring into a full coffee cup. One officer checked every inch of her house and looked for prints on the closet light switch and door knobs while the other took down all the details she could share. After repeating the information again to make certain nothing had been missed, the officer stood up. He'd almost made it to the door when the blood drained from Avery's face.

"Wait..." she said softly.

Jake gestured to the officer who had one hand on the door.

"Wait!" she screamed. Jake crossed the room in three strides and put his hands on her shoulders.

"What is it?"

"I didn't hear the beep."

Officer Dugan stood beside them. "What do you mean you didn't hear the beep?" he asked gently.

"When I got home the cat was inside, and I never leave him inside. He darted out and it scared me, but I didn't think about it till now... the security alarm always beeps to let me know I need to enter in the code, but it didn't beep yesterday. Some nut job was in my house, let in my cat, rearranged my damned closet in my bedroom, and I didn't even think to notice the security alarm didn't beep."

The officers exchanged looks and Jake nodded.

"Ms. O'Gara…"

"Dr. O'Gara," Jake corrected.

"Dr. O'Gara," Dugan said, giving Jake an exasperated look, "I think I've got everything down. If you think of anything else, give us a call, okay?"

She nodded, completely shook up.

The minute the door clicked closed and the house was quiet, she seemed to suddenly realize Jake was holding her.

Her eyes closed and she leaned against his chest, thankful to not be alone.

"I know we're fighting, but I'm really glad you're here," she confessed softly.

"We aren't fighting, Avery. I want us to be friends," he lied. He wasn't kidding himself. He wanted them to be more than friends.

She gently pulled out of his hug and went to the cabinet to pull down another mug.

"Coffee?"

"Yes, thank you."

She placed the steaming mug in front of Jake and put her hand on her hip. Suddenly she noticed how tired he looked. "Jake, your eyes look so tired. I'm sorry you were dragged into this." She leaned forward and noticed a bruise on his cheek. "Is your cheek swollen? What happened?"

"I stopped a burglary last night and caught a fist to the face."

She closed her eyes and shook her head. "I'm so glad you're safe." He watched her grab an ice pack from her freezer and wrap it in a towel before handing it to him. She picked up the mug and went back to the coffee maker.

"Jake, I don't even know how you take your coffee. Some *friend*, huh?"

Jake didn't miss the nasty emphasis she placed on the word friend. "I take it plain, just like you."

"Ah. See? You're a better *friend* than I am," she said again, loading the word with meaning as her voice was thick with emotion.

He recognized the storm brewing in her and didn't have the energy to go there. "Avery, let's not do this right now. You've been through alot already today. Well, recently," he shrugged, "and I just came off a twelve-hour shift. I'm too tired for this right now."

She nodded, but she had a smug look in her eyes. Something about the haughty way she sat down in her chair went through him like ice water.

He studied her for a moment as he felt his temper rise. She turned to face him and her eyes widened when she saw the flash of anger in his. Her features settled into a scowl, the match to his fuse.

Jake stood and towered over her. He leaned with one hand on the table, the other pointed in her face. "You know what? You want to do this now, let's go ahead. Two minutes ago you said you were glad I'm here. Now, you're giving me the cold shoulder. That's the *very definition* of what I meant when I called you hot and cold. It's like there's more than one person inside of you all the time. One is sexy, smart, and funny, and the other… the other's a hateful bitch!"

She drew her hand back as if she was going to smack his face. He caught her wrist with one hand as she did her best to slap him.

A flat smile that didn't reach his eyes appeared on his face. "Not going to happen, Avery. I'm out of here." He released her hand and turned toward the door.

Her face crumpled and tears streamed out of her eyes. She put her head down on her arms and sobs wracked her body. Jake made it as far as the door when he looked back as she looked up.

"Please don't go," she said softly. "I'm so, so sorry." Her head shook from side to side as he watched her from his position by the door. "Jake, I'm so sorry."

He was torn between walking out that door, never to give her another thought, and wanting to sweep her into his arms and keep her safe. When she hung her head and cried, he made his decision. He couldn't walk away and leave her like that. She was such a screwed up mess.

Jake walked to her chair and crouched down, his face inches from hers. He took her face in his hands and said quietly, "Avery, I'll stay, but don't you ever act like you're going to slap me again."

She shook her head again. "I'll never do that again, I'm

so sorry. I've never hit anyone. I'm so scared right now that I'm about out of my mind. My nerves are shot, my emotions are raw - I just don't know what to do anymore. My life has turned into some kind of nightmare, and I don't know what to do to make it stop." A defeated sob ripped from her body.

He rose and sat in the chair beside her and pulled her into his lap. He placed her head on his chest and pressed a tissue into her hands as she cried. Avery was such a stubborn, headstrong woman. By the way she was crying he wondered when the last time had been that she let herself lose control of her emotions. His mother had always said there was nothing better than a good cry. While it wasn't a method of coping he preferred, it seemed like an idea that made sense.

When she finally quieted down, she gathered up the wad of tissues she'd used and wiped ungracefully at her nose. "Sorry, this is disgusting."

"Trust me, I've seen worse."

"I can't even imagine…" she said, attempting a smile.

She pulled two bottles of water out of her fridge and sorted through a cabinet until she found a pain reliever. "I've got a headache out of this world," she said, dropping two little pills in her mouth and washing them down with a healthy gulp of water.

"I'm not trying to be coy here or anything, but I've got to lie down. Will you come with me and we can talk?"

Jake nodded and walked to the door to check that it was locked. He followed her to the bedroom and stretched across the bed while she grabbed a cold washcloth for her face. Her eyes were swollen from crying, and her face was splotchy and red.

"Here, lay down," he said, pulling the covers back for her. He stacked two pillows so she'd at least be propped up while she rested.

"Thanks." She adjusted the washcloth over her eyes and managed to be quiet for about five whole seconds. A corner of Jake's mouth lifted as Avery plucked the cloth off of her face and turned toward him.

She rolled to her side, propped herself up on her elbow. "Look, I'm not a fan of the damsel in distress thing. My life has turned upside down and it galls me to no end to have to depend on other people -- for anything. I'm not even really used to people being nice to me. And small talk? I hate it. In case you haven't noticed, I'm one small leap away from being a hermit."

A small laugh escaped him. Jake was a little in awe as he watched Avery's face show all the emotions whirling around in her mind. It was like watching a thunderstorm build from a distance. There was a part of him that envied her transparency when she wanted to show it.

Avery exhaled and briefly pressed her eyes closed before turning their blue brilliance on him. "I grew up in a rough neighborhood with a horrible mother. She was more interested in getting drunk, high, and laid than she ever was in raising me." Avery took a breath and braced herself. "When I was fifteen I ran away from home after one of my mother's boyfriends broke into my room in the middle of the night. He attacked me. Raped me." She watched as Jake shut his eyes and put his hand on her waist.

When he opened his eyes she saw all the good parts of his character shining through them. He had a caring heart and a burning desire for justice. "Avery, I'm so sorry."

She nodded. "I literally ran away to my grandmother's house and she willingly took me in. I finally had the kind of love and support and parenting that a kid should have. Until yesterday I hadn't even seen my mother since I ran away."

Jake's eyes opened wide as the gears started turning. "You saw her yesterday? What happened?"

Avery sat up in bed and leaned back on one arm. "She wanted money. She rolled up out of nowhere after all this time and expected me to hand over money. That's not even the worst part. She expects me to give it to her or she'll 'air my dirty laundry' about the attack."

"Unbelievable." Jake sighed and pulled her down to him. Her head rested on his shoulder, and he pulled his arm around her side. "That's so screwed up."

"I told her that the only part of my history I had to be ashamed of was her, and that nobody in this town would think differently about me over something I couldn't help. I assume that's true. I'd hope it's true."

"Of course it is. She sounds like an awful person."

She huffed. "Exactly. She wasn't anywhere to be seen

today, thank goodness, but with all this crap going on," she flung her hand toward her closet, "it feels like I've got a bullseye on my head."

Jake wasn't sure what to say. He placed a kiss on her forehead and held her close.

"I need to apologize. You're right. Although I hate the word, I have been a bitch."

"Avery, stop. I shouldn't have said that."

"No, give me a minute, please. To be fair, I did snap. I did try to smack you, and I'm sorry. I've never done that before in my life. I'm completely strung out right now. Jake, on a good day - far removed from all this bullshit going on in my life - I'm not a warm and cuddly person. I never have been. I could attribute it to my childhood, but I'm not sure that's it. It might just be how I'm wired. With the exception of my grandmother and my friend Cade, there's not a single person I've ever let myself need.

Throughout my life I've watched people do terrible things to one another. Every single day that I see patients I get a deeper sense of just how horribly one person can scar another. Half the people I see are messed up because of a parent or spouse.

I've never allowed myself to want to be with anyone before. It scares me to death that you're the person I think about when something happens in my day that I'd like to share. When I'm happy, I want to tell you why. When I'm scared, I want you to hold me. That scares the living daylights out of me."

Jake looked down into her wide blue eyes and had no idea what to say. He placed his hand on her cheek, leaned on his side for a better angle and placed a soft kiss on her lips. To his surprise she pulled her head back after a moment.

"Look, the kissing, the sex, we know we understand each other perfectly in that way - I need to know more about the rest of you."

He closed his eyes, and a heavy sigh left him. Jake shifted uneasily, so Avery moved back to resting her head on her hand. She watched him run a hand over his face and struggle to find the right words. "This isn't easy for me."

She crooked an eyebrow at him, and he realized she didn't understand what he was getting at. A frustrated growl escaped him. "Something that I admire about you is your ability to put a name or description to everything you feel. You may not like needing or wanting people, or me," he said with a squeeze of her knee, "but you can at least… express it.

"I have trouble with that. I mean, I feel things, of course, but it's more like… God. Even this part is hard. If I get mad, I'm not thinking to myself, 'mad mad mad mad mad!'" He grinned as she laughed.

"I'm being serious here, give me a break. I feel the emotions, I just can't get the damned words out easily."

"Okay, I think I sort of understand. You're a crap communicator."

He laughed in relief. "Yes. I'm a crap communicator," he repeated, bugging out his eyes. "I guess that sums me up."

She ruffled his hair with her fingers.

His face grew serious again. "I can tell you this, though. My ex did a real number on me. She was a deceitful, vindictive person, and when it all came down to it, she was just interested in getting money out of me. It's hard to let myself care about you without, I don't know, without feeling like I'm waiting for the other shoe to drop or something. Do you know what I mean?"

Avery smirked up at him. "I think so. It means we are two people with trust issues, a man-hater, a woman-hater, emotional blockage, and crap communication. Sounds like a recipe for disaster, doesn't it?"

A laugh escaped Jake before he could stop it. "It does. An absolute disaster. But, there was one way you said we understood each other perfectly... correct?"

Her eyes bugged out at his suggestion. "Are you serious? I look like a train wreck."

"You're beautiful. Plus, this counts as make-up sex. I can't miss a chance for make-up sex."

"Make-up sex? I've never tried it." At his shocked expression she replied, "What? I never let anyone close enough to fight with, let alone make-up with."

"Well then, you're in for a treat..." he said, rolling her onto her back and settling his body halfway onto hers as his lips nuzzled her neck.

An hour later, sated and sighing, Avery said, "You're right. There might be a good reason to keep you around. If we can't communicate, at least we'll get to fight and do that again." She rolled to her stomach and wiped the sweat from her forehead.

Jake gave a self-satisfied, inherently male smile.

"What? Still nothing to say," she teased.

He growled at her, "Come on, enough of that. I do have something to say, though. This might be a little awkward, but I want you to come stay with me until we catch whoever keeps getting into your house."

Avery stared blankly at him. "What? At your mom's house?"

Jake rolled his eyes. "Yes. I know. Remember, I'm not some louse that still lives with his mommy. I'm building a house, for Christ's sake. Next door to yours, if you remember."

Her lips pressed into a straight line as she mulled it over. "It's not a bad idea. I mean, it goes against virtually every independent bone in my body, but honestly, I'm scared shitless here now. The only reason I'm not packing my car up right now is because you're here with me."

"Where would you go?"

"Hotel? I don't know. I just don't want to be here," she said, exhaling loudly. "That completely irritates me. This place has been my sanctuary since I moved in. I'm not super materialistic, but every single thing in this house means something to me. I don't like clutter, and I only keep things that remind me of something I've enjoyed in my life, like trips or I don't know... or they made me feel happy or relaxed, I guess."

His fingers traced invisible circles on her back as she talked.

"You said *made* instead of *make*," he said. "How do you feel now?"

"Anxious. Terrified. Unsettled. Unsafe."

"That settles it. Come play house with me, then. Mom will love it."

Avery laughed. "Oh, I bet. Won't we scandalize the town, shacking up in your mother's house?"

"Nah, she'll keep me in line. You'll get my room. I'll either get the squeaky daybed in Mallory's room or the couch when I'm not working nights. When I am I'll sleep in my bed while you're working."

"She won't mind?" Avery asked, concern filling her face.

"She won't mind. I'll call her now if it will make you feel better."

"Thanks." Avery found his naked-walk just as entertaining as the first time as she watched him leave the bed and gather up his clothes on the way to the bathroom. She heard the murmur of his voice behind the door and questioned her sanity while he talked to Ruthie on the phone.

He entered the room with a smile on his face. "See? I told you she wouldn't mind. I had to get off the phone when she started rattling off questions about the menu for the week. Are you a picky eater?" he asked, quirking an eyebrow.

"Not a bit. As long as I get enough green veggies, I'm easy to please," she answered with a grin.

"Green veggies. Got it. So, can I help you gather your things?" he asked, sitting on the corner of the bed.

Avery stretched and smothered a yawn. "That would be great. I've got some suitcases in the garage. I'll just pack enough for the week.

Jake noticed as he walked to the garage that Avery was right. She didn't have much clutter, but what she did have was an interesting reflection of her personality. There were lots of blues and grays and neat little statues here and there. He paused in front of a bookshelf and noticed a framed picture of Avery and Cade. They were standing in front of a temple of some kind. Cade had his arm thrown around her shoulder and Avery's mouth was thrown open mid-laugh. He knew he had no right to feel the way he did, but he sort of hated Cade. Jake was taken aback by his jealousy and laughed at himself as he continued to the garage.

He looked around until he saw the suitcases and turned to walk back to the house when something caught his eye. The circuit board of the alarm system was positioned near the garage door and the wires were cut. Jake pulled his phone from his pocket and called it in. No wonder Avery hadn't heard the alarm beep when she entered the house last night. The son of a bitch had disabled the security system.

seventeen

RUTHIE PACED AROUND THE KITCHEN as Avery recapped the situation with her mother and the break-in. "I just don't understand how something can happen like this. We barely have any crime!" Ruthie exclaimed.

"Beg your pardon?" Jake asked, crooking an eyebrow at his mother. "Explain that to the dude we busted last week for running a drug ring."

"You're right, you're right, Son. I know. It's just that we have almost never had serious crime in our area and it's just hard to wrap my mind around," she said as she wrung her hands. "I just hate it. I'm so sorry, Avery."

Avery patted the hand Ruthie placed on her shoulder. "It's an awful mess, that's for sure. Thank you so much for letting me stay here. I hope it doesn't cause you any trouble, you know, with gossip."

Ruthie smiled and walked over to the whistling tea kettle. "I'm finally at the glorious stage of life where I don't have to give two shits about gossip. It's the one perk of getting older."

Avery smiled as Ruthie placed a steaming cup of tea in front of her. "Well, thanks all the same."

"You're welcome here. Plus, it'll be nice to get the opinion of someone who still gives a hoot what I think of them," Ruthie said, wiggling her eyebrows.

"Oh boy, what does that entail?" Avery asked.

Ruthie shrugged a shoulder. "Well, I just went on my first date in a million years, and I do believe I'll have another soon. Jesse and Anna give me more trouble than help when it comes to choosing outfits, and maybe you'll be a bit more useful. You know, if you're home. I mean here."

"I'm glad to help. Maybe I can get your opinion on something," Avery said tentatively.

Ruthie grabbed a tin of cookies and placed them in front of Avery. "Shoot. If there's anything I've got, it's opinions. What's up, kid?"

"Well, when my mother barreled through my door and threatened to use my rape experience against me, it gave me an idea. What if I started a support group for victims of sexual abuse? I might be able to kill two birds with one stone." Avery saw the questions in Ruthie's eyes and went on. "I could head off potential gossip by getting the word out first, and more importantly, I could offer support to a market of women who might not otherwise get help."

"Sis, I think that's amazing. Take something ugly and make something good out of it. Good for you. How can I help?"

Avery's heart was warmed by Ruthie's support. "I'm not sure yet. I have some groundwork to do first. This will be a good way for me to channel some of my energy. I need to stop focusing on the shit show my life is becoming… sorry… but I need something new to think about so I don't lose it."

"I'll feel better when the police figure out who the creep is that's getting into your place. I'm sure they'll catch them soon, dear." Ruthie was up and clearing away the tea and cookie dishes. Avery noticed the woman never sat still for long, and it reminded her of her own grandmother.

"I need to excuse myself and make some calls to my patients. I've got some apologies to make for missing appointments today. I'll probably lose a few of them over this."

Ruthie gave a tired sigh as she looked out the kitchen window over the sink. "There's one thing to be sure of, kid. The world is full of people who need help. If you lose a few, you lose a few. There will be more."

"Thanks, Ruthie."

"Make yourself at home while you're here, okay? I'm going to go to Eadie's for a while and run some errands. Jake usually sleeps till about three or four when he's got to work nights. You're welcome to use my room if you need to lie down. Or not!" Ruthie clasped her hand over her mouth at her own joke.

Avery nodded her thanks and tried to put out of her mind that the woman had basically just encouraged her to go sleep with her son. *We're all adults here, Avery*, she scolded herself.

The idea was a good one, though. She could just sneak in and sleep beside him… but what if she woke him up and then he wasn't on top of his game during his shift. She shook her head and tried to stop the negative train of thought she'd started down. Her watch seemed to tick slowly as she plotted to wait another hour before creeping up there. Till then, she could make calls to her clients and then maybe look around a little to see what she could learn about Jake.

When calling her patients, one mentioned that if she had not shown up for an appointment she would have been charged a copay. "Do you want me to send you $40 to make up for me missing our appointment because my house was broken into, Sheila?" Avery had asked against her better judgement.

"No, Dr. O'Gara. I was just noting the double standard."

"Thank you, Sheila. Would you like to reschedule for Friday?"

Thankfully, the other calls were a little less cagey. Her clients were sorry to hear of her trouble and said they'd work with her to reschedule. *Half an hour to go*, Avery thought as she glanced back at her watch.

The moment she found the note in her closet kept

flashing in her mind. Avery needed a distraction. A set of shelves in the living room caught her eye. It proudly displayed trinkets, books, and the milestone photo moments a proud mother would want to look back on over time. There before her was a timeline of Mallory's and Jake's lives in a handful of photos. On the top shelf there was a wedding picture of Ruthie and Alek in their 1970s garb. Ruthie was pretty in her simple wedding gown. Her eyes seemed to glimmer with excitement as Alek stood proudly beside her. Avery was shocked at how much Jake resembled his father. Both had dark hair, broad shoulders, and strong jaws. Thankfully, from what Jake had shared, that was about where the resemblance ended.

She picked up a frame that held a picture of Jake walking in a diaper with a pair of cowboy boots and a fairly bald head with Mallory smiling in the background. She couldn't help but smile at the little boy, astounded that such a sweet little fellow could grow into a strong, fierce, and brave man one day. There were skinny little league pictures as well as as tough, unsmiling football pictures from the 90s next to Mallory's volleyball and basketball pictures. Jake's high school graduation picture featured a glowing Ruthie and a glowering Alek. His police academy graduation picture showed Mallory and Ruthie proudly wrapping their arms around Jake. *His father must've passed by then, she reflected.* It was clear in the way that Jake spoke about his father that it was almost relief that he was gone. She had enough life experience even outside of her career as a therapist to know that even when relationships were damaged and strained, there was usually an undercurrent of regret that things hadn't been different. She could certainly understand those feelings.

There was one way Avery knew she could be certain to keep her mind busy for a while. She snuck over to the backdoor to turn the lock and peeked out the window to be sure Ruthie's car wasn't in the drive. She glanced at her watch one last time, and a smile spread over her face. She crept up the hall to Jake's room and opened the door. Her clothes barely made a sound as they fell the floor, and she had almost made it under the covers soundlessly until she reached over for a condom in the half-open drawer.

Jake rolled to his side and grabbed Avery, pulling her on top of him. "What are you doing in here… don't you know you're not supposed to wake a sleeping bear?"

"I was willing to take the chance. Your mother said you usually wake up around three or four o'clock."

He shook his head. "When you're naked in my bed, the only two words you're not allowed to say to me are 'your mother.'"

A giggle escaped her lips. "Got it. Anyway, I was hoping I could help wake you up. You know, help your evening get off to a good start."

"Nicely done." He nodded with a smirk.

"Thank you," she replied as she placed her hands on either side of his face. "You're getting scruffy," she said, smoothing his beard with her fingertips.

"And you…" he reached down to pull her leg up against his and ran his palm up and down her thigh, "are not."

A wanton sound escaped her, and he took the opportunity to pull her lips to his. One hand wrapped gently around the back of her neck while the other moved down her spine. Every inch of her was pressed against every inch of him. The light blocking curtains gave the room a sense of confusion as to whether it was day or night. Avery's mind didn't wrestle for long against the conflict of light and time. She was quickly distracted as she shut her eyes and gave herself over to the powerful sensations of Jake teasing her with his lips and hands.

"THAT WAS ONE HELL of a way to wake up. Want to grab dinner tomorrow night?" he asked as he dressed in his uniform. "I'm off the next three nights."

Jake was sexy in just about everything she'd seen him wearing, but when he was dressed in his uniform, it nearly undid her. "That sounds great. Tomorrow's my late night, so I won't be able to leave the office until seven. Is that too late for you?"

"That works out well. I've got meetings with the builder to go over some final things. Lighting, cabinet door handles, and whatnot. That kind of thing. Why don't we meet at the Hawk's Nest?"

She raised an eyebrow at his choice of restaurants. "You sure? Last time we were there you were pretty ticked off at me."

He sighed an irritated sigh and said, "Avery, this town is so small, we can't start avoiding places where we get ticked off at each other. We won't be able to go anywhere at all." She rolled her eyes and agreed.

"Okay, if you insist."

He crooked an eyebrow. "I insist."

"You're so bossy. Sounds good. I'll probably cut out early in the morning, so I might miss you. See you tomorrow night." She leaned up and placed a kiss on his lips. "Be careful."

"Will do. Don't let my mom talk your leg off."

"We'll be fine. I'm thankful she's allowing me to stay. I'll call you if I hear anything from the detective."

His knowing smile confirmed her suspicion that he would know details about her case even before she did.

"Have a good night. See you tomorrow evening."

When she walked out of the house, Avery stopped short when she saw a Mercedes parked at the end of the driveway. For an instant she was terrified that the person behind the tinted window would be her mother, but she quickly realized there was no way her mother could worm her way into a car that nice. The window rolled down to reveal a gorgeous woman. Avery began walking toward her vehicle but kept one eye on the car. She wouldn't be able to pull out of the driveway until the woman moved.

The woman didn't say a word but stared at Avery from behind sunglasses. Avery sighed and threw up a quick prayer for patience.

"Excuse me, would you please move your car?"

"Excuse me," the woman said with a sneer. "Would you please stop screwing my husband?"

"Ahh," Avery said. "You must be Juliet. What an *interesting* way to make an introduction," she said, taking a step toward Juliet's car. "Unless, of course, you consider the bizarre, threatening message that you left for me at my office number our first exchange."

"Threatening?" Juliet said, her forehead slightly wrinkling as her eyebrows rose higher. "That was nothing." And with that, she drove away.

Avery's hands shook, not so much from nerves, but from her temper. She called to leave a message for the detective about the conversation. She'd absolutely had her fill of being threatened and made to feel like a sitting duck. She touched her hand to the gun in her holster hidden beneath her shirt. Avery didn't like feeling as if she had to be prepared at any moment to defend herself, but the days of only keeping a gun beside the bed were long over.

THE LOW LIGHTING in the Hawk's Nest was inviting after what had begun as a stressful day. Avery nursed a martini at the bar while waiting for Jake to arrive. She fiddled with the olives on the cocktail pick, trying to decide whether to eat them now or savor them at the end of the drink. The vodka was doing its job, and she had entered a nice state of relaxation when Jake dropped a sugar packet next to her elbow on the bar. "Did you drop your name tag?"

She laughed despite herself. "Jake, that's terrible."

"Hang on, I've got another one. How about this?" he said, then cleared his throat. He arched an eyebrow and gave his best smoldering look. "Do you like your ego massaged or your ID shaped?"

Avery outright laughed at that. "Better. Nice touch, Freud."

"Is that a slip?"

"Okay, okay…" She smiled, popping an olive into her mouth.

"Let's grab a booth." She nodded and grabbed her drink as he pulled her chair back when she stood.

They settled into a booth at the back, and Jake chose the seat that gave him the best vantage point over the bar. Avery noticed and wondered if that was something taught in training, instinct, or coincidence. Of course, he did get jumped by a goon in an alley recently. She wondered if he felt anxious or if he was used to the dangerous element of his job. A self-professed terrible communicator, Avery doubted she'd ever know unless she outright asked.

"So, I spoke with Detective Jones today. Most of the fingerprints they pulled were crossed with yours, like the doorknobs and light switch, but they did find one on the rod your clothes hang on. They were able to confirm it matched the set pulled from the night the man took the pictures inside your house, but they are prints that aren't in the system yet, so we still don't know who it is."

"You said the man who got in… how do you know it's a man?"

"Well, after the tone of the texts questioning where you were and who are you with, I assumed it was a man."

Avery took another sip of her drink. "Well, let me tell you about an alarming female I encountered today." She recounted the details of her experience with Juliet between interruptions from the well-intentioned waitress.

Jake raked his hand through his hair and leaned his head back against the back of the booth. "She's getting out of control. She's got to be on drugs or something. We've been divorced for months, apart for longer. Hell, she was screwing around most of the time because she was so tired of me, and now? Why is she doing this now?"

All Avery could do was shrug in response. "I don't know, but I did call it in. At this point I'm making certain there's a paper trail for every spooky thing that happens."

"I don't blame you. That's probably a good idea. Normally, I'd say that she's more of an annoyance than a threat, but at the rate things are going here lately, it's probably better to be safe than sorry."

He covered her hand on the table with his own. "I'll call her and find out what the heck she's doing here anyway. She has no good reason to be down here."

"Good. Be careful, though. She's spooky."

"That she is."

"Hey, before I forget, there's a birthday party for my cousin Jesse's step kids this weekend. Would you like to go with me?"

She felt surprised that her immediate reaction was yes.

Avery wasn't one for social gatherings, or people for that matter, most of the time. This guy was growing on her.

"Let me guess, family shindig at Jesse's?"

"You're getting the hang of it."

She took a bite of her sandwich to buy time while she thought it over. His smirk told her that he was on to her.

"You don't have to come if you don't want to, but I'd like to spend time with you."

"We're basically living together…" she said with a roll of her eyes.

"Oh, I'm sorry," he said wryly. "Has it been so awful?"

"I'm just teasing. I'd like to go. I'm just a little embarrassed because of last time."

He took a bite of his cheeseburger and nodded. "I get it. This stuff isn't your fault, though. Please don't be embarrassed. Trust me, you won't be the center of attention."

Avery was confused. "What are you talking about?" she asked. Then it hit her. "Oh, the kids, of course."

"No. Better," he said with a small laugh.

"What?"

"Mom's bringing a date. All eyes will be on her."

"Ohh!" Avery exclaimed. "Good for her. She's brave."

Jake nodded. "Thank God he already knows most of us. Can you imagine walking into that group blind?"

At Avery's dirty look he laughed out loud. "They are a handful. But, they're a good handful. Plus, someone else is coming to the party."

"Who?" Avery asked, curiosity filling her face.

"My sister."

"Ah, what's she like?"

Jake shrugged. "Well, she's got a very strong personality. You'll either love her or hate her."

Avery's eyes clouded as she wondered what she was getting into.

"She's also my best friend," he said with a wicked grin.

Avery decided on the spot that she wouldn't miss the party for the world.

Later that night Avery had butterflies in her stomach as she snuck down the hall to the living room. Jake looked like a bear on a tricycle cramming himself on the couch to sleep for the night. He opened his eyes when he heard her stepping toward him.

He looked at her with a question in his eye and she gave a wicked grin.

"I'd prefer you shape my ID...definitely."

"Woman, you're going to wear me out!" he growled as he pulled her down to him.

eighteen

THE TWINS, JAMES AND HANNAH, had a terrific turnout for their birthday party. The yard was swarming with kids, adults, and the two family dogs, Harry and Oscar. Laughter rang through the air and the bugs had begun their night time serenade. The party was supposed to have ended hours earlier, but people seemed to be having such a nice time almost everyone stayed. Jesse had opted for a farm theme, and straw bales were arranged in a ring around a big bonfire.

Jake smiled and wrapped an arm around Avery's waist as they walked toward the group clustered around the group of adults busy handing out supplies for the s'mores the kids were begging to make.

"Want one?" Levi asked, handing a marshmallow and stick to Jake. He crooked an eyebrow at Avery who rewarded him with a big smile.

"Yes! I haven't had one of those in years!" she said, taking the napkin, chocolate, and graham crackers that Jesse doled out.

"So glad you guys could make it. It's been a crazy afternoon."

Avery looked around at the kids, and stage-whispered, "These aren't all relatives, are they?"

Jesse laughed. "No, the kids, except for the ones you've already met, are friends who will hopefully be picked up by parents soon. I'm nearly dead on my feet. Speaking of relatives, though, here comes one more."

Jake and Avery turned to see a woman walking up the driveway. She turned in time to see a huge smile light up Jake's face. He took her hand and walked her over to the gorgeous brunette. "Mal, good to see you," he said, pulling her into a hug.

"You too, brother. You must be Avery!" Mallory said, wrapping Avery into a quick embrace. Avery did her best not to be rigid as her head barely crested the woman's shoulder. She had to chill out and accept that the whole danged family were huggers.

She was jolted out of the hug by Ruthie's cry, "Mallory! You made it!" She barely escaped before Ruthie had pulled Mallory into her arms. A lump formed in Avery's throat as she shut down the instinctive comparison she made between the scene before her of a mother and daughter who deeply loved one another and her own toxic experience. Her own mother had left an invisible emotional residue that no amount of soap or positive affirmations would remove.

Mallory was quickly paraded around to gather hugs from the rest of the crew while Jake and Avery filled their plates with leftover birthday cake and, of course, one melty, gooey s'more. A contented and tired feeling appeared to settle over the grown-ups, no doubt thrilled the kids would all be exhausted and sleep well that night.

Avery had just settled down on a straw bale with a piece of birthday cake when Jesse, Anna, and another woman came to sit beside her.

"Brought you something," Anna said with a grin as she handed Avery a cup. "Avery, this is my best friend, Sorcha. Sorcha, this is Dr. Avery O'Gara. She's seeing Jake, but we liked her first," she added with a laugh.

"Nice to meet you, Avery," Sorcha said, smiling before turning her eyes to the crowd to track down the location of her daughter.

"Nice to meet you, too." Avery sniffed the red Solo cup Jesse handed her and smiled appreciatively. "Merlot?"

"What? It's for the chill in the air," Jesse said.

"It's got to be eighty degrees outside."

"So what? Just drink the danged wine," she said with a slap on Anna's shoulder. "We've had kids here for what feels like ten hours. It seemed appropriate to sneak some."

Mallory wandered over to the ladies and grabbed a seat.

She leaned over and sniffed Avery's cup. "Oh good, are we drinking?" she asked with a wicked grin.

"Yes! I'll grab a cup for you, be right back," Anna said, bounding to the house. In a flash she was back with a plastic cup for Mallory, who sipped appreciatively.

"Ah, just what I needed. I don't know what the deal is, but the drive from Chicago gets longer every time I make it."

Jesse laughed. "I know what it is..."

Mallory looked at her beneath knitted brows. "What? Are you going to tell me I'm getting old? If so, I don't want to hear it. I was already *ma'am*ed at the gas station today."

The group quietly laughed in commiseration. On one hand it was nice to be around polite people, but there was just something about being called ma'am that stung the pride.

Jesse whistled. *"Ma'am*ed? That blows. Nah, I wasn't going to call you old, even though you're older than me... I was just going to rag you about sticking around here, or at least moving closer."

Mallory sighed. "Yeah, yeah, older by just a few years. Not you, too, by the way, on the moving. I'm already getting it from Mom and Jake."

Anna chimed in, "It's not so bad here. I adapted fairly quickly."

"Yeah, you did," Sorcha said in sarcastic tone.

Anna elbowed her best friend. "Okay, okay!"

The ladies watched the kids run for a few minutes in silence, which Avery suspected wouldn't last long.

"They're pretty cute, huh?" Anna said, gesturing toward Ruthie and her date.

"They are," Avery agreed.

"What's Jake think about it?" Sorcha asked, looking around for the men and finding them gathered around the grill.

Avery thought about it. "He hasn't really said much, which I'm learning is kind of his thing…" she paused when the other women snickered and Mallory coughed around her barely swallowed sip. "But, I think he's glad she's got a friend."

"Me, too," Mallory added. "We've been after her for years to get out more. He must be something special for her to even consider dating."

"Hank is a pretty terrific man from what I've been able to tell so far," Anna added. "He lost his wife a few years ago. She had cancer, I believe."

"Ugh, cancer's the worst," Jesse added. "I'm a big fan of keeling over one night in my sleep."

"Agreed," both Sorcha and Anna said at once.

"Jinx, you owe me a Coke," Anna said, bumping Sorcha with her shoulder.

"What's the latest on your situation, Avery? Jake said Ruthie insisted you come stay with them for a while," Jesse asked.

"I tell you, I hate intruding on them, but it is nice not to be completely skeeved out all the time," Avery answered with a shrug.

Mallory chuckled. "Believe me, you're not intruding. My mom is in hog heaven with someone in the house who actually talks. Seriously, though, she said someone was in your bedroom?"

"Yeah," Avery said, nodding her head. "I'd handled it pretty well up until the closet. To think someone took the time to rearrange all my clothes - that's pretty jacked up. That goes beyond a fixation or harassment. That's obsession. At first, I thought it was someone who wanted to mess with me. I've had a few patients over the years that discontinued treatment abruptly. I even had to dismiss one recently. It feels like something more than that, though. My gut tells me it's not someone that intends to harm me - they've had ample opportunity. I think they - whoever they are - is trying, and succeeding, by the way, to get in my head."

"Who would do that, though?" Anna asked.

"Well, I have two ideas," Avery replied.

Anna gasped with eyes as round as saucers. "Who?"

"Did Jake or Ruthie tell you about the threatening voicemail?"

"No," the ladies answered, shaking their heads and leaning in closer.

"Well, apparently Juliet has flipped her lid and has the delusion that I've stolen her husband."

Mallory let loose a very unladylike huff. "Crazy bitch," she muttered.

"Wait, wasn't she banging her trainer or something?" Sorcha asked.

Anna's head jerked around at her friend. "How in the world do you remember that?"

Sorcha looked at her like she was crazy. "I'm a stay-at-home mom with a husband who's been home on medical leave. You people are more entertaining than soap operas. I have to take my drama where I can find it."

Jesse sighed. Avery had the impression she was well-versed in Sorcha's biting wit.

Avery continued, "Anyway, she left a message calling me a homewrecker. Then, earlier this week she was parked outside the driveway at Jake's house and told me to stop sleeping with her husband."

"Oh my gosh. What did you do?" Anna asked.

Avery threw her hands up. "I called her out on her threat, and she told me that I hadn't seen anything yet, or something similar."

"Whoa," Sorcha said.

Jesse rubbed her worry lines from her forehead. "That's just absurd. We knew she was a liar, but we didn't know she was that crazy. Who's the other person you suspect? You said there were two, right?"

Avery took a deep breath. "Well, my mother is a useless waste of humanity, and she's recently come after me for money. She might be trying to rattle me enough so that I give in."

Mallory piped up, "No shit?"

Jesse asked. "What happened?"

Avery groaned. "I hate talking about this, but I'm going to be doing it a lot soon, so I may as well get used to it."

"Hey," Jesse said, patting Avery's knee. "I don't mean to pry, I'm sorry. You don't have…"

"No, it's fine. I need to get over the awkwardness. She threatened to blackmail me over something that happened in my past. She was wasted most of my childhood and definitely through my adolescence. Mother had the typical addict traits, unable to hold down a steady job, stream of abusive men in and out of our home all the time. One attacked me when I was fifteen, and I ran away to my grandma's that night. My mom never came for me," Avery said, looking down at her feet. She dreaded the look of pity she knew would be in the eyes of her new friends.

Jesse grabbed her and held her in a tight embrace. "Unreal," she hissed.

"I'm so sorry, Avery," Anna added.

For a second, Avery felt every inch the child again, locked in her grandmother's embrace. An unsteady breath filled her, and she steeled herself against the surge of feelings.

"Well, I think I've found a way to make something good come from it, and I'm trying to get it in place before she leaks the story. She told me that unless I paid her some hush money she was going to start whispering it around town in hopes of ruining my business, or at least my image."

"But that doesn't make any sense," Sorcha said. "You're a therapist, right? If anything, it gives you more credibility because you've been on the other side of pain and abuse." Avery's heart warmed at Sorcha's insight.

"I'd like to think so, but you never really know, I guess."

"Anybody worth their salt will fall behind you rather than tear you down over something you couldn't help. If not, we'll kick their asses," Jesse said with a twinkle in her eye.

"I'll drive home and help," Mallory said as the ladies quietly laughed over the idea.

"Anyway, what's your plan?" Anna asked conspiratorially.

"Well, I was thinking about starting a support group for victims of sexual assault. It could start small, hopefully there aren't many in the area, but we all know more often than not it goes unreported."

The ladies nodded their agreement.

"I could probably start off talking with the school counselors and leaving my card. I can talk with the hospital board and area churches."

"I have a friend who works with an organization in town that might be of some help. I'll get her contact info for you."

"Thanks, Jesse."

"And I can help with the schools," Anna said. "I'm not teaching here yet, but I've managed to make some contacts."

"You guys are terrific, thanks. I was thinking of starting small, maybe one meeting a month, depending on the demand. Then, I could play it by ear."

"I think it's wonderful," Ruthie said, walking up to the ladies with Hank and Eadie by her side.

"Uh oh, were we louder than we thought?" Jesse asked, peering into her glass.

"No, I just have exceptional hearing for an old broad." Ruthie cackled.

"You're not a broad, you're a lady," Hank mused.

All the women got a kick out of that one.

"It's been a lovely party, hasn't it, Jesse?" Eadie said with a smile. "I love seeing our family gathered together with kids running everywhere again. It reminds me of when you kids were little."

"We had some fun, that's for sure," Jesse answered. "Speaking of fun, it's not going to be fun getting all these little people washed up and to bed anytime soon. I guess it's time we start wrapping it up." She caught Levi's eye and gave him the nod.

"They're so creepy. It's almost like they don't even need to talk sometimes," Anna said, leaning in to Avery.

"I think it's sweet," Avery said with a smile.

"What's sweet?" Jake asked, leaning down to plant a kiss on Avery's cheek. She jumped at the contact and reminded herself to relax. If she was going to hang with these people and actually give this relationship a chance, she'd better get used to contact. And lots of it. They were the touchiest group of people she ever remembered being around.

"The way Jesse and Levi are together," she answered.

He smiled. "They're pros at this point."

"They seem to be," she said, smiling as he extended his hand to help her up.

"Are you about ready to go?" he asked, leaning down close to her ear.

"Shouldn't we see if they need any help?" Avery asked, looking around to see what needed to be put up.

"Get out of here, you guys. We've got it under control," Jesse said, shooing them with her hands.

"That's right, you have to be around us at least another month before we work you like a dog. You're still the new kid," Anna joked.

"Fine, fine. It was a lovely party. Thanks for inviting us. Happy birthday, Hannah. Happy birthday, James," Avery said into the chocolate-and-marshmallow-covered faces that had just run over to Jesse.

"Thank you!" Hannah answered.

"Thank you," James said with a scowl, rubbing his arm where Hannah elbowed him for not answering fast enough.

"Come on, guys, let's go tell your friends goodbye," Jesse said, wrapping an arm around each set of shoulders. "Night, you guys."

"Night," Jake said. "Mom," he paused and looked down at his watch. "What time will you be home?" he asked with raised eyebrows.

"Oh, get out of here," Ruthie said with a hoot. "Hank will drive me home. Eadie, you want a lift?"

"That would be great, let me grab my purse. I want to go tell the kids goodnight. Be right back." Eadie stopped halfway across the yard and patted Levi on the back, no doubt praising the success of the birthday party.

"It'd be nice if she'd find a nice friend," Ruthie said to Hank. "You have any brothers?" she added with a smile.

"No brothers, but I might have a friend in mind. Let me know when you think she might be ready. It's still early yet," he said with a gentle pat on Ruthie's hand.

"You bet. See you later, you two," she said toward Jake and Avery. "Be careful getting home."

"Yes, ma'am. See you in a bit," Jake said, placing a kiss on top of his mother's head. "Hank," he added with a nod.

"Jake," Hank nodded back.

"Nice to meet you, Mallory," Avery said as Mallory pulled her into a one-armed hug.

"Same to you, see you guys in a little while."

"How long are you home, Mal?" Jake asked. "Do I need to haul in a suitcase when you get home?"

She shook her head. "Nah, I have to leave tomorrow evening."

"Damn. That's a long drive for such a short trip," he said with a frown.

"Yeah, but it was worth it. I was getting a little homesick."

He nodded in understanding. "Been there, done that, moved back."

Mallory sighed in annoyance. "Not again, Jake…"

He grinned and waved her off. "Fine." He pulled Avery to him and walked back to his truck.

"Well?" he asked as they backed out of the drive.

"It was nice," Avery answered. "They are a touchy bunch, aren't they?"

"It's not all bad, is it?" he asked as he placed his hand on her knee and squeezed.

Warmth started to build as he slowly inched his way up and down her thigh.

She gave a sideways grin. "No, it's not all bad."

nineteen

ONE NIGHT LATER, JAKE PACED NEAR his cruiser after he parked it outside his house. In the back of his mind he remembered his mother telling him to save the bad news until morning; she hated to go to sleep worried. However, this was news that wasn't going to be able to keep.

"You want me to do the talking?" Officer Henderson asked after parking behind Jake.

He shook his head. "No, I can tell her. Just give me a minute." He leaned over the cab of his car and ran his hands through his hair, bracing his elbows on the roof. "Okay. Let's get this over with."

Henderson patted him hard on the shoulder. "I'm here if you need me."

Jake had done this kind of thing many times over his years as an officer. It was pretty much the worst part of his job. He hesitated at the door, feeling as if the solemnity required a knock, even though it was his own house.

The door opened, and he heard Ruthie call out, "Hello, dear, what are you doing home?" The smile died on her lips when she saw Jake's expression, and then another officer on his heels.

"Well, Austin, what are you doing here, kid?" she said, a confused expression on her face as she quickly embraced the boy who used to be on her doorstep as a kid, running around with Jake.

"I need to talk to Avery," Jake said, his voice low.

Just then Avery rounded the corner. "Ruthie, did you say... Hey, Jake. What are you doing home already?"

When his eyes met hers, she stopped. Her hand automatically went to her chest. "What is it?" she asked, sitting down on the couch. Her brain ran wild. The only person she really cared about outside of his family was Cade. Jake wasn't looking at Ruthie though, he was looking at her. "Jake. Tell me?"

He sat down beside her. "We had a call come in a few hours ago. A body was found south of town..."

"A body?" she interrupted.

"Avery, due to identification found on her person, we determined that the woman we found was your mother."

Vomit rushed up Avery's throat, and she stood and raced to the bathroom off the hallway. When she returned to the living room she found Ruthie sobbing and Jake looking as if he had been turned inside out. The other officer stood in the corner of the room, like if he tried hard enough he might disappear from the intimate scene.

"I'm sorry," Avery said. "Did you say that my mother's body had been found? Did I hear that right?"

Jake sat beside her once she sank to the couch. "Avery, tonight at 7:46 PM dispatch received a call that said someone saw a…"

His words washed over Avery's ears like the tide lapping at a rock. They made a sound, but the meaning didn't sink in. Instead of taking in what it was he was saying, she could only focus on how many times patients over the years had described the instant they heard terrible news. The sensation had always been hard to fathom, but Avery understood now. The sound was a sort of buzzing in their ears, a white-noise that signaled that life had changed forever. She watched his face as he spoke and saw the tension in the other officer's expression. In and out she heard Ruthie's soft cries and accepted the cup of hot tea pressed into her hands. She knew she nodded here and there at what seemed like appropriate times, when the words mother, homicide, gunshot wound, and coroner stung her ears, but more than anything she felt a vivid sense of shame spread like a flame throughout her entire body.

A sense of utter relief cascaded through every fiber of

her being at the notion that the woman who failed to protect her had finally been adequately punished. The sensation was so intense Avery was sure of only one thing - she would be haunted for the rest of her days that her reaction was a sense of peace rather than distress.

Once the news had been given, the other officer excused himself. Avery gave a perfunctory nod at his departure. Ruthie had wrapped Avery in her arms for a hug, and she allowed the contact, but wasn't really grateful for the hug. More than anything, she felt like she wanted to be completely alone. Once Ruthie had gone into the kitchen to rattle around, Avery leaned back on the couch.

"Jake, what happens now?"

He cleared his throat. "Well, there will need to be an autopsy, and once that has been completed, her remains will be released for burial or cremation."

"Autopsy? I thought you said there was a gunshot wound."

He sat beside her and leaned back on the couch resting his head on the back. "Well, they also check for the presence of alcohol and drugs."

A hateful laugh escaped Avery's lips. "You can bet they'll find both."

Jake gave her a sad smile. "I'm so sorry, Avery."

She rubbed her face with her hands and propped her elbows on her knees. "This is unreal. I think I need to go to bed."

"Okay, I'll tuck you in."

Avery walked back to his bedroom, stripped down to her underwear, and pulled a gown over her head. Jake pulled back the covers and waited until she was settled. He smoothed the soft blanket over her and reached down to brush her hair back from her face. Gently, he placed a kiss on her forehead and flicked out the light.

"I've got to go back out for the night, but my mom is here if you need her, okay?"

"Okay. Thank you."

He stepped toward the door when she spoke.

"Jake?"

"Yeah?"

"You're going to have to tell me everything again in the morning. I only got part of that."

He nodded his head softly. "Will do. Get some sleep."

She listened to his footsteps go down the hall and the murmur of his voice as he said goodnight to Ruthie.

"Bless her heart," she heard Ruthie say in response. "I'll take care of her, hon. Be safe, Son. Love you."

"Love you, too, Mom. Thanks."

RUTHIE WAS SHOCKED when Avery whisked into the kitchen the next morning. Her eyes were swollen, but the rest of her appearance was perfection. She wore a light pink silk shirt, black pencil skirt, and spiked heels.

"Morning, Avery. Can I get you any breakfast?" Ruthie asked, a fake smile fixed on her face.

"Ruthie, thank you so much for everything. I'd love some."

"Were you able to sleep at all, kid?"

"Not much. I've been up since 4 AM trying to decide if I should get up and get it over with or just lie there."

Ruthie sighed and placed a steaming cup of coffee in front of Avery. "I hate nights like that."

Fruit and scrambled eggs were placed on the table ,and both ladies fixed their plates. "Jake should be here soon," Avery said, checking her watch.

It took all her composure for Ruthie not to nervously tap her fingers on the table. For once in her life, she wasn't sure what to say.

Avery stared toward the window between pushing bits of food here and there on her plate. "You know, the sad thing about this is - well, I suppose most of it is sad…" she started, then jumped as Jake opened the door.

"Morning," he said as he walked into the kitchen.

"Morning, Son."

Avery gave him a wave of her fingers.

"You were saying, hon?" Ruthie encouraged. Jake grabbed a mug out of the cabinet and Ruthie fixed him a plate.

"The sad thing about this is until now, I hadn't really realized how truly isolated I am," she said, lifting her gaze to Ruthie's and then Jake's eyes. "With the exception of you both, and your family, there's really only one person in the world that I talk to.

"I mean, I have patients, but in my own life, the only person I can think of to call and tell that my mother was murdered, for God's sake, is my friend Cade. He's the only person except for you guys, Jesse, Anna, and Sorcha that know that I had a derelict, substance abusing mother." She shrugged her shoulders. "That's weird, isn't it?"

Jake exchanged a quick glance with his mother. "I wouldn't call it weird, Avery. Your experiences with your mother have been awful, so it makes sense that you wouldn't feel comfortable sharing it with just anyone."

"That's just the thing, though. I don't share anything with anyone. I mean, it's not bad. I am who I am, and most of the time I'm perfectly content to go through life alone. It just strikes me as really strange not to have a list of people to notify," she said with a shrug of her shoulder.

Avery got up and put her plate in the sink, giving it a quick rinse. "Ruthie, thank you for breakfast.

"I'm off tonight. Would you like to go for a drive with me?" Jake asked Avery.

She barely nodded while gathering up her purse and laptop bag. "Sure, thanks. Can we go by my house and check on things? I don't like not knowing what's going on out there."

"You bet."

"It's so kind that Jesse had the boys feeding Rocky. There's no way he would've camped out over here politely."

"That's just the way she is," Ruthie said. "I'm glad you've stayed here, Avery."

"Thank you, Ruthie. Have a nice day," Avery answered, surprising Ruthie with a hug.

"You too, dear," she said when Avery turned her back. She looked at Jake and threw her hands up in the air with her eyes wide.

After the door clicked closed, she rounded on her son. "I have absolutely no idea what to say. 'Have a nice day' doesn't seem like something she's likely to have."

"It's okay, Mom. Might be the best thing to go on like normal until she's ready to talk about this, I guess. I have no real idea what to do, either."

"I think it's good you're getting her out of the house.

"I thought I might drive her out to the lake, or maybe up to see the mountain or something."

"That sounds nice, dear."

He placed a kiss on the top of his mother's head. "Thanks for breakfast. I'm going to go crash for a few hours."

"Jake…"

"Yeah, Mom," he said, leaning against the doorframe.

She walked over to him and held her dish towel in her hands. "I think you know this, but, in case you ever question it… I'm so proud of you, Son.

He pulled her into a hug in the middle of the doorway. "I know, Mom. Thank you."

As SOON AS she heard the door click shut, Ruthie was out the door on her way to her sister's house. This wasn't the kind of news one delivered over the phone so soon after a personal loss. She let herself into Eadie's house and hollered the same "yoohoo" greeting their own mother had their whole lives.

"In here, Ruthie," Eadie announced from the laundry room. "Let me get these out on the line, and I'll be right back inside. Coffee's on."

Ruthie poured two cups and went through the backdoor. She set them on the little table beside the porch swing and went to help Eadie hang her laundry on the line.

"Good Lord, what happened to you?" Eadie said, clutching her damp laundry in her arms.

"Terrible stuff, Eadie."

Eadie's shoulders seemed to set in resolve. "Help me hang this and then tell me everything, Sis."

They worked in companionable silence, making short work of the clothing.

Settling down on the swing, Eadie turned and faced her sister.

"It's Avery's mother," Ruthie said, placing her hand on Eadie's knee. "She was found dead in a field yesterday evening."

Eadie sucked in a breath and put her hand to her mouth. "Oh how terrible, that poor kid can't win for losing, can she? What in the world happened?"

"It was awful, Eadie. We were getting ready for bed. She was in Jake's room, and I was setting the coffee pot for the morning. I heard Jake come in, and he was pale as a ghost. You'd have been so proud of him, Eadie. It's so strange to see your children as professionals sometimes, isn't it? I mean, I look at Jake and see him as a chubby baby. I see him as a pimple-faced teen. Rarely do I truly see him as a police officer. He impressed the hell out of me last night. Anyway," she said, realizing she'd gotten off track. "He sat her down and told her the news. Dispatch got a call from a farmer about a woman's body in his field south of town. Gunshot wound," she said, tapping her chest.

"Poor Avery." Eadie hung her head and dabbed her eyes. "The kid is already under so much stress right now. How awful for her to lose her mother on top of everything."

Ruthie exhaled deeply, catching Eadie's eyes. "That's the thing, Eadie. They weren't close at all. In fact, her mother wasn't much of a mother at all, from the sound of it."

Eadie shook her head, her mother hen instinct no doubt mentally claiming Avery as one of her own at that very moment.

"I know, I know. The poor thing has had it rough. She had a grandma that took her in, but boy, it doesn't seem like that girl had much of a chance to be a… I don't know… a girl at all. It just breaks my heart, Eadie."

With her heart in her eyes, Eadie asked, "What's she like? I've only been around her a handful of times, and she's a little tough to read."

Ruthie shrugged. "You're right, she's very tough to read. I think she's a good woman. There's some warmth in there. At least, I think she tries to be, but maybe doesn't know how exactly. And Jake, well," she said with a snort, "he's so much like his father."

"Ruthie!" Eadie exclaimed. "Jake is a good boy!"

"What I mean is, the only feeling he seems to be able to verbalize is being pissed off. He's been that way since he was a boy. How's this going to play out? She's a therapist, for Christ's sake, and he's terrible with words... I just don't know. I like her," she said. "I do!" she said to Eadie's narrowed gaze. "He just had such a terrible experience with Juliet, that I want the one - and you know what I mean by the one - I want something easy. I don't think this is going to be easy."

Eadie started the swing off to a gentle pace. "Best we can do is love them through it, Ruthie. It's all we can do."

Her sister nodded in reply. "You're right, Sis."

"I love hearing that," Eadie said with a laugh. "So, what can we do to help her? Have any arrangements been made?"

"I'm not sure yet. She doesn't seem to like to rely on anybody, but I think she's going to need us."

Eadie nodded. "Let me know, and we'll circle the wagons," she said with a wink.

twenty

THE GRAVEL KICKED UP AS THE TRUCK meandered up into the hills.

"It's beautiful up here," Avery said softly. Jake glanced over at her, and his heart was heavy at her expression. She hadn't talked about her mother yet, and he was reluctant to push her into it.

He parked and opened the truck door. She exited on his side because the trees were so close on hers. Then Jake led her to a spot where they could sit down on a big rock and settled her between his knees, allowing her to lean back against him to take in the view. "This was one of my favorite places to come once I could drive. It's too light out to see it now, but in the evening you can see the lights from all the different towns."

"I bet that's pretty."

"It is. We'll have to come back sometime." He patted her shoulder and felt her take in a big breath and let it out slowly.

"I was able to make some of the funeral arrangements today," Avery said as she twisted to face Jake. "I'll have her remains at the end of the week. She doesn't..." she stopped to correct herself, "didn't have... any insurance, of course, so I'll be stuck with paying for the cremation, burial, and headstone. Looks like she ended up weaseling some money out of me after all," she said with a bitter laugh.

"What did you decide to do regarding a service?" he asked quietly.

She shrugged. "There's really no point. Nobody here knew her."

"They know you, though, and you're well respected in the community. I imagine there are people who would like to pay their respects if you'd have even a small service."

Avery shook her head. "I have zero interest in a service. I'd rather just get this behind me as quickly as possible."

"I'll go with you if you'll let me." She didn't answer but nodded her head a little. Jake placed his hands on her shoulders and slightly tilted his head to the side. "How are you doing with all this, Avery?"

She lifted a shoulder. "Honestly, I'm not sure. Part of me - and this is going to sound horrible - but part of me is relieved that I'm not going to have to worry about her popping back into my life to ruin it. Part of me is terrified, because now that she's gone, I kind of hope it was her messing with me to put me on edge. But, if it wasn't her, then someone else is out there trying to scare me to death," she said, wiping at a tear that streamed down her face.

"There's even a part of me that feels like maybe she got what she deserved for being such a terrible mother. I know that's awful." She sniffed as her tears ran freely. "Out of all of those feelings, the worst part is that I'm also really sad," she cried.

Jake pulled her onto his lap and tucked her head under her chin. He patted her back softly as she finally let her grief surface. He had no idea what to do to make it better, but at least he could hold her when she needed it.

"Things could have been so different. She could've not been an addict. She could have loved me more than getting high. My mom could have chosen to not allow scumbags into our house. She could've married someone amazing so that now I'd at least have a father in this world - some kind of family." She pulled back and looked into his eyes. "Jake, I'm completely alone. I have no family. My grandmother died years ago and I hadn't seen my mother in forever, but now it's different. I have no one in this world who's always known me."

Avery wiped her hands down her face. "I'm disgusting. Do you have any tissues in the truck?"

"I might, let me go look."

"Actually, can we go now? I want to have enough time to check in at my house, and I'd rather do it before it's totally dark.

He nodded. "You bet. We'll come back another time so I can show you the lights."

━━━━━━━━━━

"You know, I found out my house will be ready in a month," Jake said with a wide smile. "I can't wait to walk through that door."

"It's going to kill your mother when you move out," she said, then winced at her own word choice. He felt his eyes go wide and then tried to look normal.

"She'll do okay. I think having Hank as a distraction will help with the transition."

"Is she going to still clean for you and do your laundry?" Avery snickered.

"Gosh, I hope so," he said, then laughed when she smacked at his shoulder. The gravel crunched underfoot as they walked to Avery's doorstep. "Just kidding. I suppose I'll have to go back to the more plebeian method of doing my own cleaning and laundry."

"Plebeian? I thought I was supposed to be the pompous one in this couple," she said with a laugh.

"A couple? Well, look who's making progress," he said with his eyes wide.

"Now you sound like the psychiatrist," she said under her breath. Avery unlocked the door and listened as the alarm beeped.

"I can't believe they got out here so fast to fix the wiring," he said.

"Well, when the person making the phone call introduces himself as a cop in a loud, aggressive manner, they respond rather quickly," Avery answered, rolling her eyes.

"So what? It worked, didn't it?"

Avery nodded with a small smile. "It did. Thank you. I'm not sure how much faith I have in the damned thing, but at least it's set for now."

They walked through each room and Avery pretended not to notice that Jake had his weapon out, just in case, as they checked each nook and cranny of her home.

"Everything seems to be in place," she said, "except this." She gestured to her closet with a jerk of her head.

Jake checked his watch. "We've got nowhere to be, why don't you put it to rights."

"Are you sure?" she asked, relieved to not be alone while she reorganized her clothes.

"Yeah, take your time," he said as he sprawled on her bed.

She began to sort her clothes by color again. "It shouldn't matter, I guess, but it makes me feel like the intruder wins if I leave it this way." She worked a few more minutes and then stopped. "You know what? This is insane. I'm going to have to launder all these clothes. It disgusts me that some freak was the last one to touch my clothes."

Jake nodded. "I get it. Want to bag it up?"

"Nah, I'm going to wait. I can't bring them back to your house, your mother will try to wash them!"

He laughed. "You're right. We could be sneaky and drop it at a laundromat."

She shook her head. "No, I'm too picky. I'll take care of it when I move back in."

"When's that going to be?" he asked, pulling her down beside him on the bed.

"Soon. I need life to get back to normal."

"It has been kind of nice having you close by," he said as his hands moved slowly over her side. When he reached the curve of her hip, he dipped his head in to kiss her.

"It has been nice," she agreed. "Can you imagine how weird it's going to be when we're neighbors?"

"Weird is not the way I'd describe it. Orgasmic, maybe, but not weird."

A throaty laugh escaped her, and he pounced, pressing her body into the mattress with his weight. "What? Not orgasmic enough for you?" he teased as he listened to her laugh morph into a moan as his lips and tongue made a trail from her neck to her collarbone. His fingers toyed with the buttons on her shirt and she lifted her hips up against him.

She cupped his head as he moved his way down her body, her fingers tangling in his dark hair. His jaw was rough with stubble, and it chafed her soft skin as he explored her curves.

"Your body is so beautiful," he said in a low voice. "So soft and warm," Jake said, smiling at her sharp intake of breath. As he readied her he watched sensations play over her face and took in the sounds she made. When he realized he was falling in love with this complicated, headstrong woman, he pushed the feelings back down into a box he'd sort through later.

Fishing in his wallet for protection, he made short work of the necessary annoyance. She arched her back as he entered her, stretching and writhing to accommodate him. Their lovemaking was intense and unrestrained, and for the first time in a while, as loud as they wanted it.

twenty-one

"I'M GLAD YOU CAME OUT TONIGHT," Anna said quietly to Avery as she hugged her neck.

Avery shrugged. "It feels weird to come have fun, but my mother and I weren't close. Just a lot of bad memories."

Anna squeezed her tightly once more before letting her loose. Avery looked around at the crew of friends assembled and felt pretty fortunate, given the circumstances. Jake had called to let her know that Anna wanted to invite her out for a few hours the night before her mother's service. She had been hesitant at first but decided to give it a try.

Anna and Aidan had taken Benji to Jesse and Levi's house for the evening. Cade had been able to make it in that night and was staying at a hotel in town. They had just settled in at a big table when he walked in.

Avery met him just a few feet inside the door.

"Cade, I can't believe you came," she said, wrapping him in a hug.

He pulled her close and said in a voice where only she could hear, "Listen, your mom was a piece of shit. I love you… don't let this break you, Avery."

She shook her head no to let him know she'd be okay and then broke away.

"Let me introduce you," she said, pulling him by the hand to the table. "Everyone, this is Cade, an old friend of mine. Cade, this is Anna, her husband Aidan, and Jake, whom you've met," she said with a slight eye roll.

"Ah, someone's already done a shot," Cade said with a nod of his head. Jake answered with an affirmative nod and held up his fingers to show she'd had two. Cade smiled. "Nice to meet you all. Nice to see you again, Jake," Cade said with a hand stretched out in greeting. This time Jake accepted his extended hand.

Appetizers were served, and the drinks began to flow.

"Nice to meet you, man. So, what do you do?" Aidan asked Cade.

"I'm a cardiologist with a hospital in St. Louis. And you?"

"Ah!" Aidan said with a sharp laugh. "Avery said you were in cardio, and I swear to God I thought she meant you were a trainer."

Jake winced, and so did Anna, remembering that Jake's ex had been banging her trainer.

"So," Anna interjected, "do you work with a particular age?"

Cade indulged her for a few minutes talking about his profession. He then deflected the spotlight as quickly as he could without seeming rude, asking them about their own livelihoods.

Avery watched Jake as Cade made conversation with the group. They might have gotten off to a rough start, but Jake wasn't fooling her - he liked Cade. At least that's what she thought until the bar door swung open and Mallory walked in wearing a snug white t-shirt, jeans, and cowboy boots. She looked like some sort of Amazon goddess with a long, dark braid resting over one shoulder.

Avery laughed because she knew that Mallory was Cade's walking fantasy woman. She caught the half-smile on his face as Cade gave the incoming goddess his full attention. Without taking his eyes off of her, he leaned in front of Jake to get to Avery. He gave a low whistle and said, "Damn, those boots aren't made for walking!"

Jake cleared his throat and said, "Cade, meet my sister, Mallory."

"Aw, crap," Cade said quietly, but not quietly enough.

Avery laughed, then gave a quick hiccup. She leaned over to Jake and whispered, "This is going to be good." Jake made a note to keep a close eye on her and get the woman some water.

"Mallory," he said with a wide smile. "Missed you, Sis."

"Missed you, too!" she said, throwing her arms around

his neck before moving on to Avery. "Hey, Avery," she said, giving her a squeeze.

"Anna! Look at you, out after dark and everything," she teased, planting a kiss on her cheek.

Anna laughed. "Yeah, first time in over a year. We need to get out more. Benji's at Jesse's for the night," she said, leering over at Aidan, who grinned as he tipped back his beer and gave Mallory a welcoming nod.

"So," Mallory said with a smile as her eyes lit on the stranger at the table, "introduce me."

"Yes, ma'am," Jake obliged, introducing Mallory to Cade.

"Mallory, this is Avery's friend, Cade. He just got in for the service. He'll be leaving tomorrow," he said in a low tone.

"Oh, come on, Jake," Anna added. "Mallory, you might have some fun talking to this guy. Not only is he incredibly cute, he's a cardiologist."

Mallory's eyebrows shot to the sky. "Ah, a cardiologist, how interesting," she said, catching the eye of the bartender as she pointed to her brother's beer.

Cade nodded, feeling a bit like he'd just stepped into a trap. He wasn't much for talking about his profession unless prompted. People got weird around doctors. Not as much as they got weird around clergy or anything, but still weird.

"I'm an ER nurse," she said, holding her hand out to him like they were at a conference rather than a bar. She looked him dead in the eye and he felt a shiver build at the base of his spine. Her challenging stare excited him almost as much as her appearance. He nodded in appreciation and felt the eyes of the others move off of him as conversation picked back up.

AVERY WATCHED THE pair over the top of her water as she sipped for the next few hours. Jake had made sure she had a full glass at her disposal. She leaned over to him and loudly whispered, "Jake, this is going to turn into a thing. I can tell," she said with a satisfied smile.

A look of confusion stole over his face. "Isn't that weird for you?" he asked.

She shrugged. "Not a bit. Cade and I dated here and there in college, but mainly we were best friends. For a lot of years we've been close, but in a best friend way. Best friends that have sex once in a blue moon," she said, holding her glass up in the air in a mock toast.

"Good Lord," Jake said under his breath as he raked a hand over his forehead. "I think it's time we clock out. It's going to be a rough day tomorrow."

Solemnity settled over her face like an invisible veil. "You're right." Avery stood, and in a most un-Avery-like gesture, she hugged everyone at the table. Jake had been watching her, but she'd only had two shots and probably a gallon of water. The realization hit him that she wasn't intoxicated. She was allowing herself to relax. He decided there was a good chance that underneath the cool exterior, she might actually be warm-hearted and affectionate. What really struck him was that she dropped the walls enough to allow her friends to love her in the midst of the hurt of her mother's death.

He wrapped a protective arm around her and said his goodbyes to the group. "Mal, I'll see you at home?"

She answered by looking at Cade, who grinned. "I'll see you in the morning," she said with a wink.

Jake looked up at the sky like he was petitioning for grace, and after bidding goodbye to the friends and family around the table, led Avery out of the bar.

"I'm still surprised I let you talk me into this," Avery whispered to Jake. She looked around the grave to see the others in attendance talking in a low volume as they waited for Ruthie's pastor to say her goodbyes. The only person who wasn't a relative of Jake's was Cade, standing awkwardly to her left with Mallory by his side.

Jake leaned and bumped her shoulder slightly with his. "I'd say it was more my mom's idea than mine. I just suggested you might feel a better sense of closure down the road if we had a very small service. She sealed the deal with cooking the dinner."

"Fine, you're right. Still, I'm glad we did it. Cade, you're going to join us, right?" she asked hopefully.

He shook his head gently. "No, I'm sorry. I need to get back to St. Louis. Thank you for the invitation, though." He wrapped Avery in a great big hug and spoke in her ear, "Take care. Love you, friend."

"Love you, too. Thank you for coming down for this," she said with a smile and wiped away another stupid tear.

"Glad I could make it. Jake," he said, offering his hand.

"Take care," he said with a tight smile.

She watched as he gave Mallory a quick hug and peck on her cheek.

"I'm glad you two are playing nice," Avery whispered to Jake as they watched Cade say his goodbyes to the rest of the group.

"It was a misunderstanding," he said with a half-grin.

"I know, but still, I'm glad you two don't hate each other. That would be weird. He's my only real friend."

Jake pulled her close with an arm around her shoulder. "Ready to go back to the house? You tired?"

"I'm tired of this day…" her voice trailed off. "But, I'm thankful for you all. I can't believe Jesse and Anna and their husbands came. And your sister."

"She decided on a whim to come visit for the weekend. I'm sure my mom will be fired up about her not coming home last night. Expect a hundred or so interrogative questions about Cade over dinner."

Avery nodded in response. "I'd expect nothing less."

Jake shrugged his shoulder a little as Jesse walked up. "Holding up?" Jesse asked.

"Yes, thanks. I was just telling Jake I can't believe you all came today."

Jesse wrapped her arms around her new friend. "We care for you, Avery," she said with a concerned look in her eyes. The love of family had been an automatic thing with their bunch. Jesse gave Avery a smile to hide the hurt in her heart when she thought of how lonesome life would have been without the support of a family like theirs. She couldn't predict what was going to happen between Jake and Avery, but she was glad for at least this little part of her life that Avery was getting to experience what the love of a family could be like.

"I'm sorry you didn't get better news today," Jake said as he held the door open for Avery.

She put her purse and duffle bag on the table beside her entry. "You know, I'm not sure what I expected. She was probably out with some lowlife, or maybe she tried to buy some drugs and didn't have enough money..." Avery ran her hands over her eyes. "Who knows. I just hope they eventually catch whoever did it and stop them from hurting other people."

Jake led the way to her bedroom, and Avery trailed after.

"It's going to be a little lonesome not having you at our house," Jake said as he put Avery's suitcase in her bedroom.

"Just a bit longer and you'll be my neighbor, don't forget," she said, leaning against the doorframe. "Thank you for getting that, by the way."

"You're welcome. I'm glad you stayed a few days after the service. Mom would've rioted had you tried to leave that day."

"The woman nurtures through her cooking. I think I've gained five pounds," Avery said, patting her stomach.

"She does, and you look amazing," he said before dropping a kiss on her lips. "Listen, I've got to get to work, but don't hesitate to call if you need me."

"Got it," she said. "Let me walk you out."

On her doorstep, Jake pulled Avery into a hug. "Have a good night."

"Oh, it'll be a riot. I'm getting started on the great laundry project." She underscored her enthusiasm with a massive eye roll. You have a good night, too. Be safe," she said, planting a kiss on his cheek.

Jake waited on her porch until she stepped inside and he heard the deadbolt click. He saw her stand beside the alarm control, so his mind was a little at ease. He wished she had more protection than the little outside cat and her gun. Jake smiled to himself at the mental image of Avery in nothing but her gun holster and a smile. She was as sexy as she was complicated.

twenty-two

THE CALENDAR ON HER DESK SHOWED that it had already been a month since her mother's death. Avery tilted back in her chair and closed her eyes in an attempt to still her mind. It seemed important to stop and pinpoint the feelings swirling around about her mother. The sadness for what could've or should've been was still there. She also acknowledged the feeling of relief that her mother wouldn't appear out of thin air and try and ruin her professional life.

Avery had promised herself to not dwell on the guilt. She felt guilty not to miss her more because her mother had been a terrible person for most of Avery's life. She was over trying to justify her "not nice" feelings. That was between herself and God, and God knew what her life had been like growing up in that home.

Plus, Avery reminded herself, that horrible visit with her mother had been the impetus Avery needed to start the group for sexual assault victims that would begin meeting next month. She flipped ahead to the next month and circled the date of the first support group.

She flipped the calendar back to the current day and smiled to herself as her eyes skimmed her appointments. Today was the day Jake was going to show off his house. She pulled out a shopping list and made some notes. Tonight was going to be special.

***

"I can't believe the house is finished already," Avery said with a smile. "It's amazing. I'm so proud for you."

Jake pulled the door open. "Thank you. Come on in." He pressed a kiss to her lips and leaned over her shoulder. "What are you hiding back there?"

"Champagne," she answered. "Real stuff for me, fake stuff for you." She walked past him into an open living room. "Jake, this is seriously breathtaking. The view is unbelievable."

"Thank you. I hope you brought cups, I don't have a single thing over here yet.

Her eyes bugged out a little. "Oh shoot. I didn't think of that. What the heck. We can drink out of the bottle. Classy, huh?"

"And you worried you wouldn't fit in when you moved

here," he teased. "How about you join me on the deck and we'll enjoy our drinks before the grand tour.

"Excellent idea," she replied.   Avery's head practically swivelled from side to side as she tried to take in everything at once. "This is just glorious.   I can't get over all the light."

"Thanks.   I've always wanted to live in this kind of house, but in Chicago, *fuhget about it,*" he said in his best Chicago accent. "Not on a cop's salary."

"Property is wildly expensive there, right?"

"Right. Here, pull up a chair," he said with a wicked smile. He turned over two buckets left behind by the builders and gestured to one. "Your seat, milady."

"Very nice."   She watched Jake uncork the champagne and delighted in the strength of his arms.   She thought he might be flexing a little more than was necessary, but she wasn't going to complain.

He twisted off the cork of his sparkling grape juice and grinned. "Nice touch, by the way."

"Hey, nobody said you need to have alcohol to relax," she bantered. "I mean, I do, but nobody said you do."

They drank from their bottles and watched as the colors of the sunset began to transform the view from blue to gold.

"What time does the moving party start on Saturday?" Avery asked, pulling her phone out to set an alarm.

"I'll be at it around six, but the others are coming over at eight.   We'll strike early before it gets too hot.   Honestly, there's not much to move in.   I have a few boxes stored in Mom's garage, but the bulk of it will be delivered from the furniture store. I left almost all the furniture and house stuff in Chicago when I left.

"That'll make for an easy day, then. I'll be here to help unload."

"Sounds good, thanks." He turned his green eyes on her. "Things still okay at your place?"

"Jake," she said with exasperation.

"What?"

"You ask me every single day when we talk. I promise, if something was weird you'd be the first to know, right after the 911 dispatcher, of course."

He sighed. "I'm sorry. I just have to ask. I can't help it."

"It's turning into a compulsion..." she said in a hushed, teasing tone.

"Fine, I'll try to relax a little. With my grape juice." He placed his hand on her knee and breathed in the air from the gorgeous evening.

THEY SAT IN companionable silence for a few minutes until Jake laughed to himself.

"What?" Avery asked, her curiosity piqued.

"My sister called today..."

"And?"

Jake turned his green gaze on her with scrutiny. "It turns out she and Cade have really hit it off. Did you know about this?"

Avery shrugged. "Well, it's been several weeks since I've

talked to him, but..." she bugged out her eyes. "Wait, it's been a several weeks since I've talked to him." She tilted her head to the sky as she thought. "I can't think of a single time period that we've gone a full three weeks without talking."

Jake gave a small chuckle. "Well, I think he's been all tied up with my sister." He shivered as if he was grossed out. "Let me rephrase that. I think they're now a thing."

She slapped lightly at his shoulder. "No way!"

"I think so. You remember how they were at the bar that night, and at your mother's service."

Avery's eyes were round with surprise. "You're totally right. I knew there was a spark, but an official thing, huh? That's amazing!"

He shrugged a shoulder. "They seem to have a lot in common. You've been his...," he cleared his throat, "his *friend*, for several years..."

"Yes! His friend, come on now. You can't hold that against me."

"Fine. You've been his friend for years. Is he a good person?"

She smiled and put her hand over his. "He really is. He's brilliant, adventurous, loves to travel. And he's one of the funniest people I know. Cade is a total commitment-phobe, though. Is she the type to have expectations?"

Jake shook his head a little. "No, I don't think so. We saw our mother go through so much heartache, neither of us ever really planned to settle down. She's a year older than I am, and as far as I know, she's never really done the whole serious relationship thing. Mallory is more liable to hop a last minute flight to California if she gets the weekend off than to buy wedding magazines."

"Then they're probably going to have a great time together." Avery sighed. "Isn't that something? What a weird, but awesome, situation.

Nodding his agreement he wrapped an arm around Avery. The sound of footsteps in the grass drew their attention. Jake rose and stood in front of Avery, unsure who was coming around the side of his house.

When Juliet rounded the corner, Jake let a curse fly under his breath.

"Well that's a really polite way to greet me, Jake." She put her hand on her cocked hip and seemed to enjoy taking him by surprise.

He bit back the caustic reply that sprang to his lips in deference to Avery, and took a deep breath.

"What are you doing here, Juliet?" he asked as he crossed his arms, his body taking on a defiant stance.

"I tried calling a few times, but you didn't answer. Anyway, Jake, this was too important to talk about over the phone." Juliet placed her hand over her very pregnant belly. Her eyes drifted quickly over Avery and she looked away, clearly dismissing her of any importance.

"Cut the shit, Juliet. What the hell is this about?" Jake said in a low tone.

Juliet's face filled with joy and she cooed, "Jake, you're going to be a daddy!"

Avery stood from her seat and turned to Jake. "I'm getting out of here," she said quickly and quietly.

"No, wait. Please, you don't have to leave. This is a mistake," Jake said as he reached out to grab Avery's arm.

Despite their difference in size, she quickly jerked her arm away from him. "Listen, Jake. I have enough drama going on in my life right now to choke a horse." She gestured between him and Juliet. "I don't need this on top of it." Avery turned on her heel and walked back through his house, grabbing her purse and keys. He heard her wheels on the gravel, and his gut twisted with annoyance.

When Jake looked back at Juliet, he wished he could slap the smug grin from her face. "What is this about? That baby can't be mine."

"Now, Jake, where are your manners? Aren't you going to ask me in?" Juliet asked with a demure smile on her face.

He let out a bitter laugh. "Absolutely not, but I'll walk you to your car," he said, making tracks around to the front of his house. Juliet followed him at a slow pace. She walked past where he was standing and went instead to be seated on the step leading up to his front porch.

She did her best to paste a pained expression on her face. "You can't expect me to leave without talking about this, Jake."

Exasperated, he said, "I can't believe a word that comes out of your mouth. All you've done for years is lie to me." He raked his hand through his hair and looked down at the ground. "What is going on? The truth, Juliet," he said with a glare, bringing his angry green eyes up to hers.

"The truth is, you're finally going to be a father." She got up with exaggerated effort and walked up to him. She placed her hand on his arm and said warmly, "Jake, it's what you always wanted. A baby! A son. We're having a boy. We can be a family again." She emphasized her words with a squeeze.

Snapshots of emotion flashed through his memory of the disappointment he'd felt each time she'd get her period while they were trying. Those thoughts were quickly followed by the churning fury he'd endured when he found out she'd been having a string of affairs while he was away at night working. He took a steadying breath and stepped out of her reach.

"Juliet, how far along are you?"

"Twenty-four weeks. I found out it was a boy last month and have been waiting until I could come down and tell you face to face.

"Twenty-four weeks?" he asked, plastering a hopeful look on his face to draw her in.

"Yes! Jake, it's going to be wonderful," she said, extending her arms to wrap him in a hug.

He caught her arms in the air and stopped her approach. "There's no damned way that baby is mine. We've been apart for seven months, and we haven't had sex in eight."

She gasped in feigned horror. "Jake, how dare you, that's not true! You're wrong!"

He watched her face as she acted the part of the abandoned woman, and he felt himself turn to stone.

She must've thought his memory would be clouded with excitement - either that or she greatly underestimated his intelligence.

As she stared back at him, her face began to transform. Juliet turned red, and she pressed her lips into a thin white line.

"Seriously, Jake? I come all the way down here to tell you you're going to be a father and that you have the *opportunity* to be with me again instead of sending some damned lawyer with child support papers, and you have the audacity…"

Jake stepped up and grabbed her by the arms. With his face inches from hers he hissed the words, "Opportunity?" A chilling sound that might've been a laugh escaped him. "Juliet," he whispered, low and harsh. His voice rose with each tersely whispered word, "You lying witch. I know this baby isn't mine. We weren't even able to get pregnant with expensive fertility treatments, so how do you expect me to believe you're suddenly pregnant when we weren't even together?"

Something passed over Juliet's expression and Jake didn't miss it.

"What?" he demanded, barking so loud and close that she backed away, shaking loose from his grip.

"I'm just trying to give you what you wanted, Jake!" She sneered with an ugly expression on her beautiful face. "You're the one who wanted a baby. Here's a baby! Here! Here's your damned baby!" She pointed to her stomach. "What does it matter if it's yours or not - you know me. You want a baby. We didn't make one together. Take this one!"

Jake shook his head, incredulous. "How did you get pregnant now when we couldn't get pregnant before. All those fertility treatments and shots you had to take, God, it just made me sick to put you through that," he said, his voice getting softer.

Her face contorted to a sneer. "Expensive fertility treatments," she said with a grin. "You win, Jake. I'll leave," she said, turning back toward her car.

He circled around and got in front of her, blocking her way.

"What about the treatments?" he asked in an alarmingly quiet voice as she opened the car door.

"I never used them," she said as victory shined in her eyes.

He slammed the car door shut, making her jump. His face was clouded with confusion. "What are you talking about? We went together to that appointment. I donated sperm, for God's sake. You never let me help with the shots, you took them in the bathroom, and you were so moody because of the medicine..."

She snickered. "Think about it, Jake."

A few beats passed, and he shook his head. "You bitch," he whispered. "You liar! Did you even have the eggs implanted? Did you even try?" Juliet didn't make eye contact.

"Did you even take the shots, Juliet?" He saw the answer in her eyes when she raised her head. Shock washed over him at the half-grin on her face. His head turned side to side as he processed this unexpected, unwanted information.

"But, that's why I worked all those extra shifts… the medical bills. You blamed me for your affairs because I was always gone…"

Juliet blew out a bored sigh. She put a hand back on her car door.

"What the hell did you do with all that money?" he raged.

"I spent it, Jake!" she yelled. "You know what?" she said, pointing her finger at him. "You stay down here. Stay down here in this little town with your precious mom and your precious girlfriend. Be a little small town cop and give up everything." She nearly frothed at the mouth when she screamed, "You're giving up the city, a hot wife, and a baby for this? I hope you rot down here!"

"Wait a minute, you said we didn't make a baby together. Why did you say *didn't* instead of *couldn't*? We tried to get pregnant for two years before we did the IVF treatments," he seethed.

She settled into the car and buckled her seat belt, tucking the lap belt under her pregnant belly. "IUD, Jake," she scoffed.

He began to shake with rage. "Why did you even come down here, Juliet? Are you trying to find another paycheck?"

Fury washed over her features and she stuck her middle finger out the window as she backed out of the drive. That was it, he thought, watching Juliet drive away. She came down here because she's out of money. He sat down on the porch and put his head in his hands. He felt absolutely drained and disgusted. Then Jake did something he never did. He cried.

twenty-three

AVERY WAS ON AUTOPILOT FOR THE next few days. She
kept hoping that Jake would call her or show up at her
house, and she hated herself for wanting it. She stomped
around her house as she hung up the last few items in her
closet. There was no relief to be found in reorganizing
everything because all it made her do was think about how a
deranged person had been in her home.

"This is why you don't let people in," she said aloud as
she settled onto her couch. She plugged her phone into the
charger and pulled out her stack of patient files and skimmed
them. A few of her patients had had a change of insurance,
which was always a pain to work through. She lost herself in
the monotony of correcting patient paperwork and entering

new billing information into her program on her laptop. Avery was so immersed in her work that she didn't even notice the sun setting. Her living room was dark with the exception of her glowing laptop screen.

When she got up to grab a drink of water from the kitchen she heard Rocky make a racket like he was chasing away another animal. She'd seen a raccoon sniffing around the cat food bowl outside the night before, so she hurried to let him inside. Avery tapped in the code to disable the alarm and opened the door. In an instant, a man in a ski mask shoved his way into her house.

Avery let out a scream that could raise the dead, and the man hissed, "Shut up! Stop screaming right now!" He jerked her up from the floor where she had fallen, when he pushed his way in and pulled her close in a tight hug. He pulled her close to the door and leaned her against the wall as he used his free hand to turn the deadbolt.

"Avery, calm down! It's me! You're safe!" He spoke softly to her and patted her back to soothe her. He was so strong that she couldn't budge or get away. "Oh, honey. You're trembling. Don't be afraid."

Don't be afraid, don't be afraid -- Avery stilled her struggling as the words played on repeat in her mind. That's what the note in her closet had said.

A new flurry of rage swelled up inside her. Her fear transformed into outrage as she realized the person who had been terrorizing her for weeks was in her house. She leaned back as much as she could muster and rammed her head into the man's face as hard as she could.

He released her as he screamed, and she fell against the chair, knocking it over as her head swam from the impact.

"You crazy bitch!" he screamed as he yanked the ski mask off of his head.

Anthony Jase, her former patient, stood before her with blood streaming down his face. "You broke my nose, Avery! How could you do that to me?" he screeched as he dabbed at his face with his mask.

She took a deep breath and tried not to panic. Anthony was seriously deranged and apparently much more dangerous than she'd ever imagined. *Calm down, calm down*, she told herself, trying to formulate a plan as he blocked her way out the door.

"Come with me," he said, jerking her up by her arm. "I've got to get this cleaned up. I don't want to get blood all over our house."

Her blood chilled at the way he called it 'our' house. She didn't want to go farther away from the door so she tried to stall.

"Anthony, I'm so sorry. Here, why don't you let me grab some ice from the kitchen. I can get you cleaned up right here. I've got rags and everything. Here, let me help."

His chest heaved with his breathing as he considered it. He didn't even seem phased by her transition from terror to helpfulness. He was truly delusional.

"No, Mommy. I don't want to get blood on the floor in here. Let's go to the bathroom where you can help me."

Avery started to tremble. She recalled how many sessions

she'd endured where he talked about his relationship with his mother. Anthony alternated frequently between venting rage about the way she treated him and strange passivity and poignant grief about her death.

Her death, how did she die again? Avery racked her brain as he half-dragged her to the back of the house. She remembered vaguely that he had mentioned she disappeared one day and never surfaced. A hollow feeling of dread spread throughout her body as reality hit. He'd killed his mother.

"Mommy, let's get this wiped up. This blood is scary."

Avery didn't know what to do. If she played along with the delusion that she was his mother, would she be safer than asserting her true identity? If he had killed his mother, was it more dangerous to go that route? Her hands shook violently as she pulled the first aid kit from under her sink. She decided to try to talk as little as possible in hopes of not setting him off either way.

When she tried to open the kit she dropped it, spilling the contents all over the bathroom floor.

"Here, I'll help," he said, holding the mask to his face to catch the blood. All he managed to do was get the smears all over her floor. She saw bloody handprints where he had turned on the light and braced his hand against the wall when he leaned down to help.

She righted herself and pulled a washcloth from the shelf. She ran it under hot water as her mind raced. Anthony just stood there patiently, like a child waiting to be tended. Disgust and fear raced through her body, and she tried to push those feelings back. She couldn't think if she were panicked. As she cleaned off the blood as carefully as possible, her eyes caught the sight of her gun safe by the bed. It was closed, so she'd have to get her hand on the biometric reader. Thank God she'd had the foresight to keep it loaded.

Anthony sighed with relief once his face was cleaned up. "Thank you, Mommy. I've got it all down my shirt. I need to change."

"I'm sorry, Anthony," she said, forcing her voice to sound mostly normal. "I don't have any men's shirts here."

"You've got some t-shirts in your closet, surely something will fit."

Bile surged in her throat as she imagined Anthony in her house those times. It was him who broke in and took the pictures of the inside of her house. It was him who rearranged her closet and left that note. He snipped the wires to her alarm company.

He pulled her by the arm into the walk-in closet. He flicked on the light as another memory hit Avery. Anthony worked for a security company. That's how he'd been able to get in. As soon as he got his bearings, Anthony looked around the closet in confusion.

"Avery?" he said, rounding on her. He grabbed her hard by both shoulders. "Avery, what did you do? Why did you change things?"

He shook her roughly before stopping himself. Anthony cocked his ear to the side like he was listening for something. "Did you hear that?"

She stilled and tried to listen over the sound of her own breathing. She heard a faint knocking sound, then silence. Avery jumped when the phone in her pocket began to rang.

"Who is it, Avery?" he hissed. "It better not be that cop again." She recoiled in disgust as he shoved his hand into her pocket to retrieve her phone.

"Who is Jesse?" he asked, his breath hot against her face.

She shook her head. "Just a friend. Just a friend," she assured him.

"Shh!" he shushed her. "She better get the hell out of here, or I'm going to do to her what I'm going to do to you." He pulled her down to the floor of the closet and clasped his hand over her mouth.

JESSE STOOD AT the door for a few minutes before returning to her SUV. She'd run over to borrow some sugar for a cake she was whipping up, rather than drive back into town to go to the store. She stopped at the edge of the driveway and looked back at Avery's house. Something didn't feel right. The lights at the back of the house were on, but Avery didn't answer. Jesse was about to decide that maybe she was just in the shower, when she happened to look the direction opposite from where she came.

Parked in the shadows of the trees at the foot of Avery's driveway was a truck that Jesse didn't recognize. *This is weird*, she thought. She pulled her phone out and called Jake. Her call went to voicemail, so she hung up. As she pulled back into her driveway, she called him again.

"Hello?" he answered.

"Hey, sorry to bother you. Are you home?"

"No, I'm working tonight. What's up?" he asked.

She frowned. "Well, probably nothing. Have you talked to Avery today?

He let a big sigh out, and a knot of worry began to form in her belly.

"No, we're not exactly talking right now."

This is awkward, she thought.

"This is probably nothing, but I just went to borrow something from Avery, and she didn't answer the phone or the door. Lights are on at the back of the house, though."

"Maybe she's taking a bath or something?"

"Could be, but it feels weird. There's also a truck that looks empty parked off almost in the trees between your house and hers."

"I'll be right there. Go home and lock your door, just in case, okay?"

"Be careful, Jake," she said into the phone as she heard the call end.

AVERY WINCED AS Anthony laid on top of her with his hand over her mouth. She'd never been a fan of tight spaces. The combination of his weight on her body, being crammed in the back of her closet in the dark, and the tremendous amount of fear she was in pushed her over the edge.

Though she fought for calm, the more she tried, the

worse she felt. Her heart was racing, and her breath was coming in short gasps. Her body shook, slick with sweat. She closed her eyes to try and focus. Her physical reaction was so strong that Anthony took notice.

"Avery, Avery, are you okay?" he asked in a frantic, high-pitched voice. He got up and flicked the light on in the closet and stood over her. He wrung his hands, shifting his weight from foot to foot. She opened her eyes, and the sight of such a clearly unhinged man looming above her caused her chest to feel like it was caving in. She was beyond being able to control the volume of her frantic gasps for air. The sound was like a shrill wheeze cutting the silent night.

In her mind she was repeating the mantra, "You're okay, you're okay, you're okay," but the truth of the matter was, she was very much *not* okay. Scenes flashed in front of her eyes of the moment she got the text from this madman while at Jesse's party. She saw herself on the floor absolutely stunned by the fact someone was photographing the inside of her house. Avery pictured the voice of Juliet threatening her by voicemail and then again in the driveway at Ruthie's house. She played the scene back in this very closet where Anthony rearranged all her clothes and crept around her house. Most of all she saw Jake's face telling her of her mother's murder.

The pressure of her chest and the hyperventilating caused her to feel weak. Her eyes rolled back in her head, and she gasped for air. She felt Anthony reaching under her and lifting her up. She couldn't fight--she couldn't breathe--she was the very epitome of a victim at that moment, and the shame built up inside her like a wildfire.

When her eyes flickered open, Anthony was pacing around her bedroom and she was lying on the bed. He must have placed her there after lifting her from the closet floor. She watched him carefully with her eyes barely open. Anthony paced with his hands straight down at his side, and he marched back and forth near the door, a few feet from her bed. She watched as he flicked anxious glances her way every so often, muttering to himself.

Avery slowly moved her hand toward her gun safe. She thanked God in heaven that she had silenced the alarm that previously beeped when the biometric scanner recognized her fingerprint. A very soft click sounded in the air as the two hydraulic lifts opened the safe.

Anthony turned from his position near the door when Avery leveled the gun and fired, hitting him squarely in the right shoulder. He dropped to the floor, and his mouth shaped on a soundless scream as he grabbed at his arm.

There was no way for Avery to run from the room without getting close to him, so she bolted for her bathroom instead. The door had a lock, however that didn't offer any peace. She was jerking up the window pane, trying to decide if she could wiggle out of it, when she heard her front door burst open.

It was impossible to hear what was happening through the door and over her thundering heart until the yelling started. Anthony screamed, and the next thing she heard was a man yelling, "POLICE! Get on the floor with your hands over your head, now!"

It was Jake. Avery slid down the wall, and tremors rocked her body. She heard mumblings of Jake calling dispatch. More than once he had to yell at Anthony to quiet down, and then she heard a loud thump.

When a yell sounded on the other side of her bathroom door she was certain her spirit had momentarily left her body.

"Avery? Avery, are you in there?"

For a second, all she could do was nod her head yes, but the sounds wouldn't come out.

"Avery! Answer me!" he yelled through the door.

"Jake! Yes, I'm here! I'm here!" she said around the sobs that erupted from her chest. She reached up to unlock the door, and in the next second he was crouched over her.

"Are you hurt?" he asked, his eyes roaming over her body.

"My God, there's so much blood," he said, as Avery realized that Anthony had bled all over her when she broke his nose. "Are you sure you're not hurt?" he asked while he pulled her up to a standing position.

Sirens ripped through the air, and reflections of the red and blue lights flashed through her window. "You stay here, okay? Let us get him out of here before you come out."

SHE NODDED FURIOUSLY, wanting to avoid locking eyes with Anthony Jase ever again.

Her ear was pressed to the door as she listened to the police enter her bedroom.

"You were supposed to be dead!" Anthony screamed at Jake.

"What the hell are you talking about?" he said in a calm manner.

"I paid that idiot five thousand dollars to kill you! He failed! That was my mommy's money!"

Jake looked at the other officer, and he held his hand up for him to pause before carting him out of the room. He took a step toward the blubbering, insane man. "You're the one that paid Dan Rogers to attack me?"

"Yes! And he failed!" Anthony moaned, in a full psychotic fit. Something glazed over in his eyes, and he jerked his face toward Jake. "I killed my mommy to get all her money. I killed Avery's mommy, too!" he said, and then threw his head back and laughed wildly.

"I've been watching her, you know," Anthony said quietly to Jake. "I was even outside one night when you dropped her off at home. I stood outside her window until the sun came up. It was easy, you know."

"What was?" Jake asked tentatively.

"Getting inside. I even watched her sleep a few nights. She sleeps on her right side, all curled up under her blankets. Such soft blankets…"

"How did you get inside?" Jake asked, biting back the bile that rose at the back of his throat as he envisioned this sick screw up watching Avery in the middle of the night.

"It was easy. I work at the security company. You can't imagine how I laughed when I figured out my baby was buying a system from my company. I couldn't sleep for a week because I was so excited. I wanted to watch her all the time. My baby."

Jake's stomach turned while Anthony started screaming Avery's name as he clutched at his wound. "Get that son of a bitch out of here," he said to the other officers.

When he went back to the bathroom door he opened it slowly. Avery was pressed against the far wall, as pale as the white paint behind her. Tears poured down her face, and she wasn't sure where to look.

Jake sat down on the floor next to her feet, and she slowly slid down the wall next to him. She wiggled around until there was enough room for her to lay her head in his lap then she sobbed.

He didn't know how long it went on, but by the time she stopped, she couldn't have had another tear left in her. Jake rubbed his hand along her arm and back while she vented the hurt, betrayal, fear, and anger. He'd seen some terrible things over his life, but the vision of her nearly defeated, coupled with the sounds of grief and terror, was almost more than he could take.

When she had quieted to the point of little hiccups, he rose and ran a washcloth under cool water.

He held out his hand to help her up, and then pulled her into a hug. "Here you go," he said gently as he handed her the cool cloth, which she immediately pressed to her eyes. "We need to get you to the station, Avery."

She sighed heavily. "Can I at least take a shower?"

"I think it would be better to go as you are. They'll need to take some photographs and ask you questions about what happened tonight. As gruesome as it is, these pictures could help put that psycho behind bars," he said, the banked rage still burning in his eyes.

She nodded, disgusted to have Anthony's blood on her body, but she knew he was right.

"I can't believe you came," Avery said, reaching to touch his hand as they walked back into her bedroom.

He exhaled. "We have Jesse to thank for that. She stopped by and saw a truck parked down by your drive."

"Thank God," she said quietly. "How did you know I needed you?" she asked, looking into his eyes.

He let out a breath and briefly squeezed his eyes shut, still in disbelief that she was unharmed. "I could see through the door that your chair had been knocked over, and there was some blood on the floor."

She shook her head, unable to wrap her mind around what had just happened. "I have been alone with him so many times during our sessions. I knew he was disturbed, but I never dreamed…"

His big hand squeezed her shoulder as they made their way through her house. "People are good at hiding things, Avery. I'm just so glad you're safe."

His words caused a fresh round of tears as she thought

back to her mother, who had been murdered by that madman. "Come on now," he said, "let's get this part over with."

twenty-four

As Jake and Avery pulled into the station, his phone started blowing up. He didn't even bother to answer since he was in the parking lot. When they hit the lobby, Officer Henderson nodded in greeting.

"We've met once before, I'm Officer Henderson," he said, then opened a door to an office. "Come on in, guys. There have been some developments."

Avery sagged a little; she couldn't fathom what else could've happened, or even how much more she could take.

"What's going on, Henderson?" Jake asked as he pulled out a chair for Avery.

Henderson put a glass of water in front of Avery before taking his seat. He took a deep breath and put his hand over his face before explaining.

"On the way into the hospital, Anthony Jase broke loose from the officer taking him in. He was screaming and carrying on like he was at her house, and the hospital security guard drew his weapon. Jase charged the guard and the guard fired before we could stop him."

Jake stood to his feet. "Are you serious? Is he alive?"

Henderson shook his head. "Negative. The guard is on his second shift of work and was terrified - and clearly, unqualified."

"Unbelievable," Jake said, dropping back to his seat and turning to Avery.

"I don't understand," she said, her brow furrowed. "How is this anything but a good thing?" Avery asked.

It was Jake's turn to be confused. "Because he deserves to go to jail for what he did to you, to your mother. To his own mother! He doesn't deserve an easy way out!"

"Jake," she said as she reached out and put her hand on his knee. "This way I never have to see him again. I never have to wonder if he's going to get out of prison and come back for me. He's - he was - completely delusional. He's not the type to rehabilitate and get a second chance in the world. He's extremely sick. *Was* extremely sick," she corrected.

Jake gave her a nod, but he still didn't feel justice had been served. He had wanted Anthony Jase to suffer for the turmoil he'd put Avery through. "So, what do we need to do here?" he said, directing his attention to Officer Henderson.

"We've got to get a statement from Avery detailing everything that happened tonight, then you're free to go."

She drew in and released a big breath. "Let's get started," she said, straightening her posture.

Jake watched her and felt a little in awe to listen to her recap the events of the night. Her voice was strong and, despite looking like death warmed over, she appeared confident. Maybe she was right, he conceded. At least the nightmare was over.

As THEY DROVE back toward her home, Jake put his hand on her leg.

"Avery, will you stay with me tonight?"

She nodded. "I'd love that. I want to take a shower at home, though. I can't go into your mother's house looking like this," she said, weariness showing in her face.

"Of course," he said as he pulled into her driveway. "That's fine. I've got to get someone to replace your door, anyway. It's nearly midday, so Shep's Lumber is open." Jake walked to her door and opened it. "Oh, and we don't have to go to my mom's house. The crew delivered my stuff today."

"Oh my God. Today was your moving day, and you were stuck with me," she said, shoulders dropping.

"Hey," he said as his hand squeezed her shoulder. "Don't even think about it. I've helped them before; fair is fair. There really wasn't much to do. The furniture store delivery guys handled the big stuff and appliances," he said with a shrug.

"His truck has been towed off," she mentioned, staring out the window as he turned off the engine.

"The department tries to handle as much as they can in regards to the mess, but there will be work left to do."

Avery paled as the full meaning of his words sank in. His blood would still be in her home. "Fine. Not today, though. I want to be in and out of here as quickly as possible." Jake nodded in agreement as they made their way into her house.

"Guess this was a huge waste of money," she said with a sarcastic tone as she gestured to the alarm panel by her door.

Jake picked up the chair she had plowed into as Avery stepped around the blood stain on her floor. His gut twisted as he imagined the scene in his head. It made him sick that Avery had been so terrified when Jase pushed his way into her home. They paused as they walked through the hallway getting closer to her bedroom.

"Let me go in first," he said, relieved when she didn't fight him for once. Jake stepped through the doorway and paused, assessing the mess. Avery closed her eyes and listened to his steps passing back and forth from her bedroom to the bathroom. Jake stopped before her with an armload of shampoo and toiletries.

"Is this enough stuff?" he asked, eyebrows drawn high on his forehead.

A half-smile shone on her face. "That's perfect, thanks." She took the burden from his hands and made her way to the guest bathroom so she could avoid the mess.

"I'll grab some clothes for you to change into and to pack for the night."

Avery nodded in response and ran the shower water in the other bathroom. Over the sound of the water she heard Jake say that he could get the name for a clean-up crew from one of the guys at the station. Hot water washed over her as she tried to think of how she'd ever be able to relax in this house again. Scenes from the past 24 hours whirled in her memory like a demented slideshow. Images of Anthony flashed before her eyes, and she felt her throat constrict as her pulse raced. She tried to focus on the scent of her shampoo and body wash, now that her skin had been scrubbed clean of the remnants of the night. The water in her shower floor ran clear. She fought the oncoming panic attack with every fiber of her being, but a sob wrenched itself from her throat.

Jake was by her side in an instant. He'd been hovering awkwardly outside the bathroom door, torn between giving her privacy and not wanting to miss a word she said if she needed him. The sound that erupted from her lips tore his heart in two.

"Come here, baby," he said, wrapping Avery in a towel and half-dragging her sagging form from the corner of the shower. He held her up with one arm and turned off the water with the other.

"You're going to be alright," he said softly, gathering her into an embrace.

Avery sucked in one ragged breath after another, her exhales loud but controlled. Jake had been around enough people in crisis situations to recognize a panic attack. He held her while she cried and prayed silently that she would be alright.

He patted her back in a gentle rhythm that women in his family had been using on their children for generations. *Pat, pat, pause, pause, pat, pat.* An invisible smile tugged at one corner of his mouth as he recognized the sound he hadn't heard in years. Her breathing returned to normal and her sobs gradually returned to hiccups.

Avery pulled back from him with a red, puffy face. "My God, how embarrassing," she said as she wiped her face roughly with her palms.

"Don't be embarrassed. Let's go home. I'm going to put your things in the vehicle while you get dressed."

She nodded in reply. "You're going to look like crap tomorrow," she said critically to her reflection. Her eyes always swelled up after a crying jag. Hastily, she dressed in the clothing Jake had left for her on the counter and flipped the lights off. She flicked her eyes up to his as he waited by the door for her and did her best to smile, though she thought it might've looked more like a grimace.

Jake noticed that Avery barely glanced at her surroundings until they made it to his truck. They made it as far as the mailbox when she gasped.

"Rocky!" she said, her hand covering her mouth. "I forgot all about him! Can we go back up to the house?"

"Sure, no problem," he said, putting the truck back into drive as he eased back up the driveway. She was out of the door like a shot once he parked. He watched as she walked around the yard, calling to the cat. She disappeared out of view and he quickly stepped out of the cab. By the time he got around to the bumper, she was back in sight with the cat in her arms.

"Jake, this is so stupid, but…"

He nodded his assent. "Load him up. It's fine. I'll grab his food out of the house. Be right back."

"I mean, it's idiotic, right?" she hollered after him. "You'll probably just come back over here as soon as I let you out of the truck, won't you, fella?"

Jake climbed back into the cab, settling the little bag of food between them. "After all you've been through, you can let that cat sleep in our bed if you want."

She grinned despite herself. "Our bed?"

"My bed." He grinned. "Sorry," he added, his smile turning slightly devious.

"I can't wait to get into it, no matter whose it is. Any chance you have curtains up?" she said, wincing at the bright daylight.

"I'll throw some blankets up over the windows. I could crash for a week, myself. I can't imagine how you feel."

She nodded, relieved that his home was so close. "It does really look like a glass shoebox," she said, seconds later when they pulled into his garage.

"They nailed it. I'm really happy with how it turned out. Let's get you inside."

Avery followed him into the house with a perplexed, meowing cat in her arms. She whispered comforting words to Rocky and released him once Jake shut the door behind them.

"Wow," she said once her eyes landed on his furniture.

"Wow is right. It looks pretty danged good in here, doesn't it?" he asked as he kicked off his shoes. She quickly removed her own shoes and moved them to the mat beside the door. His furnishings were mainly dark wood and earth tones. Cardboard boxes were stacked in front of floor-to-ceiling bookshelves that had been installed in his living room since she was there last. A hefty selection of large potted plants stretched upward in front of one of the large panels of windows.

"You keep plants alive and you're a reader?" she asked, rounding on him with wide eyes.

"Yes, I'm not just a pretty face," he said incredulously, a teasing smile on his lips. "I'm going to go shower. You'll be okay settling in?"

Her fingers grazed a lower leaf on the huge fiddle leaf fig, yet her eyes were watching him. "Thank you, Jake. For everything."

He pressed a kiss to her forehead before walking through the open space back to his bedroom. Avery felt the last 24 hours settle on her small frame. She dug around in his cabinets until she found a mug and a paper plate. She dished out some food and a cup of water for Rocky.

"Don't you dare poop or pee in his house," she whispered to the cat. She'd let him out soon, she told herself. Avery heard the shower kick on after a few minutes and made her way back to his bedroom. A huge king-size bed sprawled under a fan. A bedside table lamp was on, but the windows had been covered with blankets. She was struck by how sparse his furnishings were. It was a minimalist's dream. She pulled the covers down and settled onto the side of the bed furthest from the door. The sound of the shower in the bathroom combined with the whirring of the ceiling fan instantly relaxed her exhausted mind and body. She felt Rocky hop onto the foot of the bed and pace around before finding the perfect spot. His purr was the last sound she registered before she fell asleep.

Jake emerged from the bathroom to see Avery fast asleep in his bed. He stood still for a minute, taking in the scene of her in his bed with the cat curled up at her feet. He walked back through the house to double check that his doors were locked. He sent a quick text to Jesse to let them know he had Avery and she was safe, sound, and resting. He sent another to his mother with a similar message, but asked that she get in touch with Mallory so that she could notify Cade about what had gone down. He let her know that their phones would be off for a while so they could get some rest. He flicked on the mute buttons on both of their phones and ambled back into the bedroom nearly dead on his feet. He scowled at the cat when Rocky begrudgingly gave up his spot so that Jake could curl around Avery. He reached across to turn off the light and settled into a deep sleep beside her.

He awoke to a sharp elbow thrown into his stomach as Avery jerked herself from the bed.

"Hey, it's okay, it's just me. It's Jake," he said with a groan as he flicked on the light to illuminate the inky dark room.

She sat down heavily on the bed. "I'm so sorry. For a second I didn't know where I was. I thought he..."

Jake pulled her down into his arms. "He's gone, Avery. You're safe. You're safe with me," he said softly. She tucked her head beneath his chin, and Jake felt his heart expand.

"Listen, Avery," he said, pulling back so that he could see her face, "I'm not sure if my timing is perfect or terrible with this, considering what's just happened... but timing has never been my forte anyway. So much of this kind of thing hasn't ever been my forte, but that's never stopped me before."

"Jake," she said, putting her hand against his cheek. "You're rambling. What are you trying to say to me?"

He exhaled deeply. "Will you move in with me?"

Her eyes went as round as saucers. "Jake," she said softly, shaking her head side to side, "we barely know each other. And you have a baby on the way. God, we haven't even talked about that..."

"She lied," he said, his voice rasping around a sudden lump in his throat.

Avery's head whipped around. "What?"

Jake half-shrugged, and Avery watched the clouds roll into his eyes. "She lied about everything. It's not my baby. I mean, I knew that. Mathematically, it couldn't have been. She lied about a lot more than that, though."

Her hand covered his, and she gave it a squeeze.

"Basically," he cleared his throat, "the entire marriage was a lie. When we couldn't get pregnant on our own, which was untrue - she was on birth control. Anyway, when I thought we couldn't get pregnant, she wanted to try in vitro. I worked my ass off in overtime to pay for that. She wasn't really getting the shots. She just said that she was, and I bought it. I believed everything," he said.

Avery took his face in her hands and gave him a kiss. "I'm so sorry. That's so cruel."

His chest lifted with a breath, and her heart broke for him. "Jake, did you want a family very badly?"

He nodded his head. "I did. I love kids and always thought I'd have a few. There are so many people in this world that take their children for granted, it just doesn't make sense." Suddenly a blush of embarrassment filled his face. "Avery, I'm sorry, I didn't think…"

She shook her head, dismissing his comment. "You're right, it doesn't make sense. I never understood how my parents took their job so lightly."

"What do you say, though, Avery?" As she barely shook her head in doubt, he reached up. His fingers stilled her head and tipped her chin up toward his, where he planted a soft kiss. "We aren't fools, Avery. We can try this. If it doesn't work out, it doesn't work out. I mean, it would be terrible, but we're tough. We can take it. Move in with me. I want to be with you. Every single day."

Her head absolutely swam with conflicting thoughts and emotions. She loved him but didn't ever want to depend on him - on anyone. "Jake, we haven't said the words out loud, but I love you." He smiled and kissed her lips. She placed her hands on his shoulders and pushed him back a little. "Let me finish." She continued quietly, "I love you, but I'm scared to jump into this."

Jake's heart broke when he saw Avery's eyes fill with tears. "Why are you afraid?"

"I saw my mother turn herself inside out trying to please whichever man she was with at the time. The men always came first. I was in the way. I don't ever want to need anyone that badly," Avery said, taking in a ragged breath.

"That's the difference, Avery," he said tenderly. "You don't need me. You're amazing. You're independent as all hell. You're stubborn as a mule." He smiled at her half-hearted glare. "I'm not here to change you. I just want to share my life with you. I don't want to change you."

"I've worked hard to keep people out, and you're changing that, Jake. What if this doesn't work? I don't have any intention of getting married. Your family is pretty traditional. They would be disappointed."

Jake looked at her deeply, making Avery feel that he saw beyond her emotional scars and baggage, right down to her heart. "That's the good part of being in my 40s, Avery. I don't have to care if my family approves. That being said, they will. They're crazy about you. You are almost an honorary member of the family anyway. Let's make it one more step toward official."

"But not legal..."

"I get it. You don't want to marry me." He grinned. She

couldn't resist running her hands through his hair for the pure excuse of touching him. "To be honest," he continued, "I'm not sure I'll ever be ready to marry again, either, after that last flaming disaster of an experience. I'd be happy just to wake up next to you every day. It's enough for me to know I love you, and that you love me back."

A smile spread across her face before it faltered. "Jake, I love the idea, but I'm not really sure what the fallout is going to be from all of this. I had a panic attack in the shower today. I don't expect to wake up after a good nap and pretend to be normal all of a sudden."

"Avery, I nearly lost you in the last 24 hours. I don't want to look back on this life and regret not getting every moment with you that I can. You're a pill, but I'm hooked."

Avery rolled her eyes at his pun. "Nice," she said, smoothing the blanket with her hands, suddenly self-conscious.

"Come on. Move in with me," he said, brushing a stray hair behind her ear.

She traced her finger down his bare chest as her options raced through her mind. She could get a hotel room, sell her house, and buy another one, which would all take time. No matter where she was, she wanted to spend as much time with Jake as possible. The idea was crazy and impulsive, totally not her style.

Avery took a bracing breath and closed her eyes. She focused on one thing and silently asked herself the question she asks her patients as they weigh a new relationship. *Does he bring positivity and light to my life?* Memories of their brief time together flashed, and she saw herself smiling, laughing, and relaxing. Avery didn't ever relax -- until Jake.

"I have another idea," Avery said with excitement twinkling in her eyes.

He wrinkled his brow at her and leaned in. "What?" he asked pretending to be grumpy. Jake felt like she was trying to redirect him, and he didn't like it.

"What if we went on a trip together first?" she asked, tilting her head to the side. Her hair spilled down her shoulder as he ran his fingers over her arm.

"What have you got in mind?"

"Well, how do you feel about the beach?" she asked, reaching up to grab her phone. She was searching for something while he mulled her question over.

"I love the beach. I haven't seen an ocean in years. I think I'd like seeing you in a bikini even more than I would like to see the ocean."

She frowned at him. "Come on now, I'm serious. What do you think about Fiji?"

"Fiji? Honestly, I'm not even sure where that is on a map. Let me see," he said, reaching to take the phone from her hands. Bungalows hovering over the bluest water he'd ever seen filled the small screen. "That's amazing. I'm in," he said, wrapping his hand around her neck and pulling her into a deep kiss. When they finally surfaced for air he smiled a sexy smile.

"When can we go? I want to put in for vacation ASAP."

He drummed his fingers on her hip as she twisted to pull her calendar from her bag next to the bed.

"As soon as I can manage it," she said. "I need an escape from my own head. I think you in a bed in a bungalow might do the trick." He watched her face as she flipped back and forth on her calendar. "It looks like I can be wide open! Let's check flights to get a better idea."

Avery's mind reeled as she pulled her laptop onto her lap, and Jake propped himself up beside her in bed. She checked several sites and tried to not be self-conscious as he watched her closely. He pulled out his phone and checked his emails while he waited for her to find the best deal. She heard his smile before she saw it. "What's up?" she asked, turning her attention to the sexy beast beside her.

"Do you remember me telling you about the little guy we found with the mother that ended up coding at the hospital?" he asked, a sadness settling in his eyes as he described Toby's situation.

"Of course. You've mentioned him several times. Is he okay? He's in foster care, right?" Avery asked.

"Right. Chloe, the foster mom, and I went to school together. She and her husband are saints. They've taken in probably twenty kids over the last decade, and from what Mary, his case worker, shared they treat the children as good as any she's ever seen in her career. They weren't able to have their own, so they sort of threw themselves into raising kids in desperate situations."

"That's wonderful. I know there are so many kids in

need of a good family. If I hadn't had the grandma I had, I'd have ended up in foster care, I'm sure." Avery touched his cheek lovingly and thanked her lucky stars for this man. "How's he doing?"

"Chloe said he's doing well. She sends me updates here and there on how he's doing." Jake ducked his head and confessed, "I send her donations sometimes to help with the kids, for holidays and birthdays, little stuff when I can."

Avery's heart split wide open at his bashful admission. Jake continued. "Chloe said Toby is still very timid and quiet. I don't know what it was about this kid, but he broke my heart. I think I saw in him what my life could've been like if my mother hadn't been fighting for me and Mallory every step of the way," he said with a sad tone to his voice.

Had she not already known she loved him, she would've known in that moment. There he was, big and tough, and yet sensitive to the hearts of kids right down to the soles of his feet. "I'm glad he's in a good place," she said softly.

"Me, too," he said softly. He inhaled and released a huge breath. "Now, show me what you've figured out, and I'll put in for time off as soon as I get to the Chief's office." She pulled up a flight and bungalow reservation one short week away. Jake's heart pounded at the idea of having her alone in as little as a week.

The morning light streamed in through the curtains and woke Avery from sleep. "Oh my gosh, Rocky! I forgot about him!" She jumped off the bed and walked through the house while simultaneously searching for the cat or any surprises he might have left. When she rounded the corner to the living room she gasped. Rocky was straddling both sides of a pot holding a fiddle leaf fig.

"What's the matter?" Jake asked, snaking his arm around her waist.

"Found him. He's, um, doing his part to tend to the plants."

"Crap!"

"No, just pee," she answered. "I'm scared to interrupt him, I don't want it to go everywhere."

"I can't believe we're standing here watching this," he said, looking down. "That's not all he's done."

"What?" she asked, looking all over the floor.

"There, by the kitchen sink," he answered, gesturing with his pointed finger.

Avery screamed and jumped when a scared Rocky streaked past her feet, abandoning his post in the plant. He sat beside a dead field mouse, proudly preening over his present.

"Little jerk is earning his keep already, isn't he?" Jake said, stooping to scratch the cat on the head. "Good boy."

"At least it's not in your cabinet, I guess?"

"I guess. I hate mice."

"Wait, you can catch a criminal, but you are freaked out by mice?" she asked incredulously.

"They're my kryptonite," he said with a shiver, picking up the dead mouse with a paper towel. "I'll take this little guy outside."

"I'll bleach the, uh, crime scene." She opened the cabinet under the sink to see a sparse selection of bottles of cleaning supplies Jesse or one of the ladies must have left for Jake.

Jake returned to the kitchen and washed his hands.

"Speaking of crime scenes, I sent a message when we got home to someone who can help with that. It's probably been taken care of while we were sleeping."

"Thank you so much."

THE NEXT NIGHT the phone jarred Avery awake, and her first instinct was to panic. She answered the phone, expecting the worst. Instead, Jake was on the other end, and his excitement was palpable.

"He gave the approval," he said into the phone.

She pressed her head to the pillow. "What?" she asked in a froggy voice, confused by the fact the phone had rang at 1 AM.

Jake chuckled, envisioning Avery frowning at the phone. "I heard back from the Chief. He gave approval for the time off," Jake said excitedly.

Her heart skipped a beat as the fog started to clear from her mind. "He did?"

"He did. Book those tickets. I'll pony up tomorrow."

Avery smiled. Jake had no idea that she had every intention of treating him to this first trip. He could get the next one. She fully expected there to be a next one. "I'll get on it. Five days in paradise, coming up."

AVERY'S FINGERS FLEW across the keyboard as she booked flights and accommodations in a fancy hotel featuring bungalows and every conceivable amenity known to man. This would be a vacation to remember. She couldn't wait to check Fiji off her bucket list. The moment she saw the huts in a photo, she knew she had to go see it. Her mind drifted to imagine the smell of the ocean surrounding their bungalow, the gentle lapping of the waves, and the sensory overload of the man who would be sharing her bed. It was almost too good to be true. Not one to tempt fate, Avery booked the reservations and settled back into the covers, ready to dream of good things yet to come.

twenty-five

HER SKIN WAS SLIGHTLY TENDER from the sun when she rolled over in the crisp, white sheets. Before she even opened her eyes, Avery opened her ears to the sound of the waves gently lapping the foundation of the bungalow. Jake snored softly inches away from her, having stayed up most of the night teaching Avery the finer points of making love while floating on top of the ocean. There wasn't an inch of each other they hadn't covered.

She faced Jake and watched him sleep. His hair stuck out in all directions, and his beard was scratchy. His skin was deeply tanned, a contrast to her own fair, pink features. They'd made the most of their week in paradise, and Avery was thankful to discover that she and Jake did seem to be very compatible. Of course it was easy to be compatible in paradise, she reasoned. She slipped from the bed on tiptoe to start the coffee. By the time she made it back with two mugs, Jake was rousing from sleep.

When his hair was mussed and his voice was gravely upon waking, he set Avery's world on fire. His green and gold-flecked gaze was almost her undoing. She traced the day-old growth of scruff on his cheek and chin and relished the feel of him.

"Good morning," Jake rasped, pulling Avery toward him after she placed the steaming mugs on the bedside table.

She gratefully allowed herself to be tucked against his naked body. "Jake?"

"Yes?" he said sleepily.

"I'll move in with you."

A smile split his face, and he pulled her against his chest so that she was mostly lying on top of him. Jake's chin rested on her head, and she listened to the sound of his heart beating while his hand stroked her arms and back.

"I didn't think I'd ever fall in love again," he said in a low tone.

"I didn't think I'd ever love, period," she answered.

He tilted his head to the side so that she could see his eyes. "I'm not perfect, Avery. I'm not even close. As a matter of fact, I promise I'll do some things that annoy the living hell out of you."

She laughed and no doubt started to make a smart comment when he hushed her. "I'm serious. I can promise, though, that I'll never do anything to intentionally hurt you." Jake dipped his head to kiss her lips and then pulled back, anxious for what she'd say next.

Avery smiled softly and promised, "I'll do my best to learn as I go. Trust and dependency have never been my things."

Jake looked deeply into her eyes. "Do we need to label it as dependency? Can't it just be love?"

She lifted a shoulder in answer. "I'm used to labeling every feeling or thought. Healthy, not healthy, depressive, anxious, manic, dependent, co-dependent..."

He rolled his eyes and flared his nostrils at her. "Avery!"

"See? I'm bugging you already!" she said, pulling up into a sitting position.

His fingers moved to her ribs and tickled her a little. "I'm just teasing. We've got to be able to tease each other sometimes."

She relaxed against him again and shared, "I'm not sure I know how to do this, but I want to try."

"We'll figure it out as we go, okay?" Jake drew in a big breath and let it out, the unanswered questions untangling their iron grip on his heart for the first time since they'd spoken about living together. "Should we call the family and let them know know you're moving in?" Jake asked, wiggling his eyebrows.

Avery was torn... she was so afraid they were making a mistake that she was anxious to tell anyone, because then they'd just have that many more people to inform when this thing inevitably exploded. But, she was also excited because she knew they'd all be so happy. They really were the most welcoming bunch of people Avery had ever met.

"How about this? How about we keep it to ourselves for one night and tell them tomorrow."

"Okay," Jake said, gently tightening his hold on Avery. "So, you're telling me you want to sleep on it?"

She caught the wicked gleam in his eyes and felt proof of his intentional wordplay as he pressed her body against his. "Sleep on it, yes. As a matter of fact, I'm pretty tired. Let's go back to sleep," she said, turning abruptly and peeking over her shoulder as she pulled up the covers.

"Oh no, you don't!" he said, rolling her over to straddle him. "Just think about it, now that you're living with me they can finally relax around you." Avery hooted with laughter at the thought that his family could be any more relaxed around her. They celebrated their new milestone and reveled in the fact that they were safe in each other's arms.

twenty-six

FALL HAD TURNED TO WINTER, AND THE fresh snow falling outside the large windows in Jake and Avery's house created an invigorating sensory experience when contrasted against the heat from the wood-burning fireplace. The sound of the wood crackling in the fire was almost as relaxing as the comfortable temperature in the room as people bustled back and forth. Jake brought in another load of firewood as his mother raced toward him.

"You're going to get all dirty, Son!"

"It's okay, I promise," he said, brushing off the little specks of dirt from his blue button-down shirt. "You look beautiful today, by the way," he said, taking her hand in his and holding it out like he was admiring her in her wine-colored, beaded dress.

"Oh, hush!" she chastised, even as a blush heated her cheeks. She held out the suit vest for him as he shrugged into it and the suit jacket. "What about Avery, Son, doesn't she look gorgeous?"

He glanced to the kitchen where Avery was gathered in a cluster with the rest of the women in his family. "She does. That's a good color on her." Dressed in a blush-colored lace and satin sheath, she looked like some kind of fair, blonde angel.

"Are you nervous?" Ruthie asked, brushing invisible lint from his suit.

"Nah, I always hoped I'd get a chance to do this," he answered with a grin.

"Always, huh?" she repeated, lightly smacking his arm.

He shrugged. "For a long time, anyway."

Ruthie released a pent up breath. "Well, honey, love is special and rare. When you find it, you have to grab it and make it yours."

"Yes, ma'am," he answered. "Now if you'll excuse me, I'll go see where the guys are at. It's about time to get this thing started. Any word on the pastor?"

Ruthie nodded. "Yes, she got here a few minutes ago and will be ready any minute."

Jake glanced at the ladies in the kitchen, letting his eyes linger on Avery's knowing smile as he walked to the porch. She was whispering conspiratorially with Mallory. Jake decided he'd have to get to the bottom of that later.

"Hey, guys, it's time. Let's go," he said with a jerk of

his head, indicating it was time to come inside. He heard the clinking of shot glasses and held his hand out. Aidan pressed a shot of whiskey into his hand and Jake shook his head, returning it. "No thanks. Ready?"

"Ready," they answered.

His family filed into the chairs that had been set up in his living room and draped with burlap and holly leaves on the makeshift aisle. The pastor took her post, and Jake walked back to the bedroom. "Everything's in place," he said.

Ruthie took his arm and walked at his side from the hallway to the living room. Jake gave her a kiss on the cheek and turned to extend a hand to Hank, who grinned like a man who had won the lottery.

"Take care of her, Hank," Jake said, his eyes both warm and stern.

"I will, son, I will." Hank smiled down at Ruthie and put her hands in his own with a gentle pat.

Mallory stood at Ruthie's side, and Jake stood beside Hank. The family watched Ruthie take her vows as she gave love another shot.

"It was a beautiful ceremony," Eadie said, wiping tears from her eyes.

Ruthie smiled and pulled Eadie into a hug. "I hope we can have a few years together and have a marriage like yours and Walt's, Eadie."

"I hope so, too, Ruthie. I hope so, too." Ruthie gave

Eadie's arm a squeeze and kissed and hugged her way down the line of family waiting to see them off after the little reception.

"I never thought I'd see my mom leave for her honeymoon," Jake said, pulling Avery into a hug.

She grinned up at him. "Wasn't that the sweetest thing you've ever seen?" Avery asked.

"You getting ideas, lady?"

Her eyes went wide. "Me? No! I'm still firmly anti-marriage, but I will say this…" she said, her voice dropping off.

"What?" he asked, furrowing his brow.

"I never dreamed I'd love living with someone the way I do with you."

"Same. We've got a good thing going. It looks like they do, too," he said, nodding toward Mallory and Cade.

Avery narrowed her gaze as she watched them. "Think they'll be next?"

"I don't know. She's a wildcard. Impossible to predict. Him?"

She sighed. "Tough to say. He's in St. Louis and she's in Chicago. It's amazing they're able to make it work at all."

"Yeah. Guess we'll have to wait and see." They stopped speculating as Jesse approached them.

"You two look pretty cozy hiding in the corner," she said, wiggling her eyebrows at them. "Making plans?"

"More like speculating. Trying to get a read on Cade and Mallory. Think they'll get more serious?"

Jesse laughed. "I don't know. They both have incredible jobs that they love, make a ton of money, have few things tying them down. As much as they travel, I'd be shocked. Maybe it's more about quality than quantity of time together."

"Maybe so," Jake agreed.

Jesse grabbed her phone as it buzzed in the pocket of her dress. "Hello? Hey, Marie, so nice to hear your voice! It's been a few months." She listened intently as she turned to watch the snow fall out the window next to Jake and Avery. "Leave of absence?" she asked, listening to her friend on the other end of the phone. "Yeah, there are cabins about an hour away down on the riverfront. They're gorgeous. Are you sure, though? You're not very... well, you're not very nature-y." Jesse rubbed at the lines that appeared between her eyes when she was questioning the sanity of people saying crazy things. "You bet. I'll get the number to you right away. I can't wait to see you. Bye, Marie." She turned to Jake and Avery. "Huh. That was weird. My friend from work, Marie, is taking a leave of absence and wants to rent one of those swanky little cabins down on the Ohio."

"That would be really pretty in wintertime," Jake answered.

"Yeah, but her idea of roughing it is staying at a four-star instead of a five-star hotel." Jesse shrugged. "Something is off about this. I'll figure it out when she gets down here." She pulled her wrap around her shoulders and slipped her heels back on at the door. "I'm going to go help Anna and Aidan get Benji and all the baby stuff into the car. I'll round my kids up after that and give you guys back your house. It was a beautiful ceremony," Jesse said, giving them both pecks on the cheek.

"Sometimes I think her brain has a stronger bandwidth than most," Avery said quietly to Jake. "She seems to collect everyone's problems and rapid-fire processes how to make things better for everyone all at the same time."

"She's pretty incredible," Jake said with a smile. It was a lot to get used to, but deep down he was so pleased to be back home with friends and family. They finished tidying up the living room and setting it back to rights as Jesse whisked in and out again with her children in tow. "This was probably pretty tough on Jesse's mother, Eadie. Walt hasn't been gone that long. Unlike my mother's marriage, hers was pretty much the ideal situation. He was a good man," he said with a sad smile as he pulled Avery closer. "I hope she'll be okay."

"Not much can be done about grief aside from waiting out the worst of it, from what I've observed," she said with a small shrug.

"Well," Jake said, sneaking his lips down to the crook of her neck, "that sucks."

His breath on her skin tickled her down to her toes, but she stifled the shiver given the nature of the conversation. Avery nodded somberly. "It does."

Her hand found his as they made their way together into the kitchen to talk with the others who had jumped into the cleanup for the party. The catered food from the town's favorite cafe was being divided up between all the families, and the background music had been turned down to a quiet murmur as the wedding celebration wrapped up.

"I think it's all picked up now," Sorcha said, pulling Avery and then Jake into a quick hug. "This turned out perfectly, I think. Don't you?"

"I do," Jake answered. "So glad you, Evan, and Clara could come. He seems like he's getting around a lot better."

Sorcha rolled her eyes. "Yes, thank goodness. That broken femur about did us in. All of us," she said, with a wicked grin. "Shame on me, that poor man. I give him a lot of trouble, but between us, sometimes I'm so choked by thankfulness that he survived that rockfall that I can't breathe." She turned to watch Evan scoop their daughter up to carry her out to the car. "He's my everything," she said with a light hearted shrug. "Night, you two," she said with a squeeze of Avery's arm before making her way out the door.

Mallory was the last guest to leave. "I'm sorry Cade couldn't make it today," she said to Jake and Avery. "He's always up for a party."

"Any excuse to get dressed up, am I right?" Avery laughed.

"He does take longer to get ready than I do," Mallory agreed. "So, did you tell him?" she asked Avery, gesturing to Jake.

"No way, that's more your news than mine," she answered.

Mallory turned to face Jake. "Well, I didn't want to tell Mom yet and get her all flustered, so keep this a secret. I interviewed over the phone this week and took a job at the hospital."

Jake's brows gathered in confusion. "Which one?"

She gestured. "Here. This one, dummy. I'm moving back home."

"Mal!" he cheered, pulling her into a hug. "Mom's going to be so excited."

"And..." she led on, drawing out the anticipation, "I'm going to rent Avery's house next door until I decide if that's where I want to be - or if it's too close for comfort."

Jake's face split into a big smile. "That's great news. It's an adjustment for sure, but I think you'll like it. It'll be good to have you close by."

Avery took in the scene with a smile on her face. She was in awe of the family dynamic with this bunch. They rarely argued and genuinely loved each other. It was very different than her own experience, and she was happy to be a part of it.

"Avery, I'll call tomorrow to sort out the details. Sound good?"

"Sounds good, talk to you then," Avery answered.

After Mallory closed the door behind her on her way out, the house was oddly silent. Though it had been filled to the brim with people and strong emotion for so much of the day, suddenly it felt as quiet as a tomb. Jake locked the door and flicked the light down low. He wandered over to the barely audible stereo and turned the music up a tiny bit.

He held Avery by the elbows as she kicked off her heels and sighed with relief.

"Dance with me?" he asked as he wrapped her in his strong embrace.

"How could I resist?" she asked, tipping her lips up to his.

His kiss was warm and soft as his fingertips danced up and down the satin of her dress and across her skin. "I'm not sure which is softer, the dress, or you."

"Hmm, I'm not certain myself. I do have something I want to talk about before you get me all carried away," Avery said, nuzzling her lips against his neck.

"What's that?" he asked, pulling his head back from hers.

She fidgeted with her hands, a dead giveaway that she was anxious. He placed his own hands over hers and looked into her eyes. "What is it, Avery? Is something wrong?"

She shook her head before she got the words out. "No, not a thing. That's what I wanted to talk about. Do you feel this is going well, Jake?" Her eyes looked deep into his soul, and for a second he felt panicked. He had never been happier in his life than during the time Avery had been living with him.

"I think it's been wonderful having you here. I love you. How do you feel?" he asked, his heart in his throat.

"Wonderful is a good word. I'm so glad we feel the same way," she said anxiously.

"Avery, you're killing me here. Spit it out," he said, pulling her closer with his hands on her upper arms.

"Jake, you've been very clear that you've always wanted a family. While I have not ever planned on having children of my own, my heart is more than open to foster care or adoption."

Avery saw Jake swallow a lump of emotion as she continued. "You talk about that sweet little Toby all the time, and I was wondering if you think now that we know we're going to do well living together -- Jake, do you think we could look into adopting Toby?" Avery's eyes were shining with tears, and she had never been more anxious in her entire life.

Jake crushed her against him, and she heard him choke on a sob. He struggled to control his emotions, unable to relax his hold on her until he had composed himself. He leaned back and nodded his head. "Yes, I would love to check into that. Avery, are you sure? It would change everything. Are you willing to do that?"

It was her turn to tear up. "Yes. You said once that you could have easily ended up in the same kind of scenario he was born into if your mother hadn't had the ferocity to fight for you and Mallory. I want to do that for Toby. I want us to give him a good home, love him, and be a family together."

They held one another for several minutes as the music washed over them. A few songs later, Jake's lips moved near her ear and dipped down to that spot at the juncture of neck and shoulder. Avery rolled her shoulder to give him more access, and he made that satisfying, masculine groan that made her want to drag him back to their bedroom.

He sank into the overstuffed chair and pulled Avery down across his lap when the song switched to "Say Goodbye" by Dave Matthews Band. "I always loved this song."

She sighed. "I haven't heard this one in years. It's not your way of giving me a signal, is it?"

"Nah, you're not listening to the words. Stay for the night, but get lost in the morning." He faked injury when she delivered a playful slap to his arm. Avery leaned forward and righted herself over both of his legs, hitching her dress up high to accommodate the yards of blush material. His fingers traced lines up her thighs as she leaned her face into his, nose to nose.

"Get lost tomorrow, huh?"

His fingers curled at the base of her neck, loosening the hair pulled up in an elegant twist. "I'll not hear of it. I want you here to stay. Forever."

"You do, huh?" she said, stiffening her spine and eliciting a moan from his lips as she brushed her lips against his. "You should be so lucky."

"Lucky? I like the sound of getting lucky," Jake answered as he ran his fingertips beneath the strap that grazed her shoulder and dipped down to the modest neckline of her dress. As his fingers traced the satiny edging of her dress, she lifted her eyes to his. One look was all the encouragement he needed. He tucked his fingers beneath her hips and hefted himself up to a standing position while her legs wrapped around him.

Avery grinned as Jake walked her back to their room, pressing kisses to her mouth, her throat, and her shoulder as the strains of the song changed to "Crash Into Me." Her body slowly sank down his as he allowed her feet to find the floor. She turned her back to him and looked back over her shoulder. Jake placed one hand there beneath her chin as the other lowered the zipper from her shoulder blades down to the top of her hips. He greeted each newly exposed inch of skin with a kiss.

With each touch of his lips Avery sent a prayer of thanks up to the God she wasn't entirely sure existed, but she thought the chances were pretty good. She was so thankful to have this man in her life. He treated her with equal parts reverence and tolerance. Avery knew she was a handful. She had more baggage than the average bear, but then again, so did he.

A soft laugh escaped her lips as Jake turned her gently by the shoulders.

"What's so funny?" he asked, nuzzling her neck and the spot directly below her ear. Her hands found the buttons on his shirt and worked their way down slowly as she answered. "I was just thinking…"

He pulled his lips away from her collarbone long enough to to mutter, "Thinking what?"

She pulled her head back and laced her fingers in his dark hair as she answered, "How ironic it is that a man-hater fell in love with a woman-hater so quickly."

Jake straightened and ran his hands down to each side of her hips as he looked into her eyes. "Well, you're not most women," he said, dodging her fake-slap on his arm. "And," he said, ducking his lips down to hers, "I'm not most men." At that, he pulled her up off the floor and deposited her onto their bed, sending a disgruntled Rocky running from the room. She scooted up to the top of the bed as he crawled after her and took her in his arms.

"You're right about that, Jake," Avery answered, as he brushed a lock of her golden hair away from her face. "You're not like most men. I love you."

A smile pulled at his devilish lips. "I love you, too, Avery. My turn to talk." Her eyes jerked to his as he narrowed his beautifully dark eyes at hers. "You have the right to remain silent…" he said, slapping her on the hip as his hungry mouth enveloped her laughter. Avery was happy to oblige.

Acknowledgments

To my family, thank you so much for your patience for all the time I spent chained to the computer trying to get this book out of my head. It's a magical feeling to have a story to tell, and I hope you all have something to do every single day that gives you this much joy.

Cori Dugan and Alison Han, thank you for fielding random questions over and over again as I use you both as my ultimate springboard for storylines, character details, and best of all, how far I can push a character before they are unlikeable.

My beta readers are the best at reigning me back, offering feedback, and poking holes in the stories where they are needed. To my mom, Cherrie Harris, and my dear friends, Amy Gibbs, Sarah Hart, Jerri Harbison, Julie Natzke, and Krystal Wilson, you did some great work and Avery, Jake, and I appreciate it. To friends and family that allowed me to ask questions about law enforcement and child services, thank you for sharing your experiences and expertise. I hope I did your admirable professions justice.

Sarah West at Three Owls Editing, thank you for your patience as I stalk your cursor, following along as you clean up my stories and help them put the best foot forward.

Cassy Roop at Pink Ink Designs, I nearly cried with relief when I found this cover for Poets Pass. I knew I'd know it when I saw it, and yet again, you've nailed it. Your formatting is top of the line and I'm so happy to have your hand in this book as well as the others in the Coal Country Series.

To my new author friends who have fielded a million and one questions, I've enjoyed our new friendship almost as much as I've loved reading all of your books! Anne Conley, Erica Cope, Autumn Doughton, Hazel James, and Stacy Kestwick, I hope you realize how appreciative I am of your kindness. Thank you for your time, consideration, and for not rolling your eyes so loud at my inane questions that I can hear it through the computer.

To every blogger who shares books they enjoy with their readers, thank you from the bottom of my second-chance romance loving heart. Your enthusiasm makes a terrific difference for those of us who love to tell stories. Thank you for sharing your passion for reading novels with your readers. Your reviews make our world go around!

Most of all, to the readers who have come to love the characters in the Coal Country Series, you'll never know how much your support means to me! It's one thing to have the joy of getting these characters out of my head and on paper (or eBook) but it's quite another to bring them to life for you as well. Your reviews help get the word out about our books and are the greatest gift you can give an author! Your support, comments and recommendations to friends are so appreciated. It means so much to me. Thank you!

books by
Hillary DeVisser

Fishing Hole (Coal Country Series - Book One)
Copper Creek (Coal Country Series - Book Two)